THE S HEA

Volume 2 of The Silk Tales

A NOVEL BY

JOHN M. BURTON QC

Edited by Katherine Burton

This book is sold subject to the condition that it shall not, by way of trade or otherwise, be lent, resold, hired out, or otherwise circulated without the author's prior consent in any form (including digital form) other than this in which it is published and without a similar condition being imposed on the subsequent purchaser.

TEXT COPYRIGHT © JOHN M BURTON QC, 2014

ALL RIGHTS RESERVED

John M. Burton QC has asserted his right under the Copyright, Designs and Patents Act, 1988 to be identified as the author of this work.

This novel is a work of fiction. Names and Characters are the product of the author's imagination and any resemblance to actual persons, living or dead, is entirely coincidental.

First Edition 2014.

Books by John M. Burton QC

The Silk Brief, Volume 1 of The Silk Tales

The Silk Head, Volume 2 of The Silk Tales

The Silk Returns, Volume 3 of the Silk Tales

The Silk Ribbon, Volume 4 of The Silk Tales

The Silk's Child, Volume 5 of The Silk Tales

Parricide, Volume 1 of The Murder Trials of Cicero

Poison, Volume 2 of The Murder Trials of Cicero

The Myth of Sparta, Volume 1 of The Chronicles of Sparta

The Return of the Spartans, Volume 2 of The Chronicles of Sparta

The Trial of Admiral Byng, Pour Encourager Les Autres, Volume 1 of the Historical Trials Series

Treachery, The Princes in The Tower.

FOR MY MOTHER AND FATHER WHO ENCOURAGED MY STUDIES AND GAVE ME THE SUPPORT I NEEDED TO EMBARK ON A LEGAL CAREER

Table of Contents

CHAPTER 1
CLAPHAM COMMON, LONDON 11

CHAPTER 2
CLAPHAM COMMON, LONDON, THE INVESTIGATION BEGINS. 18

CHAPTER 3
CLAPHAM COMMON, LONDON, THE INVESTIGATION CONTINUES 25

CHAPTER 4
SOUTH WESTERN POLICE STATION 30

CHAPTER 5
THE BOYFRIEND 41

CHAPTER 6
THE SOLICITOR 49

CHAPTER 7
THE EX-WIFE 52

CHAPTER 8
AN UNEXPECTED CALL 61

CHAPTER 9
TEMPLE LANE CHAMBERS 68

CHAPTER 10
THE EVIDENCE STACKS UP 79

CHAPTER 11
THE FIRST CONFERENCE WITH THE CLIENT . 84

CHAPTER 12
FURTHER INSTRUCTIONS 92
CHAPTER 13
THE WINE FRAUD 98
CHAPTER 14
THE CHRISTMAS PARTY 113
CHAPTER 15
THE MORNING AFTER 118
CHAPTER 16
CHAMBERS AFFAIRS 125
CHAPTER 17
THE NEW HEAD 135
CHAPTER 18
THE WINE FRAUD PLEA 141
CHAPTER 19
THE FIREMAN'S CASE 147
CHAPTER 20
THE TRIAL COMMENCES 155
CHAPTER 21
THE FATHER'S EVIDENCE 173
CHAPTER 22
THE VIDEO AND AUDIO EVIDENCE 185

CHAPTER 23
THE POLICE AND THE EMERGENCY SERVICES 189
CHAPTER 24
SCENES OF CRIME 200
CHAPTER 25
CHAMBERS 207
CHAPTER 26
THE NEIGHBOUR 215
CHAPTER 27
THE OTHER BOYFRIEND 224
CHAPTER 28
THE EYEWITNESS 231
CHAPTER 29
CHARLIE'S NEIGHBOUR 244
CHAPTER 30
THE NEWSAGENT AND THE BUS DRIVER 253
CHAPTER 31
THE FIREMAN AND THE NURSE 264
CHAPTER 32
THE JUNIOR TENANT 273
CHAPTER 33
DINNER WITH WENDY 281

CHAPTER 34
THE PATHOLOGIST 284
CHAPTER 35
THE BLOOD EXPERT 295
CHAPTER 36
THE PHONE EVIDENCE 309
CHAPTER 37
A LATE APPLICATION 316
CHAPTER 38
THE OTHER BOYFRIEND 322
CHAPTER 39
THE OFFICER IN THE CASE 338
CHAPTER 40
THE FINAL CONFERENCE 345
CHAPTER 41
THE DEFENCE CASE 347
CHAPTER 42
CROSS EXAMINATION 361
CHAPTER 43
THE WEEKEND WITH WENDY 378
CHAPTER 44
THE THERAPIST 381
CHAPTER 45
THE PROSECUTION FINAL SPEECH 399

CHAPTER 46
THE DEFENCE SPEECH 416
CHAPTER 47
DELIBERATION 434
CHAPTER 48
VERDICT AND AFTERMATH 444
CHAPTER 49
THE HEAD OF CHAMBERS 450

CHAPTER 1

CLAPHAM COMMON, LONDON

"I hate that bitch and wish she was dead!" said Roger Wright out loud.

He was driving home to Clapham Common, South London, and his outburst was directed solely to himself.

It had been another long day on the road for him. It was Friday, 15th June, 2012. He had awoken at 3:45am and, after a slice of toast and marmalade and a cup of tea, he drove to his firm's depot just off the Wandsworth Bridge Road. He picked up his lorry and drove the 200 miles to Manchester where he dropped off his load and rested a little before making the tiresome journey back.

Throughout the day, his wife's words to him the night before returned like a bad song. She had told him she was going to cook a roast dinner for him and the children that night, but she also explained that it would be the last meal she would ever cook for him. She had had enough. She expected him to move out of the house in the next few days. Their marriage was over, she had told him. The meal would be to explain the situation to the children, as gently as they could of course.

As he drove home, he thought about his marriage. They had been very happy at the start. He was now 39, and he had met Sheila 16 years earlier. She was 18 when they met in a nightclub in Central London and, after what had been intended as a "one-night-stand" he met her again and soon fell in love. She was soon pregnant and the following year they were married. Within a few short months of marriage their first child, Susan, was born. Two years later their second child, Billy, arrived.

He thought their relationship was a happy one. Sheila had looked after the children and home whilst he provided them with the essentials and a few occasional luxuries, courtesy of his employment as a Heavy Goods Vehicle driver. With the assistance of a substantial mortgage, he had purchased a small three-bedroomed terraced home in Clapham. It had a small back garden and an even smaller front garden, but it had been adequate for their needs. However, the last two years had been very difficult, firstly with Sheila complaining about her lack of social life and holidays, then with her asking him to move into Billy's room. He had not wanted to disturb Billy when he got up early, so he had spent most of his weekdays sleeping on the couch in front of the television.

He had suspected that Sheila was having affairs, as there were signs of her infidelity scattered around the house, suggesting she had a frequent male visitor. He noticed two wine glasses on the draining board one early morning when he had returned from a night of long-distance driving from Holland. Another day he found a pair of her sexy black stockings on the floor under the bed, on his side. She had always taken great care of the few expensive items she had and this suggested a recent event that he had not been part of! Then there were the cigarette stubs he had found. Of course she always denied this, but he knew she was lying.

After this bombshell had been dropped on him, he had driven to Manchester in a daze, he had said no more than a few words to the Operations Manager in Manchester and then driven back still blank with shock and hearing Sheila's cruel words over and over again, as if they would not sink in.

"How dare she tell me to leave my house? She's the bitch having an affair, not me!" He shouted out again to himself. It did not make him feel any better though, but he had to shout to relieve the anger. A driver to his right sounded his horn as he had drifted too close, he answered with the traditional driver's sign and raised his middle finger, clenching his mouth over his teeth as he did so.

He thought about Sheila's offer to make the evening meal. The last thing he wanted was to share a meal with her and the children, demonstrating, as it clearly would, what a failure he was as a man!

His deep pain rapidly morphed into anger and throughout the day he convinced himself that he hated Sheila and he rehearsed in his mind what he would say to her later.

He looked down and checked his watch. It was 3:45pm as he drove up outside his home. Would this be the last time he ever entered his home? No, he was determined to tell her if she did not want to live with him, she could move out and into the home of the lover he was sure she had.

He saw his children by the door, returning from school. His daughter Susan was unlocking the front door and Billy was close behind her. It was a surprise to see them together as he knew his son should have been home first as his school was nearer, and the two children never spent any time together if they could help it.

Roger parked the car and shouted to them both. They looked in his direction and then ran towards his car. He tried to be cheerful as he did not want them to know how he was feeling.

"Hi kids, what's this, you two coming home together now?"

Susan gazed at him with a contemptuous look that only a teenage daughter could truly master, "Of course not, Dad, Billy forgot his key and for some reason Mum's not answering the door."

She's probably with her boyfriend, he thought.

He got out of his car, locked the car and walked towards the front door of the house. He caught a glimpse of a human shape on the sofa through the almost fully-drawn curtains into the lounge.

Strange, he wondered, *why are the curtains closed at this time in the day?*

As he approached the door, he decided to ring the doorbell. *If she is with her boyfriend, it would be best to avoid the embarrassment of the children seeing her with him. Hopefully, he would leave through the kitchen and out of the back door!*

After ringing the bell a few times, he used his key.

The lazy cow can't even open the door to her children, he thought angrily.

"Sheila?" he shouted as he entered the hallway. No response. The children were behind him exchanging childish insults.

He walked into the living room and poked his head round the door. He was surprised to see Sheila there, alone, sitting upright on the sofa, but he noticed her head hanging down and resting on her chest.

"Sheila, why didn't you answer the door?" he shouted at her.

Again, there was no response, and he entered the room and placed his hand on her right shoulder and lightly shook her.

"Sheila, what is the matter with you?" he asked again.

Sheila seemed to sigh in response, as her body gently fell to the left. Roger withdrew his hand in shock and noticed heavy blood staining on his palm.

"What the hell?" he exclaimed.

Recovering slightly he shouted out,

"Sheila, Sheila, are you all right?"

He looked closely at her. He could see a small cut on her right arm, with congealed blood around it. She was wearing a burgundy blouse, one of her favourites, and a mauve skirt. He found it difficult to make out any blood staining because of the colours, but he could make out a few cuts around the chest and stomach area and what appeared to be dark staining around them.

"Oh my God!" he said, more quietly this time, aware that the children were close by.

Susan and Billy were right behind him coming into the room.

"Stay out kids, your mum is …. Not well."

Susan was overcome with curiosity, and she was a stubborn girl at the best of times. She was not going to take orders from her Dad. She moved further into the room and saw her mother collapsed against the sofa.

"Are you all right, Mum?" she asked.

Billy was right behind her, "What's wrong with Mum?" he asked, leaning forward to find out what the drama was about.

Susan had learned basic first aid in Girl's Guide and she went over to her mother to feel for a pulse.

"She's got no pulse Dad!" she shouted in shock.

"I heard her breathing. Quick, we have to phone an ambulance!" replied Roger.

He picked up the house phone and immediately dialled 999. Straight away he was put through to the operator and asked what service he required. "Ambulance!" he cried down the phone, then looking at the cuts in Sheila's clothing and the lack of movement he added, "You'd better get the police as well."

CHAPTER 2

CLAPHAM COMMON, LONDON, THE INVESTIGATION BEGINS.

Roger was kept on the phone for ten minutes until police officers arrived. They were followed closely by paramedics from the Ambulance Service, who in fact arrived first but, as was standard practice when there was a situation involving a stabbing, they waited for police protection before entering the property.

Jennifer Gray, a female police officer, took the children into the kitchen whilst, Ian Battle, an officer who had attended the property with her, took Roger into the small dining room.

As they left they overheard the paramedic Catherine Ford telling her colleague,

"She's been dead at least two hours." Hundreds of questions whizzed around Roger's stunned and bewildered mind as he followed the officer.

Ian Battle had been in the police force for nine years. He was still a police constable and was never likely to rise any higher. In his opinion, there were too many 'toffee-nosed' graduates in the police force these days. They eventually took all the top jobs and, due to the 'rapid promotion entrance schemes', they also prevented the likes of hard-working, honest coppers like him, from reaching the next position in his career structure of Sergeant. He looked now at the blood on Roger's hands and, fully aware that in a domestic situation like this that spouses commit most murders, he studied him closely. Maybe he could solve this murder quickly and, just maybe, secure a justly deserved promotion for himself?

He could not fail to notice how shocked Roger looked but then most people who kill for the first time are probably shocked at themselves. He would try a few probing questions.

"Mr Wright, it doesn't look good, you heard the Paramedic. Your wife has been dead for at least two hours."

Roger looked at him blankly, "But she was breathing when I got home."

Interesting, thought Ian.

"And when was that, sir?"

Roger was trying to think straight. Less than an hour before, he hated his wife. Now all he could think of was that she was dead, he would never see her again. He caught himself realising that at least he didn't have to move out of the house now and could not help but feel a little relieved.

He recovered and considered how awful that selfish thought was. His wife, the love of his life, the mother of his children was dead and all he could think of was where he was going to sleep!

Ian Battle observed the thought processes and thought he could detect clear signs of guilt. Then Roger spoke, "I only came home a few minutes ago with the children."

Ian paused for a moment. There was an obvious inconsistency. He had said he was home when his wife was still breathing. She had died two hours ago, now he was saying he had been home only a few minutes. He scribbled a note in his notebook, "Inconsistent answer".

"But you were here when she was still breathing? Do you think you might have been here for more than a few minutes?"

Roger had no idea, "I suppose it's possible."

This is easier than I thought, Ian mused smugly.

"All right sir, it's obvious someone has stabbed your wife. I note you have blood on your hands. How did that get there?"

Roger looked at him quizzically. "I don't know", he answered, "I supposed it was when I shook her."

Ian looked up from his notebook, "When did you 'shake' her, sir?"

"When I first came into the house."

"Why did you feel the need to shake her?"

"Because she wasn't moving or answering me!"

What is wrong with this idiot, thought Roger, *asking stupid questions, he should be out finding out who killed my wife!*

"Did you see a knife when you came in the house?"

"No, I don't think so. All our knives are kept in the kitchen."

Ian smiled and asked Roger to wait there whilst he walked into the kitchen where Jennifer Gray was comforting the children.

He saw a set of kitchen knives in a whimsical knife stand, made to look like a man who had been stabbed several times. He smirked at it and thought about getting one himself. He noticed immediately that one of the knives seemed to be out of place. It was larger than the others, and although it fitted in the slot in the man's stomach, it had a differently shaped handle. He also thought he could see traces of blood near the hilt. *Gotcha,* he thought to himself, and went back to the dining room.

"I note you have one of those knife stands which looks like a man being stabbed." Ian stated in an accusatory tone.

"Yes, we do." Roger answered him looking confused and wondering what that could possibly have to do with anything, "It was a gift to my wife from a girlfriend of hers. I have never liked it. I don't think she liked me." Roger realised he was going off-point and waited for more ridiculous questions.

"Do you remember when you last touched any of the knives in that stand?"

Roger was getting quite frustrated now. *What is wrong with this officer? It's my kitchen, I'm always in there!*

"I suppose it would have been this morning when I sliced some bread for toast."

"Have you used the large knife today, sir?

Roger was becoming annoyed, "What large knife? I broke our only large knife the other day when I had an argument with my wife."

Ian's smile grew wider as he noted this answer.

"What was the argument about, sir?"

This was too much for Roger. "What can that have to do with anything? If you want to know, I suspected that my wife was having an affair with another man and that he had been round the other day. I got angry and threw the knife against the wall, and the handle broke."

Ian made a full note of this, noting the word, "confession" at the side of his notebook. This was too easy, he would solve the case before the Scenes of Crimes Officers (the SOCOs) arrived and before the Detectives even got here! That promotion was in the bag. He would now go in for the kill.

"Well sir, there is a large knife in place now and it looks to me like it might be the murder weapon." He feigned sympathy and asked Roger, "Do you want to tell me the truth, sir? Your wife was having an affair, and it was eating at you wasn't it? You could not bear the idea of that or of losing your children and your home."

Roger looked at him and nodded in agreement.

"And you just had an understandable loss of control when you killed her?"

Roger looked at him as if he was mad. "Are you a complete moron? What are you talking about? I came home from work, with my children, and found my wife dying on the sofa. How dare you accuse me of killing my own wife!"

Just as Ian was about to reply, the door from the living room opened, and Detective Sergeant Duncan MacDonald walked into the room with Detective Alex Williams. Turning towards Ian, Duncan said, "All right Constable, we'll take it from here. Can you arrange for a police cordon around the house and keep guard out front until we call for you?"

Ian was furious, he felt he was on the brink of obtaining a full confession and solving this murder, and now these "Detectives" were kicking him out and putting him on sentry duty. They would probably make a complete hash of it too, ruining his excellent questioning of the main suspect. Nevertheless, experience had taught him that it was better not to argue with superior officers, and he left the house muttering to himself.

Duncan MacDonald could not resist, "What was that you said, Constable?"

Ian quickly answered, "Nothing, sir. Frog in my throat."

Duncan grinned as Ian left the house dragging his heels. He turned to Roger and said, "Sorry about that sir, our Uniform colleagues are a bit keen at times! Now perhaps we can ask you one or two relevant questions?"

CHAPTER 3

CLAPHAM COMMON, LONDON, THE INVESTIGATION CONTINUES

Ian took up duty outside the house creating a one man police cordon and surreptitiously looking for clues that might demonstrate that Roger Wright was the murderer. Meanwhile, Duncan commenced his own investigation. Although he started with a similar view to Ian, he quickly dismissed the idea. His initial questioning of Roger had established that he had travelled to Manchester and back during the day and a quick phone call to his employers had confirmed his journey and that he was nowhere near the house when the murder probably occurred.

Duncan looked closely at the tragic scene. He had seen a number of murder scenes before in his eighteen years in the police force. Usually they were murders of young men by other youths who due to drink or drugs had only been able to articulate the finer points of their risible arguments, with the murderous use of a knife. This was different. A mother found in her own home, almost sitting upright according to the husband and children and with a surprising lack of blood despite a significant number of stab wounds. The murders he had seen before had all had the look of frenzied attacks but this looked different, almost clinical.

The Scenes of Crime Officers had arrived now and were busy trying to find traces of the murderer from fingerprints, fibres, shoe marks or DNA. Duncan advised PC Gray to take the children to their grandmother's house, Sheila's mother, which was only a mile away; whilst he suggested to Roger it would be better for all involved if they left the house and continued the questioning at the police station. "That will allow the Scenes of Crimes Officers to get on with their work to try to find traces of the murderer."

Roger left the house with Duncan and Alex and was placed in the rear of a police car. Ian smiled to himself as they left. *Well at least they have got the right man,* he thought, *even if they won't give me any credit for it!*

There were a number of neighbours gathering outside the address, drawn to the flashing lights of the police cars and the glimmer of excitement that brightened an otherwise dull neighbourhood. Ian looked at them and was determined to exhibit the full force of the authority that had been given to him. He straightened his back and exhibited his best no-nonsense face.

As the Detectives drove away with Roger, Bill Callaghan, a neighbour from across the street tentatively approached Ian.

"Excuse me, Officer."

Ian took one look at him and immediately decided that he was nothing more than a busybody.

"Move along sir, there's nothing for you to see here."

Bill Callaghan looked surprised at this response; he was only trying to help with what he had seen and was surprised at his brusque dismissal. He was about to complain but looking at Ian's expression, he shrugged his shoulders and returned across the road to his home. *Perhaps the police have it all in hand and don't want to know that I saw the murderer enter the house,* he thought.

It was only ten minutes later that the police car, carrying Roger and the two Detectives, drove into the car park behind South Western Police Station.

Roger was taken to a private room and left for about half an hour with a cup of tea and his grief-stricken thoughts for company. "Paperwork", the officers had told him. They would be back shortly they said.

Eventually, Duncan and Alex joined him again. Duncan gave him his most sympathetic smile as he said, "Are you all right sir. Is there anything we can get you?"

Roger just wanted to go home and see his children. Duncan gave him another sympathetic nod and answered, "Don't worry sir, your children are being taken care of and the SOCOs are currently at your house. They will be finished as soon as they can but these things take time. We know you will want the murderer caught so it's important that they do a thorough job. We suggest you stay with your children tonight at a relative's address and don't return home for a few days."

Roger took the news surprisingly well. Thinking about it to himself, the last place he wanted to go now was to his former matrimonial home with its conflicting memories of happiness and anguish.

Duncan resumed his questioning and soon found that Roger believed that his wife was having an affair, but he did not know who the man was or where he lived.

After another hour, Duncan arranged for Roger to be driven to his mother-in-law's whilst he started a thorough investigation of all the preliminary reports in the case.

He was particularly impressed by a very preliminary investigation of two phones that were found in Sheila's handbag. One was a small phone with a pink cover; it contained a set of text messages to and from someone who was only stored in the phone with the initial "C" and a mobile phone number ending with the numbers 3317. An initial investigation had already discovered that the phone was a Pay As You Go phone, and the purchaser had not given a name or address. The final set of messages was sent the day before Sheila's murder. The first message was received at 4-12pm and simply read, "See you tomorrow at 12 noon, C".

The next was her reply a minute later, "I told you I don't want to see you anymore, please stop pestering me."

Duncan smiled to himself. Now all he had to do was find out who "C" was!

CHAPTER 4

SOUTH WESTERN POLICE STATION

Duncan was not averse to working on Saturdays. His children were grown up, and his wife had long ago divorced him, deciding that a carpet salesman from Croydon in South London offered more than a cynical Detective Sergeant in the Metropolitan Police.

He recalled how she loved carpets and how she seemed to change theirs every few years while the children were growing up. She told him it was because the children were always spilling although he never noticed any mess. It was only in subsequent years that he realised the divorce and new carpets may well have been connected!

Work had proved a useful distraction to a dysfunctional family life then, as it did now.

At 17:00 this Saturday, he was seated at his desk in South Western Police Station looking out over the police car park and thinking about the murder of Sheila Wright. His thoughts focussed on the husband but once his alibi was established, it was clear he needed another candidate and Duncan believed he was well on the way to finding him.

He attended the autopsy carried out that morning at 09:00am by a rather young pathologist called Mr Petrov Labaski. He had been introduced to Mr Labaski and wondered to himself why it seemed that everyone was getting younger these days. Pathologists used to be wizened old men, he recalled, with an offish, and often scary demeanour, spending their days opening up dead bodies. They always seemed to show more respect for the dead than for the living. Nowadays they appeared fresh out of medical school and it was difficult to adapt to this new breed. He shrugged off these reflective thoughts and focussed on the autopsy, after all, that was why he was there.

The autopsy had not taken long and within two hours, Petrov explained to him that he had identified nine separate wounds to Sheila's body, mostly on the right-hand side. Two had been potentially fatal and, according to Petrov, had probably been inflicted first as the lack of significant blood at the scene indicated the victim's almost instantaneous death. Petrov explained that, after the first two wounds, the blood had stopped pumping through her body and the remaining wounds had not bled much.

Duncan asked him to draw an image of what the knife probably looked like. He drew a long blade about 14 centimetres long with a 2 - 3 centimetre width. Later Duncan showed him the knife recovered from the knife stand, and he confirmed that it was approximately the right size being 15 centimetres long and 2.5 centimetres wide and that it could therefore be the murder weapon.

At 12:00pm Duncan had supervised the interviewing of Sheila's children from a video room. They were interviewed for just over an hour each by a female Police Officer, DC Karen Knight.

The interviews had been a typical ABE interviews, the acronym for "Achieving Best Evidence". A trained officer had taken the children gently through their evidence whilst they were videoed. The video would later be played in court and would stand as their evidence in chief, rather than having them questioned by Prosecution Counsel. The procedure had been around a few years now in order to minimise the stress to young or vulnerable witnesses and Duncan thought it a considerable improvement. Of course, it was not perfect as the defence still got to question the witness in court, but it was a lot better.

The only thing that surprised Duncan during the interviews was how composed the children seemed and how willing they were to discuss their mother's life. Both knew that their mother and father did not get on, and both stated that their mother had a "friend" who had been a regular visitor to the house when their father had been away at work.

They had known this man as "Charlie". Billy had liked his mother's friend, whereas Susan was aware that Charlie was a "boyfriend" rather than a mere friend and had been concerned of the effect the relationship would have on her father. Crucially for Roger, she confirmed that she had never mentioned Charlie to him at any stage.

Both described Charlie as tall, with fair hair, and that he walked with a limp. They were aware he was a Fireman who had been involved in a serious accident. They had seen him using crutches and latterly a walking stick to get around. Billy had described it as 'sick' as it had a "fire symbol" painted on it. The female officer interviewing Billy had informed Duncan this was "teenage slang" for "awesome". Duncan had nodded at this new nugget of intelligence, but thought to himself, *God I'm getting too old for this, there's a whole new language out there!*

Susan told the officers that a few weeks ago her mother had "confessed" to her that she thought she may be in love with Charlie and this had led to a major argument between them.

She was not aware how her mother felt now about Charlie as she had not seen him since their argument and had not discussed the subject again with her mother.

33

Billy had been slightly more forthcoming and useful, and Duncan could not believe his luck when the boy mentioned that one day his mother took him to Charlie's flat. Billy confirmed the address and offered to take them there in a police car. Duncan checked the voting register and discovered that 'Charles Holmes' lived at the address provided by the boy. Now he had a name and address for his chief suspect. This was too easy he thought to himself.

It appeared to Duncan that no one was at the address when he arrived, and he decided to wait until the following morning to arrest Charlie. He was still concerned that unless he could put Charlie in the house on the day of the murder he would not have a case but the text message and the fact that Charlie was Sheila's boyfriend made him believe that the case was solved.

Just as he was having this thought he received a call from the front desk at the Police station. A man named Bill Callaghan was reportedly there, saying he believed he had seen the murderer enter the house on the day of the murder.

It's probably some nutter trying to make a name for himself, nevertheless, I better listen to what he has to say, thought Duncan

Ten minutes later, Duncan was in an interview room with Bill Callaghan. He claimed to be a neighbour of Roger and Sheila Wright, and lived almost exactly opposite their house.

Duncan ordered the customary tea and biscuits from a Police Constable, thinking he may as well have a break as he conducts what he guessed would probably amount to a wasted interview. Ordering tea and biscuits was a luxury he could only request from a Constable if there was a witness to interview.

Duncan was introduced to Mr Callaghan, a small timid little man, wearing cheap spectacles, who looked like he had little social life to speak of and no doubt hoped this was his big chance to obtain a few minutes of fame.

Dunking a digestive biscuit into his cup of tea and putting on his, 'I am interested in everything you say' smile, Duncan began the interview. "I understand that you say you saw someone entering the house of Sheila Wright at around the time the murder took place?"

Bill Callaghan held his cup of tea close to his chest as he blew on the hot liquid and sipped slowly. "That's right, Officer. I'm sure I saw the murderer!"

Duncan smiled patiently. "Tell me what you saw."

Bill placed the cup on the table in front of him and sat upright, as far as he was concerned he had important information to convey and he needed to focus and state matters accurately, he did not need any distractions. "Well, Officer, I

35

did try to tell the Police Constable who was stationed outside the house, but he just told me to move on!"

Duncan put his tea down and adopted his practiced 'look of concern' and then in a suitably apologetic tone, said, "I'm sorry to hear that, Mr Callaghan, can I call you Bill? Please, call me Duncan. Some of our uniformed officers are not the brightest. Please tell me the full story; I assure you I am very interested in what you have to say."

With that he dunked another digestive into his tea, keeping it under just long enough to soak through but not too long that it would collapse back into his tea and be lost forever. He managed to take his pen up whilst negotiating his tea and biscuit, ready to write down notes in his investigator's notebook on the off chance something useful might be said.

"Yes, please call me Bill, everyone does." Bill was ready to continue but he waited until Duncan had finished his digestive biscuit. This required the officer's full attention.

Realising why Bill was waiting for him, Duncan cleared his throat and smiled putting the remains of his biscuit down on his plate. He looked as attentive as he could wondering what he should have for dinner and doodling a picture of a steaming lamb chop in his notebook.

"I live alone," explained the neighbour, Bill.

No surprises there then, thought Duncan.

"I am not working at the moment," Bill continued, "I was made redundant from my last job at the Clapham Common library. You know what it's like, so many cut backs these days and people don't seem interested in reading."

Duncan nodded in agreement. *A librarian, I should have guessed,* thought Duncan. *Come on get on with it and let me get me out of here.*

"Anyway, it was sometime between 12pm and 1pm. I can't remember the exact time as I was reading and not really watching the time".

Duncan smiled and nodded again and wrote the word 'reading' on his note pad. He was doodling a drawing of a train next to it. He cocked his head to one side, scrutinising his efforts, and then added some steam, remembering with dismay that all trains are electric nowadays. *Bother*, he thought, creasing his face up in disappointment.

"I was sitting in my living room," continued Bill, "and I was in a good position to see a man across the street. My visibility was unobscured, the lighting was excellent and I had him in my view for at least a minute, so it was not a 'fleeting glimpse' situation," he added.

Oh boy, thought Duncan, *he's read too many detective novels!*

"I don't believe I had ever seen this man before but I noticed that he had a large folded umbrella with him, which I thought was a little strange, as there had only been a very light drizzle in the morning and it wasn't raining."

Duncan quickly looked up from his doodling.

"An umbrella you say. Are you sure it was an umbrella?"

"Well, I'm not sure, it might have been a stick."

"Could it have been a walking stick?" asked Duncan with mild interest.

Bill paused for a second, trying to remember, "I suppose it could have been," he answered.

Duncan warmed to this theme, "Did you notice how he walked? Was there anything unusual in the way he walked for example?"

Bill looked at him, "What do you mean?"

Duncan assisted, "Well, if he had a walking stick, did he walk normally or did he have a limp?"

Bill thought for a moment, "I suppose he must have had a limp."

"Are you sure?"

"Yes, he must have."

Duncan made a note, heavily crossing out the doodled train as he realised his notes might actually be seen by someone else. 'Witness refers to seeing man with a limp using a walking stick, approaching the victim's house between 12pm and 1pm.'

He looked up from his notebook. "Now, Bill," he asked, "this could be very important, what did you see happen next?"

Bill smiled to himself. Finally, the Officer stopped doodling and was interested in what he had to say. "The man used his umbrella, sorry his walking stick, to push open the gate to the house. He must have then 'limped' up to the front door."

Duncan took a note, 'Man used his walking stick to push open the gate and limped towards the front door.'

Bill continued, "I didn't see what happened then because I was distracted by my kettle. I'd put it on to make a cup of tea and the whistle went at that moment. I got up and walked to the kitchen, made myself a cup of tea and when I returned, the man was gone. He must have entered the house, although I did not see this, nor did I see him leave."

39

Duncan smiled and continued writing his notes, 'Witness believes the man entered the house but did not see this as he was distracted by his kettle. He did not see the man again.'

Bill gave a description of the man as average height, average to muscular build with brown hair. He stated he could not make out any further details from where he was sitting and that for most of the time he had only seen the rear of the man.

Duncan thanked Bill for his assistance and was expecting him to go when Bill added, "I ought to say that, about half an hour later, I heard a scream coming from the direction of that house. I wasn't sure if it did come from that house though because there is also a school nearby, and you usually hear children screaming around lunchtime, but I think now it must have come from the house. It must have been that poor woman being horribly stabbed to death!" he looked shocked as he realised what he could have heard.

Duncan dutifully noted, 'Half an hour later, the witness heard a scream coming from the direction of the house. He believes it must have come from the house and must have been the victim.'

Duncan felt that the case was being solved for him! He now had what could only be Charlie, entering the house shortly before the murder. This was proving to be just too easy.

CHAPTER 5

THE BOYFRIEND

Duncan looked at his watch closely - it was 4:52am on Sunday, 17th June 2012. He had had little sleep. He had organised a "dawn raid" and was with DC Alex Williams, three male, and one female police constables. They were outside the home address of Charles Holmes, which was a flat in Tooting, South London. He looked at the other officers and nodded, giving the go-ahead for the raid. One of the male constables lifted an "enforcer" off the ground, a police metal battering ram. He held it at waist height and rammed it against the front door just where the lock was situated. The lock smashed and the door flung open. The remaining officers ran straight into the flat shouting "Police! Police!"

Charlie Holmes opened his eyes drowsily and was shocked to see four uniformed police officers standing in his room, wearing thick black stab proof vests. As he tried to comprehend what was happening, he was dragged out of bed by two officers. "Christ, what the fucking hell is going on?" he shouted.

The officers did not reply, and he cried out in pain as his right hip was twisted in an attempt to get him to his feet, "Bloody hell man, be careful of my leg!" he protested.

Within seconds, he was pulled to his feet with his hands cuffed behind him and two officers holding his arms. Duncan entered the room "Charles Holmes?" he asked.

Charlie looked quizzically at him, "Yes?"

"You are under arrest for the murder of Sheila Wright. You do not have to say anything, but it may harm your defence if you do not mention, when questioned, something you later rely on in court. Anything you do say may be given in evidence."

Charlie just stared at him and then said "what are you ...?"

Before he could finish his sentence Duncan interrupted, "We're taking you down to the police station Mr Holmes. We have a number of questions for you. You'll have plenty of time to talk there whilst officers search your flat."

"Can I at least change and put some clothes on?" he asked looking down at his tatty pyjamas.

Duncan studied the suspect. He looked like a normal young man, and it still surprised him after many years in the force that murderers could look so ordinary away from the scene of their crimes. "No son, we will need to bag your clothes up for forensic analysis. We'll get you something to wear at the Station."

Two of the officers took Charlie downstairs to the waiting police car as Duncan and the other officers started to search the flat. One of the first things Duncan noticed was a walking cane propped up against a cabinet by the side of the Charlie's bed. It was a copy of the one carried by the fictional TV doctor, called House. It was black with an orange flame spreading up to the handle. He smiled to himself in satisfaction as he held it. *From a distance, this could look just like a folded umbrella,* he thought.

He began to search through the small wardrobe and the various drawers in the room, just as an elderly woman, wearing a dressing gown, appeared at the door. He looked up.

"Excuse me, what's going on here?" she asked him.

Duncan had posted the large police constable with the enforcer on the door to stop people coming into the flat and was very surprised to be confronted by questions from this woman who had clearly come in through the front door.

"I'm sorry madam but you really shouldn't be here. We are investigating a serious crime and the officer on the door should have stopped you."

She replied in an off-handed way, "I told the officer downstairs that I might be able to help you and he told me to come and have a word with you."

Duncan frowned, this was a murder enquiry, how could a police constable just allow a stranger into a suspect's address in the middle of a dawn raid? Anyway, he decided to find out what she had to say. "All right, madam, but obviously we can't talk here as my officers need to search the property. Do you live nearby?"

"Yes, next door. That's what I wanted to tell you. I'm Mrs Crawford, Betty Crawford."

She held out her hand which Duncan shook lightly. "Well, shall we go to your house and you can tell me what this is all about."

Duncan followed her downstairs to her flat, passing the constable on the door. He looked at him sternly, "PC Andrews, keep a guard on the property and don't let anybody else in!"

PC Andrews nodded. *Grumpy old sod, the woman said she had important information, what was I to do, send her packing?*

Within a few minutes, Duncan was seated in the living room next door in Betty's house. She had insisted on making him a cup of tea whilst she conveyed her important information.

She entered carrying a tray with a pot of tea, two china cups and a plate piled high with rich tea biscuits. Her month's quota appeared on the plate but she thought it was worth it. It wasn't everyday she could assist the police in a murder investigation, she thought. She sat down and began her tale.

"I woke up when I heard the door smashing next door. I was very frightened until I looked out of my curtains and saw that nice police officer at the door. I wondered when you would get here."

She nodded at Duncan to pour the tea, which he dutifully did for both of them. He looked up surprised at this comment and asked, "You were expecting us?"

"Oh yes, you see I saw the murdered woman's photograph on the local news on the television last night. As I'd seen her next door on a number of occasions, I assumed you would come to arrest him."

She snarled a little as she referred to "him", her neighbour, and Duncan immediately realised that there was some history between them. He let her continue without any further interruption.

"He wasn't always an unpleasant man. He used to be quite nice, but then he had that nasty accident and since then, well, he has become rather rude and morose," she confided sadly.

Duncan nodded politely, wondering where this was going.

"He can be very short with people, he has been with me on occasion!" she continued.

Duncan took a sip of tea whilst continuing with his practiced impression of a nodding dog.

"So you saw the young woman who was killed?" he asked.

"Oh yes, frequently. She wasn't very talkative though, always turned away if you tried to engage her in conversation."

"You said you had some important information. Was it that you had seen the woman come to Mr Holmes' flat?"

"Oh no, that's just part of it. I heard on the news that she was killed sometime in the afternoon on Friday?" She looked towards him seeking confirmation that this was correct.

"We don't know exactly when she died, we are still trying to discover that. Tell me though, what did you want to tell us?"

Betty, paused, took a sip of her own tea and then continued, "Well," she said, "our flats are next to each other, and the walls are very thin, so you can hear any noise."

Duncan nodded, pleased that finally this was going somewhere.

"I don't go out very much, I'm not a busy-body but I can always hear when he gets home. He usually comes back in the early evening and stays in. However, I noticed that although he came home in the afternoon that day, he went out again and didn't come home again on the Friday. In fact, I heard him come home yesterday afternoon at about 5pm."

Typical, thought Duncan, *about an hour after young Billy showed us where he lived!*

Duncan had tried to arrange for police officers to keep an eye on the flat to see if he returned, but he was told that, for financial reasons, police surveillance was not justified in this case.

"Tell me, Mrs Crawford ...."

Betty quickly intervened, "Please, call me Betty."

Duncan smiled, "Of course, Betty. Are you sure he didn't come home on Friday? Maybe you just missed him?"

"Oh no, I remember wondering why I hadn't seen him come home, and I did look out of the window a few times. Also, I never heard any

48

noises coming from the flat, and he does make a lot of noise when he is home!"

Duncan produced his investigator's notebook and made a note of the conversation. "Thank you Betty, you have been very helpful, I'll send a police constable round to take a formal witness statement from you if I may?"

He noticed a look of pleasure on her face, pleased no doubt to have provided important information meriting another visit from the police. Centre stage in a real life murder. She was excited and felt important.

Duncan said goodbye and made his way back to Charlie Holmes' flat. He passed PC Andrews giving him a slight frown and went back in to continue his search. He could not remember a case which had been so easy to solve and where the witnesses literally threw themselves at him, and now he had his chief suspect in custody. This was too easy.

CHAPTER 6

THE SOLICITOR

By 6am, Charlie Holmes was in the South Western Police Station, sitting in a cold police cell. His pyjamas had been taken from him for forensic analysis and he had been supplied with a police paper suit.

He was freezing and sat clinging to a smelly blanket he had been handed with the comment that it was "the only clean one available". He had been booked-in by the custody sergeant and offered a duty Solicitor to advise him, but he declined, deciding to call his old Union Representative, who had advised him to contact a local firm of Solicitors who dealt with Fire Officers' legal work. Although he suspected that they might not have much knowledge or experience of allegations of murder, he knew they would have a great deal of experience dealing with Firemen, and he felt some comfort from the loyalty that would bring.

He managed to get some sleep and was woken up at 9AM with a fried breakfast made in the Police canteen. With a history of working in the Fire Service, he was a fan of a good 'fry-up', but he could not eat anything at the moment and he declined the food, accepting only a cup of coffee.

He was offered lunch a few hours later but, again, he did not feel like eating, and he picked at the steak and kidney pie that was presented to him on a paper plate with a plastic knife and fork.

Just before 2pm, the door to his cell opened and a Solicitor, William Golding, from the company Golding and Sons, walked in to greet him.

William Golding was wearing a casual pair of trousers and an open shirt with a jumper. He did not remind Charlie of any Solicitor he had ever seen on the television or in films. He was slightly taken aback having assumed that his solicitor would be wearing the standard pin-striped suit from Savile Row.

William soon dispelled his concerns by telling him that Sunday was his day off, and he had not intended to conduct any business that day. "My firm has a close association with the Union and I have no intention of leaving a Fire Officer alone in a dank, cold police cell on a Sunday afternoon."

Charlie thanked him for coming and they discussed the allegation. William had spoken to the Officer in the Case, Duncan, who had disclosed some of the Prosecution case. William was now relating what he had been told.

"Mr Holmes, I haven't been provided with much information by the police yet, but what they have told me is that they understand you were having an affair with a married woman called Sheila Wright, the deceased. On Friday, her husband and children came home just before 4pm to find that she had been murdered. Paramedics believed she had died at least two hours before, and a neighbour apparently says he saw a man arriving at the house sometime between 12pm-1pm. That man was carrying a walking stick which he used to open the gate to the property. About half an hour later, that neighbour heard a scream coming from the direction of the house.

Mrs Wright's children were interviewed by way of a video interview. Both of them told the police that their mother had a male friend and the youngest child, Billy, provided your home address, where he said he had visited with his mother. When they came to arrest you, they found a walking stick."

Charlie looked at him in a daze and tried to answer but just stammered, "I, I, I ...."

William sat next to him and tapped him lightly on the shoulder. "Don't speak for a moment, I appreciate that you must be in a state of shock. Let me ask you a few questions, and you answer what you can. Then we will decide whether you should answer any questions in the police interview."

CHAPTER 7

THE EX-WIFE

"Thanks Sarah, you were excellent."

Sarah Montgomery shook hands with her client outside the High Court in London and thanked him for the compliment. It was Wednesday, 7th November 2012, and Sarah was feeling the effects of the frosty morning. She had managed to settle a private family case on the third day of trial, even though it had been listed for two weeks. This had produced a nice gap in her diary which she would now use to carry out some much-needed billing.

She had launched a vigorous cross-examination of the Claimant wife which revealed that she had far more assets to her name than she had disclosed to the court previously. Sarah's client was a millionaire who had been married for twenty years until his wife had filed for divorce, because of a nocturnal habit of visiting his favourite call girl. The divorce had been as acrimonious as any case could be. Both sides had made serious allegations against the other, digging deep in the dirty linen closet, ostensibly to find anything that might be useful in their financial proceedings, but in reality, just to see how much they could humiliate each other in court.

Sarah's client had rejected her suggestion of instructing a Queen's Counsel specialising in Family Law and had insisted that she conduct the case. Sarah enjoyed the challenge and the handsome fees.

She was very satisfied that she had managed to negotiate an equitable settlement between the parties. The wife had accepted much less than she had sought and that was a success for her client, and for her own professional reputation.

Neither party were truly happy though, both feeling that they had been cheated by the other. There was nothing new in that for Sarah, she could not recall the last time she had seen a truly satisfied family law client. It was not to be expected in her line of work and was of no concern to her anymore, provided they did not complain about her conduct of their case.

Sarah was 52 now and was herself divorced. Her ex-husband was David Brant QC. They had divorced a few years ago after she had found out that he had had an affair with an Instructing Solicitor when he was conducting a case in Leeds. The marriage had not been a happy one for a number of years and had drifted on until she became aware of the affair. David had confessed about his liaison, but not until she had already found out by the Solicitor concerned. She had somehow got Sarah's mobile number and sent text messages to her with lurid details of what she and David had got up to in a hotel room in Leeds.

Sarah did not tell David she had found out before he had decided to confess to her. There was, in her opinion, nothing worth saving in the marriage but there was the element of fear about a future of being alone.

During this period of reflection, she stayed one night in her Chambers, Queen's Chambers, in the Temple, crying in her room, when Geoffrey Buckle, a fellow Tenant, saw her, and offered his sympathy. This involved them sharing a couple of bottles of Chenin Blanc and a bed for the night. The rest was history.

She had decided that divorce was the only option. She had not bothered David with the details of her own affair as she believed it had only happened because of his adultery and she knew it would not assist her negotiations for a financial settlement. She may as well take advantage of David's feelings of guilt and obtain the best settlement she could, after all, he deserved it.

David did find out about her affair however, some months later, and when he did he immediately phoned her and delivered a tirade of abuse. She listened quietly and then put the phone down without a word.

Her boyfriend Geoffrey sold his flat in the Isle of Dogs, in London's up-and-coming East End, and moved in with Sarah, in her home in Kent, which used to be the matrimonial home she shared with David.

Their relationship had flourished, though she refused to get married again. Geoffrey was a Human Rights lawyer in her Chambers. He had a sizeable income. She enjoyed their love life in bed too.

Having said goodbye to her client, she returned to Chambers with her papers and sat at her desk. She completed the necessary endorsements on her brief so her clerks could easily see the results of the case today and could process and bill her case accordingly.

She also kept her own records, and was inserting the final hours she worked on the case into a Spreadsheet on her computer, when her Chamber's phone extension rang. It was Anne Holmes, a friend from whom she had not heard for years. They met when they both attended the University College, University of London. Sarah studied Law, Anne had studied Political Sciences. Sarah had carried on to study for the Bar and become a practicing Barrister, whereas Anne had met the man of her dreams and settled down and had children. They had drifted apart and only communicated once a year with the odd Christmas card. Anne always included a newsy catch up letter, which Sarah always found to be self-congratulatory and nauseating.

"Anne, how lovely to hear from you," said Sarah, sounding slightly concerned. "I hope everything is all right?"

Sarah had never given Anne her Chambers number and knew that something must have happened for Anne to go out of her way to find it.

"Sarah, thank you so much for taking my call, I just don't know what to do, I just didn't know who to call."

"What's wrong, Anne?"

"It's my son, Charlie. You remember him?"

Sarah paused for a few moments before replying, "Yes, I remember you writing to me about him. He joined the Fire Brigade and became a driver, didn't he?"

"Yes, but he had a terrible accident in March and was seriously injured."

"Oh, Anne. I'm so sorry. That is awful," Sarah paused sympathetically. "What happened?"

"He was called out on an emergency. It was a fire at a house, people were at risk and likely to die unless they got there quickly. He was driving the fire engine. He had the lights and sirens going when he went through a red light. The trouble was, there was a petrol tanker coming from his right. The driver didn't see the fire engine or hear the sirens and he smashed right into him. Charlie's right leg was badly crushed, and his bladder was ruptured. He was in hospital for weeks. He was only released in early May."

"Oh my God, that's terrible. I am so sorry to hear that." Sarah paused again before adding, "I'm not sure how I can help though, I don't deal with personal injury claims."

"No, it's not that, he has lawyers dealing with his claim for his injuries. The thing is, before he was injured, he began an affair with a married woman. He continued to see her after he came out of hospital. In early June this year she was found dead in her home by her children. The police believe Charlie killed her! He says he didn't. Oh Sarah, I know he wouldn't do anything so evil, he's just not like that!"

"My God, that is shocking, has he got a good lawyer to represent him?" asked Sarah, who was now anxious to help.

"The Fire Brigade Union recommended a Solicitor called William Golding in London, but Charlie's not happy with him. He is more used to dealing with Fireman's driving and employment claims, not criminal cases. Charlie has not seen him very often, and the Solicitor also wants him to be represented by two barristers who are employed by his firm, but I want the best for Charlie and I just wondered if you could help?"

Sarah paused before continuing, "Anne, I don't conduct criminal cases anymore. My speciality is Family Law. You need a good criminal lawyer, someone who is a really good jury advocate. I could certainly recommend someone if you like."

Sarah's Chambers dealt mainly with Human Rights and Family work. There were a few good advocates who conducted criminal work, but they mainly specialised in Appeals and European cases, not jury trials. Although many had conducted some jury trials when they started off at the criminal bar, they were "intellectuals" and didn't enjoy conducting jury trials, which requires an ability to communicate and appeal to ordinary people. They preferred focussing on points of law instead of trying to relate facts and evidence to appeal to jurors. Charlie would need someone who was not too clever, but who could address a jury and obtain their sympathy, rather than make esoteric points of law to a judge. There was one person who immediately came to mind, her ex-husband!

"Anne, you know that I'm divorced from David and that I'm now living with Geoffrey."

"Yes, I was sorry to hear about David, as I always remember you made a lovely couple when you got married. What a beautiful church that was, the Temple Church wasn't it?"

Thanks for reminding me, Sarah thought.

"Yes, well, obviously David and I have some personal issues but we have tried to be civil for the sake of the children. Nevertheless, whatever my personal feelings towards him, I still think he is one of the best jury advocates I have ever come across." *Although I wouldn't tell him that,* she thought. "He would do an excellent job and, if you want, I could ask him to represent Charlie".

"That's a great idea. He's a Queen's Counsel isn't he? That's the sort of representation that Charlie needs. He needs the best."

They exchanged mobile phone numbers, and Sarah agreed to call her as soon as she had contacted David.

She had not spoken to David for some months now. The divorce had been relatively civilised, and she got most of what she wanted out of the settlement, but there hadn't been much else to discuss since then.

She felt a certain degree of resentment that David received the flat in the Barbican as she had been the one to suggest buying that place as a retirement investment, and he had been very reluctant. Nevertheless, she got the house in Kent, and she knew she could not complain. Now she had to consider how to approach David about this case. She was aware that more and more barristers were avoiding legal aid work because of the poor rate of pay. Would David be willing to take on a legal aid case she wondered?

CHAPTER 8

AN UNEXPECTED CALL

David Brant QC was sitting at his desk in Temple Lane Chambers when he received a call at 4pm. He was happy. He had his success in the Damien Clarke murder case in September and was now working on a wine fraud, listed for trial next year. John Winston, his Senior Clerk, had as usual oversold the case to him. He had told David it should last six months when in fact it was listed for four. John had also said that there would be about a 1,000 hours preparation in the case but David had been in contact with one of the Contract Managers who managed the Very High Cost Cases (VHCC) on behalf of the Legal Aid Agency and, try as he might, she had refused to authorise more than 500 hours preparation time. He knew from experience that the case would take a lot longer than that to prepare because it involved reading over 80,000 documents. Appeals against these decisions took a great deal of time, with no guarantee of success.

David thought about the changes he had witnessed in "VHCC" cases over the past few years. They were first brought in by the Government to reduce the cost of the most expensive legal aid cases. When the system first began in 2000, the hourly rates were higher and in order to keep control over payments, the Government had employed "Contract Managers" to authorise and manage hours spent on such cases. It seemed to David, and probably every other member of the Criminal Bar, that "Contract Managers" were employed not to determine how many hours were actually required, but to ensure the bare minimum was paid to Barristers and Solicitors. They determined how much work would be chargeable by lawyers on a case even though none of the managers were lawyers, and none had ever conducted a case themselves. They therefore knew very little about how to prepare a case. Every request for hours had to be detailed, spelling out what needed reading and drafting and why. When the system was first set up, they authorised far more hours than they now did. Due to the recession, and not because Barristers could suddenly read faster, they now agreed far less hours for case preparation. It meant, in practice, he was not paid for all the work he did on a case.

He was content though that he had some work to do now to keep his mind occupied. He had also been surprised to discover that the Legal Services Commission had paid him for the case of Damien Clarke. This payment was made a lot quicker than he anticipated, and he knew his Bank Manager would be very happy to see his overdraft reduce, albeit only slightly. *A step in the right direction,* he thought, and smiled as he anticipated the bottle of Claret he would buy himself tonight in El Vinos. He would invite the lovely Wendy Pritchard out for a drink. His Doctor had advised him to reduce his red wine intake owing to the results of his recent liver function test and accordingly David had decided to moderate his drinking. After all, he was happier in himself. Although he still agreed with Churchill, who had once said on this subject, words to the effect that, "I have taken more out of alcohol than alcohol has ever taken out of me." In reality though, he was beginning to feel that the scales were falling more in favour of the alcohol at present. Nevertheless, a shared bottle of good claret would do more good than harm right now.

Just as he was thinking of how to approach Wendy for a drink, his Chambers' phone rang. He picked it up in a disinterested fashion as there were rarely any calls of importance for him in Chambers. If there was anything useful or important, the calls would usually come through his mobile phone, from his own contacts.

It was Asif, his Second Junior Clerk.

"Hello sir, I've got a barrister on the line for you."

"Thanks Asif, who is it?"

"Sarah Montgomery," he announced.

David felt a cold shudder run through his body and strike hard in his gut. He started to panic - his ex-wife, *what the hell does she want*, he thought desperately! Had she heard that he had just been paid in a legal aid case? Could she somehow know he was about to ask Wendy Pritchard out for a drink? Did she want more money out of him? So many thoughts ran through his mind, and none of them were good.

Within a couple of seconds, he realised how absurd he was being. It was latent guilt coming to its head. He did not owe her any money, the divorce had been a "clean break", meaning neither could come back with further claims, and of course it did not matter who he took out for a drink. She was, after all, living in their former matrimonial home with her lover, that pompous idiot, Geoffrey. He sat up, regained his composure and told Asif to put her through.

"Sarah! How nice to hear from you," he said, trying to sound casual and pleasantly surprised. "What do you want from your ex-husband?" he asked jokingly.

"What makes you think I want anything?" she asked a little defensively.

"Sarah, I cannot remember the last time you spoke to me and didn't want something akin to the proverbial pound of flesh."

There was silence at the other end of the line, and David instantly regretted making the comment. He still had strong feelings for Sarah, he still loved her and detested her, in equal measure, and because of those conflicting emotions he could not help but say unpleasant things to her when they spoke. It made no sense to him and never made him feel any better.

"Actually, David I was going to see whether you would be willing to conduct a murder case, but if you're not interested I will happily suggest someone else for the case."

The words, "murder case", had the desired effect.

"I'm sorry, Sarah that was uncalled for. What's this about a murder case then?" he asked cheerily.

David could visualise Sarah smiling at the other end of the line and indeed she was.

"You remember my old friend, Anne Holmes?"

David thought for a moment searching his memory through the myriad of friends that Sarah had introduced to him over the years.

"I remember the name, but I can't remember anything else about her," he replied.

"Well, she's a friend from my University days and she has a son called Charlie Holmes, who is a Fireman. Unfortunately, he was involved in a serious accident which crushed the right side of his body. Once he was released from hospital, a married woman he was having an affair with was murdered, and he has been charged with her murder. He needs a good criminal Barrister...."

She paused before mischievously adding,

"... and, as all the good ones are engaged in other cases, I thought of you".

David smiled at the phone receiver. Now it was Sarah who could not resist a little dig.

"Ha, Ha, Sarah, that is very funny. You said he is a Fireman, how is the case being funded?"

He hoped she would say it was a private case.

"He has been granted legal aid. I assume you still conduct legal aid work David?" she asked mischievously.

"Oh, I've been known to, now and again." *More's the pity*, he thought to himself. *I wish my practice was privately funded, but the vast majority is legal aid work, like most of us criminal barristers.*

"I suspect I can make a sacrifice for the right case, do tell me more."

Sarah gave him all the details she had and said she would contact Anne Holmes and make sure arrangements were made for him to be instructed. Once their business was concluded, neither could think of anything further to say so they both gave a hurried "goodbye" and put the receivers down.

David's expression changed from polite to sombre as he thought about the unexpected source of this new brief.

Why would she recommend me? I wonder if there is a catch? What is she after?

CHAPTER 9

TEMPLE LANE CHAMBERS

The following Tuesday, at about 10-00am, on 13th November, David was in his flat in the Barbican, contemplating whether to go into Chambers, when he received a phone call from Asif again.

"Hello sir, how are you?"

David thought about discussing the odd pain in his chest and the recent worrying results of his liver function test, but he felt Asif's enquiry was simple politeness and not a genuine enquiry.

"I'm fine, thanks" he said. *If only I could cut back a little on the red wine*, he thought.

Despite his good intentions he had enjoyed two bottles of red wine with Wendy Pritchard last week. He had consumed the lion's share of them, and every day this week had ended in him opening and finishing a bottle at home. His wife had always nagged him about finishing a bottle of wine. "You can put a cork in it you know, dear." She would say. Put a cork in it! He knew she was trying to be funny. He had wondered how their relationship had become so unkind, and when she had become so uninterested in him. He sighed and returned his mind to the twerp on the phone.

"That is good sir, I just want to say, we've managed to get you a murder brief!"

Another brief from Chambers, things were certainly looking up, thought David. Could it be that his Senior Clerk, John Winston, was actually working for him for a change? He knew that John had gone for a two week holiday to his private villa in Spain, on the Costa del Crime - and had assumed he would currently be sipping Sangria and playing golf, as was his passion these days. Had he done him an injustice? Had John actually been busy on the phone getting work for him?

After a pause, Asif continued, "It's a new firm of Solicitors, Golding and Co. and they are sending the papers to you. It involves a fireman who is alleged to have killed his girlfriend."

Typical, thought David, who could not help but feel a little deflated. He had been excited by the prospects of obtaining a second murder case, but when he heard who the Solicitors were, and then heard the word "Fireman", he knew it was the same case Sarah had discussed with him. Unless, of course, there had been a sudden spate of firemen allegedly killing girlfriends and wanting him to represent them?

He noted that Asif was developing certain clerking skills, essential to the success of a clerk, namely, claiming credit for a brief even when a particular barrister is requested. He had already learnt the other main rule of clerking, never accept you have made a mistake and always blame someone else. He was not going to allow young Asif to take false credit for this one, he had to be corrected, in his own interests of course!

"Yes, Asif, I know about that case. My ex-wife Sarah told me about this last week. She contacted me to ask if I was interested in taking it."

There was a pause from the other end of the line before Asif answered.

"Oh, I thought this was a case John had got for you. Must be another case I was thinking about then".

David was tempted to ask, "What case is that?" but he decided to leave it to avoid unnecessary antagonism.

"Where are the papers, Asif?"

"Papers in your pigeonhole, sir."

David thanked him and said he would be in later on that day to pick them up.

At 12:00, David strolled into Chambers, saying hello to his apparently very busy Clerks, each of whom was either talking on a phone, typing on a keyboard or shifting papers from one end of the room to another. The Clerks' room was, as usual, a veritable hive of activity that would have put an 18th century Lancashire cotton mill to shame. He suddenly thought of the old stories he had read of the odd youth having his ear nailed to a workbench because he did not work hard enough. He had a momentary image of his Senior Clerk with his ear nailed to his desk. He soon dismissed the idea and became concerned about his increasingly macabre sense of humour.

He checked his pigeonhole and took the two lever arch files out labelled 'Regina v Charles Holmes'. He left the room and paused outside the clerks' room, wondering whether they stopped working the moment he left, but no, they all still seemed busy, although it was far from clear to him what they were actually doing!

It was time for a strong mug of coffee to accompany him as he started reading into his latest case. Chambers had recently invested in a filter coffee machine. No doubt it took at least a couple of hours' discussion in the Chambers Management Committee before the expense could be agreed, but it was well worth it. *One useful thing that Committee has done,* he thought.

He made himself a steaming mug of coffee and took it back to his room, removed the pink cotton ribbon from around the brief and dove into the papers with enthusiasm.

Murder cases are always emotive for the obvious reason that someone has died unnaturally. Although many such cases involve defendants with previous criminal convictions, it was not unusual to come across a defendant who had never been inside a court before, never mind been tried or convicted in one.

This was such a case and Charlie Holmes was a young man far removed from a life of crime or David's usual run of clients, like his last client, Damien, a crack cocaine addict and woman-beater who had been charged with murdering a drug dealer.

David started by reading his client's instructions, prepared by his solicitors who had already spoken to their client. He had never heard of the firm Golding and Co. and had certainly never been instructed by them. The brief had been drafted by William Golding, the Senior Partner of the firm. David checked the firm on the Internet and noted that it did not have many partners. It was what was known in the business as a 'High Street' firm based in West London. There were five partners in total and the firm dealt with all manner of business, probate, conveyancing, a bit of company law, and crime. It employed two "in-house barristers", who had started their careers as barristers at the independent Bar before trading in the freedom of being self-employed for a full time position in a solicitor's office, forced by constant legal aid cuts, into accepting salaries and a boss.

One was a relatively senior barrister, William Jarvis-Smyth, who had been called to the Bar in 1985. Presumably, he had intended to be the leader at the trial, before David was instructed. He would no longer play any part in the case.

He had a vague recollection of the name William Jarvis-Smyth when he had been at the Bar but could recall very little else about him. The other was a barrister called Jamie Wilson, who had been called to the Bar in 2006. David did not recognise his name and did not think he had ever come across him before.

David noted that Jamie had been instructed as Junior Counsel in the case, mainly to keep the fees in the firm instead of giving them to external counsel. He also saw that Jamie had conducted an appearance in the Magistrates Court and two hearings in the Crown Court and had provided his own detailed notes.

David's instructions were reasonably detailed, which was becoming increasingly rare in criminal cases these days.

The case had all the hallmarks of a tragic one with many lives destroyed in what was probably a few short frenzied minutes.

As was his practice, he began by reading the Prosecution papers.

He read a statement from the father and the transcripts of the ABE interview of the children. He also read the transcript of the 999 call made by Roger Wright to the police and the ambulance service. The latter made harrowing reading with the voices of the children in the background being transcribed, trying to revive their mother.

He noted the statement of PC Ian Battle who had entered the address first and the comments of the paramedic, Catherine Ford, who had said that Sheila had been dead for over two hours, placing her death sometime before 2pm.

A flurry of police officers then arrived on the scene and searched the house whilst the Scenes of Crime Officers (SOCO) came in and took photographs, fingerprints and swabs for DNA analysis.

David read through their evidence relatively quickly, knowing from experience that they would list everything seen, most of which was irrelevant.

He read on, as the papers disclosed the investigation that had been carried out by the Police.

He noted that the neighbours had been contacted and provided interesting background information about the household.

The nearest neighbour, Abigail Richards, was a close friend and told the police that, about a year before her death, Sheila had confided to her that her marriage was over and that she and Roger slept in separate rooms. Abigail said that Sheila also told her that, in the last year, she had had two boyfriends, both younger than her and both were exciting and virile lovers.

She had told her that there was a fireman who she was very fond off. He was very strong and she saw him at least twice a week. She had said very little about the other boyfriend so Abigail had assumed that she was not very serious about him.

Abigail's statement went on to explain how she had been told by Sheila that both men gave her money to buy clothes and jewellery, and this had continued until the fireman had had a serious accident on the way to an emergency call. Sheila had told Abigail that she was devastated by this and had visited the hospital daily, claiming to be his elder sister.

This was confirmed by police when they visited the hospital and took a statement from Nurse Mary Young. She had been on duty at the hospital when Charlie was admitted. She had noticed visits from his "sister", Sheila Wright. She had seen how affectionate they were together and had not believed they were siblings. Apparently the visits had been every two days, except at weekends.

Abigail had learned from Sheila, that the fireman had come out of hospital after about two months but, because of the serious injuries to his right leg and bladder, he had to walk with the aid of a crutch and later a walking stick.

Sheila had told her that because of his serious injuries, sex had become impossible, a distant memory to both of them, though she had continued to see the other boyfriend who had satisfied those needs,

Abigail had never seen Sheila with either man and Sheila had not discussed either man with Abigail recently, so Abigail had been surprised to hear Sheila on the phone to one of the men, the day before her murder. She had been in her garden when she heard Sheila in her kitchen, talking on the phone at about 3:30pm. She did not catch the whole conversation, but believed she had heard Sheila say, "I've told you, I've had enough, I don't want to see you again."

Noticeably she stated in her witness statement, "I believe she used the name "Chas" but I'm not sure."

On the morning of the murder, Abigail had been in the back garden at about 09:30, when Sheila spoke to her over the garden fence. Sheila told her she was going to cook a roast meal that night for the family and needed a carving knife as her husband had accidentally broken the handle of hers. Abigail had gone and collected one and gave it to Sheila. She never saw Sheila, or the knife again and was horrified to hear that the police thought that her knife had been used as the murder weapon.

A knife had been found in a knife rack shaped like a man with a number of slots for different sized knives. It looked like a man who had been stabbed several times. It was noticeable to police though that one knife was did not match the set and a close view of that one revealed minute traces of blood and skin. This was sent for DNA analysis and found to come from the deceased, Sheila. It had also been seen by the pathologist, Mr Petrov Labaski, who carried out the post mortem, and he confirmed that it had the right dimensions and could be the murder weapon.

The police found two mobile phones at Sheila's address. Both belonged to her. They checked the numbers and discovered they were "pay as you go phones", with no subscriber details recorded.

They noted the last two text messages on one of her phones were received and sent the day before her murder, indicating that "C" was going to visit her, but that she did not want a visit.

After four hours of reading, David decided to take a rest and left Chambers to buy a sandwich.

He had a brief stroll around the Temple to clear his head, before he decided to return to Chambers. He took the time to think thought about his work and life in general before his thoughts returned to the Charlie Holmes papers.

Presumably the Prosecution would build a case based upon the fact that Charlie had been seriously injured and could no longer perform in the bedroom and so Sheila had got bored of him and decided to finish the relationship. It was likely to be their case that he went to her home, as he had in the past, and killed her as a result of his sexual frustration and her rejection.

So far, the Prosecution case looked like a circumstantial one, and a strong one at that. David began to think that, unless there was some evidence to shift the blame away from Charlie Holmes, it may be in his client's best interests to plead guilty and get the maximum credit and reduction in sentence possible.

CHAPTER 10

THE EVIDENCE STACKS UP

David returned to Chambers after strolling past the Temple Church. He paused outside its iron embossed gates and, for a moment, images of his own wedding there, to Sarah, came to mind. *Why am I thinking of her? I've walked past this church thousands of times since our wedding and never given it a second's thought! Why now?*

He recalled how beautiful Sarah had looked that day as she emerged from a white Rolls Royce, which had drawn up outside the Church in the courtyard, having only just negotiated the archway from Kings Bench Walk.

He continued to walk to chambers, trying to dismiss these foolish memories. Those days were long gone and he felt he should have moved on by now and got used to being alone. After-all, he could now immerse himself snugly into his new case and forget thoughts of a romance which had died years ago.

He returned gratefully to his papers and the sordid world of murder.

Throwing away the remains of a tasteless ham and mustard sandwich he had purchased from Fleet Street, he began to focus and read a statement from a friend of Charlie's, a chap called James Bevan, also a fireman. James confirmed that 'Charlie' had told him about Sheila before the accident and that he had strong feelings for her. He had even told him that he wanted her to divorce her husband and marry him. However, after the accident, Charlie had told him that Sheila had become cold and distant towards him and felt it was because he could not have sex with her.

A few pages on, he came across the statement of William Callaghan. He read how his house was almost directly opposite Sheila's address, and he was home the day she was murdered and believed he had seen the murderer sometime between 12-1pm that day. David noted the reference to a man carrying a walking stick and how the man had used it to push the gate open. Mr Callaghan was sure that this was the murderer because he heard a scream from the direction of the house about half an hour later!

Reading on, David came across a statement from a man called, Ashiq Ali, the owner of a newsagent near Charlie Holme's flat. Police had discovered that one of Sheila's 'Pay as you Go' phones, had been topped up with credit on the very day of her death. Ashiq Ali confirmed that he had sold a "top up voucher" that day to a man he recognised. It had been purchased at 10:37am, by a young man using a walking stick.

The police had checked the telephone evidence and found that Sheila had used the top up card at 11:35am.

Just in case the point was not suitably made, Mr Ali produced a credit card slip which showed that the man purchasing the top up voucher had used a credit card in the name Charlie Holmes.

David was wondering just how much stronger this case could get when he came across a statement from John Richardson, a bus driver who drove the 155 bus between Tooting and Clapham Junction. John had remembered a young man with a walking stick get on his bus in Tooting at about 10:50am on the day of the murder.

His bus was fitted with CCTV, and he had been shown a video of what was obviously Charlie Holmes getting on the bus. He recalled the man because, as could be seen on the CCTV, he was using his phone when he boarded the bus and the man had seemed agitated and was quite rude. The CCTV showed the man getting off the bus in the Clapham Common area at 11:12am. He later saw the man get back on his bus in the same area a few hours later.

The CCTV showed him boarding the same bus at 2:22pm. A map had been produced by the prosecution that showed that the stop he got off and the stop he got back on were the nearest bus stops to Sheila's home.

82

David next read the statement of Betty Crawford, Charlie Holmes' neighbour, who mentioned that she had seen Charlie with the victim on a number of occasions. She noted that since he came out of hospital he had stayed in his flat every night. The only night he had stayed away, was the night Sheila was killed.

It was time for another coffee before David read on in the case statements. Things were not looking any better for Charlie Holmes.

The next set of statements all concerned Charlie's 'Pay as You Go' phone. His phone had been taken from him on arrest. There was a SIM card in the phone, and telephone records had been obtained for that SIM. The police expert had managed to find the phone's unique IMEI number and had found that no calls were made using that SIM card on 15th June 2012 until 8pm. The case statement pointed out the inconsistency in the evidence here. The bus CCTV showed Charlie Holmes boarding the bus, apparently using a phone that looked like the one recovered from him on his arrest. If it was the same phone then, clearly, he had been using a different SIM card which had not been found by police when his property was searched. There was apparently a corruption in the phone's software that had meant the phone number of the other SIM card was not recorded in its memory.

David moved on to the pathologist's statement. Mr Petrov Labaski detailed his qualifications and experience. He listed the usual details of an autopsy, the weight of various organs, the absence of any medical condition that could have caused or contributed to death and then he listed the injuries he found. There were no classic defence wounds such as injuries to the hands or forearms. This suggested that Sheila had died quickly, before she had time to realise she was being attacked. The nine wounds he found were inflicted to the right-hand side of her body, most of them penetrating in a downwards angle to the right. He considered that the likely scenario was that she was seated on the sofa when she was attacked by an individual sitting on her right hand side. The position and angle of the injuries suggested that the assailant was right-handed.

The knife found wrongly placed in the knife rack, had been sent for DNA analysis. There were minute traces of blood and tissue on the blade and these matched the profile of Sheila. No DNA was found on the handle though, which David thought surprising, as everything else pointed to his client being the murderer.

CHAPTER 11

THE FIRST CONFERENCE WITH THE CLIENT

A week later, on Tuesday 20th November 2012 at 2pm, David was queuing up with other legal visitors at the security desk at the Visitor Centre in Belmarsh Prison. He signed in and was given a security pass. He sat down at a table and waited for his solicitor and junior counsel to arrive.

David had read all the Prosecution papers now and noted that Charlie had not answered any questions in an interview when he was questioned by the police after his arrest.

A draft proof of evidence had been prepared by William Golding, setting out some basic details about Charlie's background, but not going into much detail about the murder allegation. He accepted he knew Sheila, that they had an affair and that he loved her. He denied that there had been any problems in their relationship. Of course, there had been the odd argument, but nothing major and she had never suggested that she did not want to see him.

He stated that the texts sent to and from her phone the day before her murder, were not to him and he did not know who "C" was.

In his proof, Charlie claimed that he had not seen her that day. She had asked him to get a top up for her phone, and he purchased one for her. On the morning of 15th June 2012 he had used his phone to contact her and send the details of the top up vouchers to her so she could use them to top up her phone.

He accepted he caught the bus that day but stated that he had not been going to her home. It was not him who entered through her gate that day using a walking stick, even though he accepted that he did use a walking stick. He was adamant he had not killed her, on the contrary, he loved her and wanted to marry her.

William Golding and Jamie Wilson arrived and after exchanging a few pleasantries, they had coffee together. David used the time to ask what Charlie Holmes was like as a person, and a client. William Golding replied, "Charlie is a nice chap. Obviously he was badly injured in the crash, and it has affected him both physically and undoubtedly mentally. He comes across as lacking in confidence and, obviously, being charged with murder has made him depressed. but he seems genuine to me. I don't think he committed this murder, what do you say Jamie?"

Jamie Wilson looked taken aback by being asked such a direct question. David realised that this conversation had clearly not been pre-planned by them to impress him.

Jamie swallowed and paused before answering, perhaps his training at the independent Bar had made him a little more cynical that William Golding. "Charlie does come across as a decent individual, but, of course, he does face a number of problems in this case."

So you think he is guilty, David thought to himself.

David smiled at them both and then asked a number of questions about the case. He finally turned to the question of the no-comment interview. "William, you were present at the interview and obviously you advised him to make no comment. What was the reason for that in this case?"

William frowned, "Why, do you think it was the wrong advice?"

David smiled his best, 'of course not smile'. "No, I'm sure it was the right advice, all I want to know is why you gave him that advice."

William returned the smile. "Of course, I understand. I saw Charlie on a Sunday a few hours after his arrest. He had clearly not been in a police cell before, and he was in a state of shock. He told me he didn't know Sheila was dead until the police told him." William continued, "He was also a little vague on details, understandably, considering the state he was in at that time. I decided that it would be better to write a prepared statement simply stating that he knew the victim, had a relationship with her and that they were in love and that he had not seen her on the day she died and had not murdered her. I then placed the statement before the officer and advised Charlie to make no comment to any questions asked. I was worried that if he did answer questions, the police would suggest different scenarios which he might unwittingly accept."

After they finished their coffee, they made their way to the main entrance of Belmarsh prison from the Visitor Centre. It took them at least half an hour to clear through security and to travel through the different parts of the prison, before arriving at the private interview rooms. They had removed their shoes, belts, coats, laptops, and been sniffed up and down by keen and excited drugs dogs.

David and the others entered an interview room where Charlie Holmes was already seated. Charlie began to stand as they came into the room, but David immediately responded with, "Please, don't get up."

Charlie thanked him and remained seated. Introductions were made, and David shook hands with his client. He was not surprised to find that Charlie had a firm handshake. After all, he had been a strong fireman. Also, his injuries would have meant that, for a time, he had to learn to get around using crutches and David's experience of such matters was that people with such injuries develop considerable upper body strength. Unfortunately for his client it was also a power that could be said to be useful to wield a knife!

David treated the conference very much as a meet and greet exercise rather than going into great detail about the case, but he nevertheless wanted to cover a few important points.

"Charles, or is it Chas or Charlie?"

"My friends call me Charlie."

"Does anyone call you 'Chas'? asked David innocently.

"No."

"Good, then I'll call you Charlie, if that is ok."

Charlie smiled and nodded at David. David smiled back and carried on with his questions. "Charlie, there are a few matters I want to deal with at this stage. Obviously, I am going to see you on a number of occasions before the trial, so I don't intend to go through everything today, but there are one or two matters I need some assistance on now."

"Certainly, ask me anything." offered Charlie. He looked like he had not slept well for days but was keen to assist, which was encouraging.

"Well Charlie, I've read all the Prosecution papers, in this case and I've read your draft proof of evidence and indeed your Defence Statement that the Courts require these days ..."

He paused and turned towards Jamie and added, "... and may I say you have done a masterful job of drafting that document. It appears to be full and detailed but actually says very little. I am a firm believer that we should provide the Prosecution with the bare minimum when possible!"

Jamie blushed slightly, but it was clear to him that David was genuine in his praise. Jamie had learned during his time at the independent Bar that Defence lawyers did not like to have to provide Defence Statements outlining what the defence was, as the Prosecution often made substantial use of them in Court. Less was definitely more for the Defence in most cases and it was a skill to be able to submit a Defence Case Statement that could satisfy the disclosure rules and leave the defence open to manoeuvre during trial. So the least said, the better, was the view of most.

"Having read all the documents in this case, it is clear that there are a number of difficulties WE face."

It always helps to show we are in this together, he reasoned to himself.

"There are a few matters that I want to cover now," he continued.

"Could you tell me whether you are right or left handed?" David paused for an answer.

Charlie looked at him quizzically, "I'm right-handed. Why?" he asked nervously.

David immediately thought about the Pathologist's evidence that the murderer was right-handed. *Right, that puts an end to that possible defence!*

"Thanks for that, now there are three further matters I want to ask you about.

Firstly, why were you travelling by bus that day and where were you going? That does not appear in the papers I have read."

Without pausing, he moved on.

"Secondly, it appears clear from the evidence that your phone used two SIM cards. One was found inside the phone, but the second has never been found. Where is it?

Finally, your neighbour, Mrs Crawford, states that you returned home every night. However, she states there was an exception to your usual routine and that was on Friday nights. Why was that?"

Charlie looked at David with concern. *Surely he had some answer to these basic questions,* he thought.

CHAPTER 12

FURTHER INSTRUCTIONS

Silence fell over the small group in the interview room, with Charlie looking at William Golding for guidance. David sat quietly and observed. Finally, after what seemed an uncomfortable age, but was only in fact a few seconds, William Golding spoke to Charlie, "You must tell Mr Brant everything Charlie."

Charlie nodded and after a pause explained, "Okay, well I was travelling by bus that day and it is the bus I would have caught if I was going to Sheila's address."

He paused before adding, "I was on my way to her address, but I never got there."

David was taking a note of the answer in his Counsel's notebook, the standard blue lined notebook that all barristers used. He stopped and looked up, the answer was different to his instructions, but, before he could ask a question, Charlie continued.

"However, I received a call from her just as I was getting on the bus. She told me not to come that day and said she would see me next week."

David now wondered whether his earlier praise for the limited information in the Defence Statement had been misplaced. It would surely have helped to make this point early on. He looked towards Jamie, who had a look of surprise on his face. David decided to ask another question. "You nevertheless got off at the bus stop closest to her address. Why was that?"

"I'd got on the bus, intending to get off there, so I just did. I didn't go near her house though, the bus stop is a few roads away from Sheila's address and I just wandered around for the next few hours."

David nodded as he noted down these comments. "Did you go anywhere where you might be recognised, or buy anything where you might have obtained a receipt, showing when you were there and at what time?"

Charlie paused and seemed to think about this. "I bought a cup of coffee or tea at a kiosk, but I just paid cash, they didn't give me a receipt."

"Might the person who sold the coffee recognise you?" asked David, pushing the point.

"They might I suppose but I doubt I'd recognise them!"

David turned to William. "It's really a long shot after such a length of time but could you check this out?"

William nodded and reluctantly replied, "Yes, of course we will."

Turning to Charlie, he asked, "Can you tell me, where was the kiosk, approximately what time did you buy the drink and who served you?"

Charlie stroked the stubble on his chin as he thought about this. "It's a kiosk on the east side of the Common, just opposite Ingrams Newsagent, by the traffic lights. It was probably around one-ish, it was a man who served me, but I can't remember anything else about him."

David moved on to his second set of concerns.

"Alright Charlie, can you tell me whether you had two SIM cards, and, if so, why did you use them both that day? And what has happened to the second SIM?"

Charlie started to scratch the stubble of his chin again, this time more quickly. "Yes, I did have two SIMs, Mr Brant, I used one because it makes very cheap calls to the Nimbus mobile phone network and that was the network that my mother and other members of my family used. That was the SIM that was in the phone when the police arrested me. I used the other because it makes cheaper calls to other networks, including Sheila's."

David nodded, it seemed a sensible answer to him. "What happened to the second SIM?"

Charlie didn't hesitate, "I don't know Mr Brant. I took it out of my phone in the evening to change it so I could phone my Mum. It should have been in my wallet which is where I usually keep it. The police seized my wallet, I saw it at the station. The SIM card must still be in there."

David looked at him closely. He had better warn him what he intended to advise. "Charlie, the Prosecution are claiming that a text message was sent to Sheila's mobile from a mobile phone ending 3317, and she replied to that text, to that same number, on 14th June."

"Yes, I read that Mr Brant. My number didn't end in 3317."

"What was your number?"

"I can't remember the exact number, but it ended 83. I remember that because it was the year I was born."

"Charlie, it is in your interests that we find that SIM card. We will need to ask the Police where the wallet is and what the contents are. Do you have any problem with us doing that, because the first thing they will do if they locate the SIM card is check the number and then check the calls that were made to and from it and discover the approximate location of those calls. They will also try and discover what text messages were sent from that number."

Charlie looked at him with a look that suggested he was surprised by the question. "No, Mr Brant. I want them to find that SIM card. It might help me."

David smiled and then asked, "Charlie, if they don't find the SIM card is there someone we can call as a witness who will recall what your telephone number was and hopefully have it programmed into their phone?"

Charlie looked down at the table before answering, "There are a few people, but I don't want to trouble them."

"Charlie, I don't need to tell you, you are facing a very serious charge, you will receive life imprisonment with a recommendation that you spend anywhere up to 25 years or so in prison before you can apply for parole. I doubt in those circumstances that people will feel too 'troubled' coming to court to tell the jury what your phone number was!"

"No, Mr Brant, I don't want anyone approached," Charlie replied adamantly.

David looked at him surprised, he decided to re-visit this on another occasion.

"Very well Charlie, can you help me with the third matter. Why didn't you go back home that day? That appears to have been your normal routine?"

Charlie looked down and wouldn't answer.

William Golding now joined in the questioning. "Come on Charlie, Mr Brant is here to assist you. He needs to know everything. He is not here to judge you, and we will decide, in your interests, what to reveal to the Prosecution and the court. You should answer the question."

Charlie's scratching of his chin became more vigorous drawing a little blood before he answered, "I'm sorry Mr Brant, I'm not going to answer that question. I'm never going to answer that question."

CHAPTER 13

THE WINE FRAUD

Charlie had continued to refuse to answer the question and the conference ended soon after. All three lawyers advised him to think about this and to consider that, if he gave evidence in court, the prosecution would undoubtedly press him for an answer and a refusal to answer in the witness box would probably be held against him by the jury.

He agreed to consider their advice but he would give no further information as to where he had gone that night, or why. David returned to Chambers and decided to return to the papers on his wine fraud case, as he was due to have an in depth conference with the client before Christmas.

The case had not made good reading so far. The more David read, the more insurmountable the case appeared to be and the more obvious the client's guilt.

On Thursday 20th December at 2pm, David was in Chambers waiting for his client and the solicitor to arrive.

The solicitor in charge of the case was Jimmy Short, a partner in the firm Rooney Williams LLP, which had also instructed David in the

Damian Clarke murder case. Jimmy was an ex-policeman who had become disenchanted with the police force when, as he put it to anyone who would listen, his seventeen year old son had been 'fitted up' for a robbery by police officers from a different area.

He stayed with the police force long enough to study law on day release courses, and qualify as a Solicitor. Why police officers had decided to "fit up" a policeman's son was not clear though, and David, no doubt cynically, assumed that what he actually meant was that the police officers in question had refused to let the matter go and give his guilty son a "get out of jail card". However, David had never seen any reason to debate the subject with Jimmy who, after all, had been a good source of work over the years.

Jimmy's career change had not been an easy one. His time in the police force had given him an unhealthy disrespect for defence lawyers. Like a few of the less enlightened members of the Police, he believed all criminal lawyers were bent. He had therefore decided to adopt a similar approach when he became a Solicitor and was surprised when others lawyers did not share his relaxed view of professional ethics.

The wine fraud was similar to all other wine frauds that David was aware of. A number of individuals had created the company, Healthy Organic Red Bordeaux Investments Limited

'HORBIL' for short. They had cold-called potential investors offering them the "wonderful" opportunity to invest in fine "first growth" red Bordeaux wines. The sales pitch was always the same, invest in a young wine which would not be sold for five or ten years. Then investors could expect a 200-400% return, easily outperforming many other investments available. To avoid inconvenient UK duties your wine would be placed in a bonded warehouse where duties were not paid until the wine was sold to a consumer. A certificate would be issued, detailing where the wine had come from, when it was bottled, the date it could be consumed and documentation from the bonded warehouse, naming the wine, the case number, where it was stored in the warehouse and at what temperature.

Of course it all looked highly professional, as it was intended to. The problem was the wine did not exist, nor did the bonded warehouse. No one had discovered the fraud until the passage of five years when some investors had wanted to literally 'liquidate' their investment. By that stage the company was in administration and millions of pounds had disappeared.

David's client was Geoffrey Hunter. He was described as a "fine wines" expert who had been arrested due to a number of emails that he had sent to investors in his name. He had been interviewed by Fraud Squad officers and had accepted his solicitor's advice to make no comment to all questions asked.

David had now read the most important documents in the case, namely those that concentrated on his client rather than all the other Defendants. He had been informed by the solicitors that his client had been an "innocent dupe". Geoffrey had believed that the wine existed it had never been his responsibility to check this with the Bonded warehouses. His sole function had been to find investors. He had done an excellent job and a few hundred individuals had invested thousands of pounds sterling into the wines, on his recommendation.

The difficulty was that there were a series of emails found on the company's servers which suggested he was involved in the fraud. One in particular was from a senior manager in the company, addressed to Geoffrey Hunter and quite simply stated:

"Hi Geoff, I enclose a list of potential stooges for you. Good job the poor saps don't know anything about wine! Often wondered what they'd think if they knew the wine they had invested in distinctively lacks a bouquet!!

Martin"

Geoff's reply had been even more illuminating,

"Hi Martin,

Thanks for the list, I'll start working on it soon. These wines do have a distinctive bouquet, similar to a load of hot air!!

Yours,

Geoff"

It still never ceased to amaze David, regardless of the size of a fraud or its complexity or the efforts made to disguise it, that fraudsters frequently had the need to confess and leave a documentary trail leading straight to themselves! Of course, to be fair, the only known fraudsters David had any dealings with were his clients and they had all been caught because of stupidity and greed. He presumed there were fraudsters out there who never made such mistakes and hence were never caught.

Having read a number of other documents that all pointed to Geoff's guilt, David decided it was time to have a conference and see whether his client should go to trial or plead guilty.

His junior in the case was Wendy Pritchard and his first step was to contact her and ensure she shared his views on the case. Bitter experience had taught him that it did not help to have a junior disagree about an approach to a case. A bottle of Organic Bordeaux was shared with her the night before the conference, as he detailed his doubts about the case.

He need not have worried though, Wendy had read all the papers and reached the same conclusion. She had tactfully waited until he had formed his own opinion before expressing hers.

After discussing the case for an hour or so, Wendy had to leave as she had arranged a meeting with some girlfriends that night. David was sorry to see her go but his mind drifted back to the case and he thought that perhaps the case should be a trial. After all, he could then spend more time with Wendy and maybe his relationship with her might develop, along with the case.

He put aside the idea almost as soon as it occurred to him and decided to order another bottle of the wine. At least he knew where he was with a bottle of red.

On 20th December, just after 2:15pm, Geoffrey Hunter and Jimmy Short were ushered into the large conference room at Temple Lane Chambers by Ryan, the Chambers gopher clerk. David was already seated with his papers and trusty laptop spread out in front of him, switched on with and his notes up on the screen. Wendy sat to his right with her papers and laptop. Ryan offered them all a coffee and, after a moment's reflection, David accepted. Ryan's coffee making had improved of late, someone had taught him how to switch the filter coffee machine on and had also taught him the difference between a tablespoon and a teaspoon. Anyway, a conference with a solicitor and client was the only time that David was offered coffee by his clerks, so he felt he should accept. Having taken orders for drinks, Ryan left the room, closing the door behind him.

Jimmy Short made the introductions and David shook hands with Geoffrey Hunter. David took his first look at Geoffrey and the vision confirmed the image he had assessed from the papers. Geoffrey was a large man, about 6 feet tall, 20 stone with a well-tailored Saville row suit and shirt, wearing a large cravat. He had a ruddy complexion with numerous broken veins on his nose and cheeks, tell-tale signs of a man who had enjoyed drinking his product instead of selling it. For a moment David wondered whether he himself might develop such a complexion. He immediately decided he must cut down on the wine again.

Geoffrey was the first to speak. "Sorry if there's a bit of a smell Mr Brant. I was working in my garden before I changed to come here. I was up to my ankles in manure. David politely smiled and thought, *sounds to me like a typical day in my Chambers*!

The conference commenced with David allowing Jimmy to give his thoughts on the case first. It was not wise, he had learnt, to meet a client for the first time and immediately announce that they should plead guilty!

After a few minutes of listening to Jimmy, it became clear that he had either not read the papers or simply had no concept of the weight of the evidence against the client. Worse still, he was probably just interested in squeezing as much out of the case as possible, regardless of the client's interests. His opinion on the evidence was simply unbelievable, thought David when he heard him speak.

"They've got nothing, David. This is a pathetic case and I don't know why they charged Geoff at all. They can't make a case against him and we should apply to dismiss all the charges."

David looked at him and smiled. He would have to be subtle and not show Jimmy up in front of his client.

"Jimmy, I can understand why you say that, but we do have to be realistic about Geoff's prospects. Applications to dismiss are never easy. A Judge will only dismiss a charge if it appears to him that the evidence against Geoff "would not be sufficient for him to be properly convicted."

In deciding whether that is the case the Judge will assess all the inferences that the prosecution will ask a jury to conclude and he will only dismiss the charges if he concludes a jury could not properly draw those inferences from the evidence.

Now, in Geoff's case there are a large number of emails that would cause a judge to conclude that a jury may properly draw an inference of guilt. Of course, Geoff may have an answer to those emails at trial, but the Judge wouldn't be interested in that answer at this stage of the proceedings."

Jimmy looked at David as if to ask him, 'Are you mad?'

David felt the necessity of pointing out the problem emails. He noted how Geoff reacted. It was obvious he had no answer to any of them. Jimmy's reaction was even more interesting. It was obvious he was unaware of the emails but, nevertheless, he said, "We know about those David, but it's no problem, Geoff has an answer to them and I don't think they stop us making an application to dismiss."

David looked at Jimmy closely and smiled. Jimmy lived up to his name, he was only about 5 feet 4 inches tall, though he was heavy for his size, probably about 15 stone. He had relatively long unkempt grey hair and his suit looked like he slept in it regularly. David decided to confront the issue. "Well Jimmy, I'm interested, what is Geoff's answer to those emails?"

Geoff remained noticeably silent, so Jimmy replied to David.

"We'll provide a full proof of evidence in due course, but we need to think about the application to dismiss."

David knew at once there would be no answer forthcoming and the client was being given false hope.

"Jimmy, we have to think about this from the Court's point of view. Once the Judge reads those emails, he'll decide there is a case to answer and the trial will go ahead. All we will do is make the Judge think our applications are unrealistic, which may affect his judgment when we have a reasonable argument to advance. What do you think Geoff?"

Geoff muttered what sounded like some sort of agreement with David's assessment.

David turned to Wendy, "Wendy, do you agree?" he asked.

He would not usually put a junior under such pressure but he thought Jimmy might try and put her on the spot, at least this way she would only be seen to agree with her Leader.

"I do, David, I think an application to dismiss will undoubtedly fail and we ought to concentrate on the trial."

David was impressed. Jimmy had begun to open his mouth to express his opinion but stopped after Wendy voiced her opinion. David decided to move in quickly before he recovered.

"I agree, Wendy. Let's set aside the question of an Application to Dismiss and focus now on the trial.

Geoff, I understand that you are pleading not guilty to the charges. Obviously we are duty bound to explain that if you are guilty and you intend to plead guilty, the sooner you do so, the higher the discount will be from your sentence. It starts at one third of the sentence you would receive after a trial, reducing to 25% as the trial approaches, and then it's a ten per cent discount if you plead guilty on the day the trial is listed."

Geoff took notice, "ten per cent?"

"What do you think my chances of a not guilty are, Mr Brant?"

"Well, I haven't seen your instructions yet. The Prosecution's case is that you were a knowing participant in this fraud. Clearly you were a participant as you were involved in obtaining investors for the wine. The question is whether you knew you were involved in a fraud. Those emails I have mentioned suggest you did know. Of course, I don't know what your answer to them is."

Even David was taken aback by the quick response.

"I don't have an answer, Mr Brant. When I first became involved I thought it was a genuine business. However, after a few weeks I learned there was no wine. By that stage I was being paid a lot and I couldn't afford to get out of the scheme. But, I certainly didn't know it was fraudulent at the start."

David nodded, before continuing, "Geoff, it doesn't matter when you became a knowing participant. That's just mitigation which may affect your sentence. You became guilty of the fraud when you became aware of it, and continued to participate in it regardless."

As he said this he noticed Jimmy's face turn a deep shade of red, rivalling the colour of the non-existent wine, but he remained silent.

It was Geoff who decided to speak next. "All right Mr Brant, "I'm guilty then. I told Jimmy ages ago that I was willing to plead guilty, but he told me you're a good brief who could get me acquitted!"

David decided to use one of his favourite metaphors, "Geoff, I've always thought that barristers are like marksmen, supplied with the best rifles and facing a target a hundred yards away. Give me the right ammunition and I will hit that target every time, but if you don't provide me with the ammunition the rifle is useless and there is nothing I can do to hit the target with it, except throw the rifle itself."

Jimmy groaned a little as he had been caught out giving false hope again. Geoff nodded at David, understanding the reality of his situation. David caught a glimpse of Wendy looking down at her papers trying to hide a smile.

Jimmy felt he had to defend himself, , "Look, David, we all know that sometimes the best mitigation for a client comes out in a trial. When the court clearly sees what roles people played in a fraud and I think Geoff should plead not guilty, have a trial and we put all our mitigation before the judge during the trial."

David looked at him with a smile and thought to himself, *you can always tell which lawyers do not spend any time in a court room.*

"Geoff, it is right that in some cases the mitigation can come out in a trial, but that happens when someone has claimed they have a defence and are then found guilty. If we run a trial lasting over three months when we have no defence we are likely to aggravate the situation, not mitigate it. Large costs will build up which the Judge will blame you for and no doubt seek recoupment from you and you will not benefit from any credit for a guilty plea.

In my opinion, as you are admitting guilt in this case, the best course for you is to allow me to negotiate a basis of plea with the prosecution, minimising your role where possible. You will then get the most credit and reduce your liability for the costs of the proceedings."

David's advice was met with a scowl from Jimmy. He wanted a trial out of this case! Geoff on the other hand nodded at the proposed course of action.

Eventually it was agreed that David would discuss the case with the Prosecution and seek a negotiated basis of plea which would hopefully reduce his sentence.

The conference ended shortly afterwards and two hours later, just as David was about to leave Chambers for the day, he received a call from Jimmy Short. He could tell from the laboured wheezing and slurred voice, that Jimmy had immediately retired from the conference to a local pub, and sounded like he had consumed a bottle or two of real Bordeaux, rather than the product his client sold.

"David, I'm not best pleased with your advice. You were completely negative with the client about his chances of success and now he's pleading to what is a very weak case against him. I feel you forced him into doing that."

David paused, trying to be remain calm and polite. He really wanted to tell Jimmy what he thought of him, but the realities of life at the Bar, namely, relying on Solicitors to provide work, meant he had to be diplomatic. "Jimmy, I have to disagree with you. It is my job to properly advise a client about the strengths and weaknesses of a case, and that is what I did. I only became 'negative' about his prospects of an acquittal when he told me he had no defence and said he was guilty!"

Jimmy was clearly not in the mood to discuss the matter in an amicable fashion and after an attempt at abuse and threatening to withdraw his work from Chambers, he promptly put the phone down.

Oh well, thought David, *no more instructions from that source!*

It was David's experience that it was often counterproductive doing the right thing, and resulted in lower fees and less work, but it was the professional thing to do and he would not be forced to act differently to solicit or keep cases. As he pointed out to friends and family, it had taken thirty years of hard work for him to be awarded Silk, and he did not want to lose his hard-earned title in just over thirty months!

CHAPTER 14

THE CHRISTMAS PARTY

The following day was Friday 21st December 2012. It was that time of year again when Chambers had its Christmas party. A time for all the tenants to meet over a few drinks and nibbles, to demonstrate their camaraderie, discuss careers, bemoan the further reductions in legal aid, the lack of work, the greater use of solicitor advocates and in-house barristers in the courts and the general lack of a future at the Criminal Bar and of course to have a good time!!

David was not looking forward to it. He knew from bitter experience that, if he was not careful, he would drink too much and then remember very little about the later stages of the party, until the memories slowly resurfaced and he would have to compile a mental list of people he had to apologise to when he returned to Chambers in the New Year. *Better not to turn up this year*, he thought sensibly, but he knew he could not do that as that would be regarded as a snub, and it would be far more difficult to secure forgiveness for that, than for a few embarrassing moments which everyone enjoyed.

He stayed in his flat in the Barbican throughout the day and only travelled into Chambers in the early evening, arriving just before 6pm. Chambers had effectively closed at lunchtime for the Clerks to have their Christmas lunch. Consequently, the Clerks' room was not its usual noisy hive of activity but a quiet room.

The three conference rooms had been cleared of furniture, save for a few tables which had been decorated with red tissue paper and covered with bottles of Champagne and wine and various tempting treats. David's fingers twitched as he spied the greasy sausages covered in bacon.

David walked into the main conference room and came across the Head of Chambers, James Wontner QC and his wife, Virginia, both sipping Champagne and talking to a Senior tenant, Graham Martin. Virginia was pointing to one of her latest pieces of art which now adorned the wall in Chambers. It looked to David like it was a picture of a black tunnel. He had never asked anyone about it and did not want to now, so he tried to back out of the room.

Just as he was negotiating the turn, Graham Martin shouted out to him, "Ah! David, good to see you, come and join us, Virginia was just explaining to us the thought processes behind her latest masterpiece!"

David stopped in his tracks, turned towards the group and smiled at Graham. *You Bastard,* thought David.

Graham smiled back at him, reading his thoughts.

David joined the group, "Graham, Virginia and James, how nice to see you all. Don't let me interrupt you, you seemed deep in conversation."

"Good grief no David," Graham fought back, I have detained James and Virginia for far too long, and I just need to go to the Clerks room and check my pigeon hole to see what might exercise my attention over the holiday period. I'm sure I am leaving them both in good hands."

Double Bastard, thought David.

David's smile grew wider as he looked at Graham, "Are you sure you have to leave Graham? You can always check your pigeon hole later."

Graham's smile almost dropped but he then recovered, "No David, knowing me I'll forget. Back soon," he said casually.

I bet you will, thought David.

Graham left the room whilst Virginia started to tell David the inspiration behind her painting. David pretended to listen and made suitable noises when required, whilst he poured himself a glass of Champagne. *I'm going to need a lot of this tonight*, he thought

After what seemed like hours but in truth was measured by the number of glasses of Champagne he had drank, namely four, David was able to make his excuses and move around the room, which had now become occupied by a large number of the Chambers' tenants. He saw Wendy Pritchard in a corner looking delectable in a smart cocktail dress. She smiled at him, and he quickly went and joined her.

She was the proverbial 'breath of fresh air' after discussing the dubious inspiration behind a black hole on the wall. Of course, they could not resist 'talking shop'. They discussed the conference the previous day. It was Wendy who mentioned it first. "David, if you don't mind me saying, you handled that client excellently yesterday. I thought the solicitor was a complete idiot, suggesting that the client plead not guilty, run an expensive and lengthy trial and that as a result the client, as opposed to the solicitor, would benefit from that strategy!"

David agreed and after consuming a few more glasses of Champagne, he added, "Wendy, you are looking absolutely beautiful tonight."

As soon as the words were out, he regretted them. He had stepped over the line. He saw Wendy's expression change, and she seemed to step back looking quizzically at him. He quickly tried to change the subject. "Anyway Wendy, tell me, what you have got on for Christmas? I've arranged to see my children at some stage and my parents in Lancashire. I imagine your Christmas will be a lot more exciting than mine?"

CHAPTER 15

THE MORNING AFTER

David woke just after 9am. He had intended to have a lie-in after the Chamber's party but now a splitting headache, a terribly dry mouth and a full bladder intervened in his plans. He slowly raised his head off the pillow, hoping by gentle movements to minimise the drumming inside. *Why did I drink so much Champagne? Again!*

As he rose from his bed he immediately stopped. *Oh my God, Wendy!* He remembered them falling into a cab and then struggling into the flat after the party.

He looked to his left and saw under the sheets of his bed, a naked Wendy, sleeping next to him. She looked particularly beautiful as she slept, seemingly unaffected by the copious amounts of wine that undoubtedly led her to his bed. *Oh my God, what have I done*, thought David. Will she scream when she wakes and realises where, and with whom, she is?

He tried to move quietly, so as not to stir her. Of course, as soon as he paused, Wendy opened her eyes. He was expecting her to sit bolt upright but instead she moved a curl of hair away from her face, smiled and said, "Good morning."

David knew that this was the time to say something amusing, erudite and clever, demonstrating to her that she had been right to spend an evening with a man almost twenty years older than her.

"Morning", was all he came up with. "Cup of tea?" he asked.

God, how boring he thought to himself, smiling at her. She nodded, yawning and re-arranging herself against the head board. *Beautiful*, he thought, as he noticed her breasts shift with her body under the sheets.

They spent the rest of the morning together, both sympathising with the other as they slowly recovered from the excesses of the previous night. Wendy left just after 1pm, agreeing to meet for a meal later that night.

As she left the flat, David felt a pang of guilt. Was he taking advantage of a young junior tenant? She had just turned 33 in October 2012 and he had attended birthday drinks with her and a few others. He was now 56 years of age, old enough to be her father! What would Sarah think? What would his parents think? What would Wendy's parents think? *God they're probably younger than me*, David did the maths in his head.

He considered the matter for a moment and had a vague recollection from the night before.

Wendy had hooked her arm through his and when asked by Sean McConnell, a junior tenant in Chambers, why she was doing that she had said, in a slightly slurry voice, "Because, he's gorgeous!"

So what if he was older than her. She was not a teenager, she was a grown woman, aged 33. She had been a Solicitor before being called to the Bar. He was not taking advantage of a junior tenant, was he?

He rapidly dismissed such ideas, he was happy with himself, looking forward to seeing Wendy again tonight and sharing an intimate meal with a stunningly attractive woman.

As these thoughts were passing his mobile phone rang. He recognised the number straight away, it was his daughter Katherine. *Damn, I forgot about the children*, he thought. Katherine and Robert were 25 and 23. *What are they going to make of me going out with someone just a few years older than them*, he felt uncomfortable at the thought.

He picked up the receiver feeling more guilty than when he had discovered Wendy asleep next to him. "Hello Katherine, how are you love? So nice to hear from you."

He had emphasised the word nice. He had not meant it to come out sarcastically, but both children still blamed him for the break-up of the marriage and rarely contacted him, unless they wanted something.

"That's not very welcoming." Katherine replied with clear irritation. Her Dad had sounded a little sarcastic. He obviously assumed she wanted something. *How cynical*, she thought, *and how typical!*

"I'm sorry, Katherine, I mean it, it is nice to hear from you." *True, but what does she want*, he wondered.

"That's better Dad. I just wanted to phone you for a catch up and to tell you my latest plans." She said enthusiastically.

Ahha, thought David, *there is it. Their latest plans obviously involve money..!*

"Giles and I are buying a house together, and we are hoping to move into it in the New Year," she continued innocently.

David fell silent, he had met Giles. He was a weak, insipid banker who was part of Katherine's crowd. He had never thought for one moment that his daughter would take the relationship seriously.

"Dad? Are you still there?" she asked.

"Of course, Katherine, sorry. We had a Chambers' party last night, and I'm still recovering."

"Oh, I see." Katherine recalled a few Chambers parties and how her father had come home having consumed copious amounts of alcohol. She also recalled that he had an affair in Leeds with a Solicitor, and she could not help but add, "I hope I'm not interrupting anything, there's no one there with you is there?"

"No, no, of course not." David wondered if he had spoken a little too quickly with his denial.

"Anyway, Dad we are going to have a few people round for drinks in the New Year to celebrate the new place. Obviously we didn't think it right to invite you and Mum together, but we would like you to come round and have a drink with us sometime."

I don't even get to go to my daughter's house-warming. Pity, I could have taken Wendy, he thought mischievously.

"No problem, Kate, I shall look forward to seeing the flat. Anyway, I was hoping to see you over Christmas."

He heard silence on the end of the line.

"Sorry Dad, we have had to change our plans because of the new house. We are hoping to get away for a few days just after Christmas Day, but it will be great to see you in the New Year."

I bet she's seeing Sarah and her obnoxious boyfriend, he thought.

"That's ok Kate. I hope you will be able to see your Mum though?" he asked inquisitively.

"Oh yes, she's invited us round for Christmas dinner. We will be going away the next day, on Boxing Day."

David's mind wandered as he thought of his ex-wife and her new boyfriend spending Christmas with his daughter at the house they had all lived in together as a family not so long ago! *How the kids could still blame me for the break-up I don't know*, he thought bitterly. *How perfectly cosy for them all*, he thought bitterly. *And he, left out in the cold at Christmas*! But then he remembered Wendy and smiled.

"Oh, that will be nice for you all." He could not hide the sarcasm that crept involuntarily into his voice.

"Now, now, Dad!" she warned. "Anyway I just wanted to ask you a favour. Giles' salary isn't as high as it was, he's not getting any bonuses from his bank this year. We need someone to guarantee the mortgage. It shouldn't be a problem. I would ask Mum, but it doesn't seem fair as she and Geoffrey have helped us with the deposit."

And I was worrying about the opinions of my loving children, he thought! *Now my eldest is not interested in seeing me over Christmas but instead wants me to guarantee her and her idiot*

125

boyfriend's mortgage! She knows I can't refuse because Sarah and her obnoxious boyfriend have contributed to the deposit! What a clever girl my daughter is, he thought.

"Of course Kate, no problem, delighted to do so, until Giles earns a better salary…" He paused for a moment, tempted to tell her about Wendy but decided not to. *After all, she might dump me tonight,* he thought, *and I don't want Sarah finding out!*

CHAPTER 16

CHAMBERS AFFAIRS

David's Christmas was infinitely better than he could have hoped had expected. He managed to see his son Robert and catch up over a few pints in a pub in Central London. Robert had finally forgiven him for the divorce, and David enjoyed meeting him. He managed to see his daughter Katherine for half an hour over a cup of coffee, but the purpose of that meeting had solely been for him to sign a Mortgage guarantee form. His highlight was his relationship with Wendy which had blossomed and he was surprised and happy to see that it had proved to be a departure from his annual Christmas party mistake!

In fact, he and Wendy had spent Christmas together, and enjoyed a happy festive season. Both had decided not to trouble the others in Chambers with news of their union, unless it became necessary due to any professional conflict of interest. Both were aware of the Bar Code of Conduct that would prevent them appearing against each other in such circumstances, and they agreed to avoid such a problem and to tell the Clerks if that issue ever arose.

David visited his elderly parents who lived in a village near Manchester, but he only stayed a few days as he looked forward to the warmth of Wendy's arms back in London.

For the first time in years, David felt good about himself. He was always happy in his work, it was his personal life that had caused some loneliness and sadness. He had always chosen to ignore it and find solace in a glass of red wine, but now, he seemed to have it all! He was relatively busy with work, his finances were much better than they had been for a long time, and he had a young and vibrant woman in his life.

It was 4:20pm on Friday, 11th January, 2013 when David received the news.

He was in his flat in the Barbican looking forward to spending an evening with Wendy. They had kept their relationship a secret in Chambers and David had yet to tell his children. The only person who knew was David's cleaner who had arrived early one morning to find Wendy there. She offered Wendy a knowing smile and then gave David a look as if he was a dirty old man. This did not bother him in the slightest. He had long become used to Mary's disapproving and judgmental looks. She often gave him a look, as if to say he was so unbelievably messy, and why couldn't he tidy up before she comes to clean the house! He tolerated it because she was a half decent cleaner, and he knew how difficult it was to find one in this part of London.

David was reading in his sitting room when his mobile rang. It was Chambers, "Hello?" he asked hoping it wasn't Wendy cancelling on him.

"Hello sir, its John, I've got some bad news."

It was his Senior Clerk, John Winston, no doubt freshly back from one of his many holidays. *Does he know about Wendy,* wondered David.

John continued, "I'm sorry to say it's about Mr Wontner. We've just been told he collapsed in the Silk's robing room in the Bailey. They think it's a suspected heart attack, and he's been rushed to hospital."

David's immediate reaction was one of relief when he realised they did not know about Wendy. He then realised he was being totally thoughtless. "That is terrible news, how is Virginia doing?"

"We arranged for her to be picked up from home by cab and taken to the hospital to be with him."

"That's good, obviously if there is anything I can do then do call me."

"Certainly sir, we are calling every member of Chambers to tell them. Unfortunately, we've been unable to contact Ms Pritchard, and we wondered whether she is with you?"

They do know, thought David.

"No, she's not," he replied simply.

"Well, if you see her tonight can you tell her the bad news, please?" John asked.

They definitely know, David thought, wondering how they found out. He doubted Wendy told anyone.

"Of course I will John." he said casually.

A week later David was sitting in a Chambers' meeting whilst the most recent news of James Wontner was being discussed. Graham Martin took the lead, "I'm afraid it sounds bad news for poor James. As you have all heard he collapsed last week in the Bailey. They thought it was a heart attack and indeed he did have a mild one, but that has led to complications and he has had a series of small strokes. He is stable, and his life is no longer under immediate threat, but there is no question of him coming back to Chambers for some considerable time, if ever.

The strokes have left him slightly paralysed on the left side of his body, and although the Doctors believe that he will eventually regain use, they say he cannot practice at the Bar for months to come. They blame his current condition on over-work and the stress of leading Chambers in these troublesome times."

There were many nods from tenants around the room. The general perception of James Wontner QC was that he always wanted more work, but never read any papers in a case. Members of chambers also felt he did not actively administer Chambers but allowed the Clerks to run it, and keep his diary full. However, in the circumstances, no one felt like expressing this opinion.

David looked quickly at Wendy, who avoided his eyes just as quickly. They were trying to avoid discussing their relationship with anyone, even though they suspected everyone knew. He also noticed a junior tenant, Julian Hawker, looking at her in what could only be described as a predatory way.

Julian Hawker was a relatively new tenant in Chambers. He moved recently from another set in the Temple. David had never heard of Julian and had not opposed his application for tenancy, though there had been some resistance from some of the female tenants, who claimed he had a bit of a reputation. Those objections had been overruled by the tenancy committee because he had produced a full diary of work, a large aged debt and good income figures for the last three years, all signs of a successful barrister. Judging by the way Julian was looking at Wendy now,

David wondered whether he should have tipped the scales with another "no" vote against Julian joining them. He then realised he was acting like a jealous child, and he forced his attention back to Graham's comments.

".... of course that does mean that James cannot act any longer as a Head of Chambers. The Clerks did ask Virginia whether we should appoint a temporary Head until James is better, but she was adamant that should James return to the Bar she does not want him taking on the stress of that position again.

It follows that we should elect a new Head of Chambers and in order to have continuity it should be as soon as possible."

There was general assent around the room to this idea as Graham continued.

"In reality the Head of Chambers needs to be a Silk. We have four Silks in Chambers, James who can no longer be a candidate. We also have Bill."

Everyone looked towards William Bretheridge QC. He was 75 years of age and in his time had been at the top of his profession, but the last five years had been tiring for him. He had been given less and less work until his practice had almost completely dried up. No one could actually remember when he had last appeared in Court.

Bill seemed to wake from a deep sleep when his name was mentioned.

"What was that?" he asked.

Graham looked at him, "That's all right Bill, I was just explaining how we need a new Head of Chambers and I was saying how I know you do not want the job."

Bill paused, *what is this youngster talking about?*

"No, of course I don't want the job, in any event I probably don't have many years left in this job, I'm thinking of retiring soon."

A few people politely objected to this idea as Graham continued, "We then have Tim."

All eyes turned to Timothy Adams QC. He had just taken Silk last year and, like David, was struggling to make a name for himself as a QC.

"I know Tim feels too junior to be Head." Graham continued.

Tim looked surprised at the comment, he had never expressed this opinion to anyone and indeed it was not how he felt.

"That leaves just David who can take on the role. I have known David for many years now and I think you will all agree with me, he would do an excellent job and I suggest we appoint him immediately."

There was a round of applause around the room. David was truly dumb-founded. Graham had not mentioned this to him before the meeting. No one had canvassed his opinions. The last thing he wanted was to be a Head of Chambers. He had always likened the role to pinning a target on your back and letting people take shots at you. It also required a lot of extra work, no one was ever happy with what you did and, because the Head of Chambers is self-employed like all other members of Chambers, the role did not necessarily come with an increase in income. Indeed, often it meant a reduction in income because there was so much Chambers administration to carry out.

"Graham, sorry, no one has mentioned this to me and quite frankly I don't think I'm the man for the job. It should be someone who really wants to do this and is willing and able to put the extra hours in."

Graham smiled a knowing smile at David.

"That is precisely why I suggested you and didn't tell you beforehand. I knew you wouldn't want the position. To me we should never trust anyone who wants the job because no one in their right mind would want to be a Head of Chambers unless they can see something in it for themselves. Everyone knows you're not like that which is why you are the ideal candidate for the post."

Almost everyone was in agreement, the noticeable exception was Tim Adams who said nothing but few noticed as David received a few slaps on the back with the odd "Well done!" David noticed Wendy smiling at him. He tried to fight back. "Look, everyone, I really am flattered but I'm not convinced that you have to be a Silk to be a Head of Chambers."

He heard Graham shout out "Nonsense!" David continued, "It is a big step for me and for Chambers. Someone has to oversee a real transformation in Chambers if it's going to survive the next few years with further legal aid cuts on the horizon."

David was referring to the latest idea by the most recently appointed Lord Chancellor, , who had just announced that he wanted further cuts to legal aid amounting to 30% off fees for VHCC cases and about 17.5% off fees for all other criminal cases.

Despite his arguments, it did not seem that anyone was actually listening to him so he changed his tack.

"Very well, I am honoured, but I would like the weekend to think about my decision."

Even Graham thought that was fair and so it was left that Chambers would give David the weekend to think about whether to accept the post. He decided to add just one caveat, "Could I ask you all not to tell the Clerks as I don't want them to put any added pressure on me!"

It was agreed by all present that no one would tell the Clerks. David walked out of Chambers, to Temple tube station and then he walked north to consider what had just happened in Chambers. Within ten minutes his mobile phone rang. It was his clerk, John Winston.

"Congratulations Mr Brant, I understand you were offered the position of Head of Chambers. I think you are the only one who can do the job and I am happy to see you take over the reins of Chambers. Well done sir!"

CHAPTER 17

THE NEW HEAD

By Monday, there was no doubt who the new Head of Chambers was going to be. David reluctantly accepted the role, mainly to stop the endless phone calls from people encouraging him to accept the job. The only call that had been made to discourage him was from Timothy Adams QC who had told David he would take the role if David did not want the position. Like Graham, David did not trust anyone who actually wanted to be a Head of Chambers, and he knew Tim had wanted the role solely to promote himself and secure more work.

As David accepted the poisoned chalice that came with the job, he was determined to do his best in the role, and he could not help but exhibit a little self-interest and think that maybe his relationship with his Clerks would be a better one in the future.

Wendy had spent Saturday night with him and most of Sunday and she had also encouraged him to take the position.

"There is no one else better suited to the job and I'm not saying that because of my feelings for you. After all, your becoming Head may mean we spend less time together, because you will be busier."

She had looked at him with a mischievous expression as she said this.

Hers had been the final argument and presented as it was with a passionate embrace, it had won the day. It was official, he was now Head of Chambers. The question was, where should he start with his new found position?

He went into Chambers early on Monday and saw the Clerks' room was, as usual, a picture of busy efficiency. The only difference was that, as he came through the door of the room, John Winston rose to his feet , walked up to him and put his hand out. "Well done sir! We are all sorry about Mr Wontner's ill-health but I think I can safely say that everyone in this room thinks you are the right man for the job."

The remaining clerks all murmured their agreement. It immediately reminded David of a sketch from the Television show, Spitting Image, which he had seen years ago. A puppet of Margaret Thatcher was sitting down to dinner with her Cabinet Ministers. The waiter asked her what she wanted and she replied, "Steak". The waiter then asked, "and what about the vegetables?". She replied, "They'll have the same as me!"

As if to emphasise his new loyalty John turned to Ryan and added, "Ryan, get Mr Brant and me a coffee. Milk no sugar isn't it, sir?"

David was taken aback, not only were his clerks making him a cup of coffee, his Senior Clerk knew how he took it! *I should have taken up this position long ago*, he thought!

He had quickly learned in life that there was no such thing as a free lunch, or a free coffee and David waited to hear what John wanted from his new Head of Chambers. John followed David to his room and began laying out his plans for Chambers.

"We have fifty-two barristers now in Chambers. The Clerks room are rushed off their feet, and it is obvious we need another clerk if we want to continue providing our high standard of professional efficiency. We only need another junior, no one higher than that, but someone who can take the pressure off Tony and Asif, allowing them to take some more responsibility in Chambers."

You mean take over some of your work so you can play more golf, thought David.

David tried to look suitably impressed by John's wholly self-serving suggestion. "John, I have no doubt there is something in what you say and certainly some would benefit by having a new clerk in Chambers." *Namely you, you lazy beggar,* he thought.

"However, this is my first day on the job and I obviously have to tread carefully before I suggest any major changes in Chambers."

John smiled a knowing smile to him before returning back to his room. He knew a diplomatic exit when he heard one. David suspected he would be back to making his own coffee from now on.

The next couple of days David was consumed by checking through numerous documents that only found their way onto the desks of Heads of Chambers. Missives from the Bar Council about Solicitors who did not pay fees and should not be extended any credit by Chambers, and complaints from Solicitors and members of the public about Tenants in Chambers.

Most of these could be dealt with by a standard letter but some may require a proper investigation by a Chambers' Committee.

One in particular was from a female client of Julian Hawker who complained about his 'inappropriate behaviour' towards her, putting his hand on her knee and making indecent sexual suggestions to her. As she had been acquitted of theft of a gold watch from a jewellers' shop, she told him she was grateful to Julian and did not want a formal investigation but she did want the Head of Chambers to speak to him about his inappropriate conduct.

David thought about the way Julian Hawker had looked at Wendy. Maybe there was something in this, maybe not, but he had better have a discreet word with Julian in the next few days.

The next two days, David looked through a number of other Chambers files, including the rent history of Chambers.

Chambers was located in the Temple which is owned by the "Inns of Court". They had taken over the property when the Knights Templar was disinterred in the 14th Century. Accordingly, Chambers had to pay a rent to one of the Inns of Court. Every barrister in England and Wales has to belong to one of the four Inns. In this case, David's Chambers paid rent to the Middle Temple Inn because of its location.

David discovered that Chambers was a late rent payer and owed about £50,000 to the Inn for reasons that were not clear to him. More worryingly, the Inn was pressing for payment. The more he delved, the more he discovered that Chamber's finances were not as healthy as he had been led to believe and one of his upcoming duties was to meet the Treasurer of the Middle Temple to discuss rent payments. He had known nothing about Chamber's financial position as it had always been represented as being healthy to

Chambers by James Wontner and the Chambers' Treasurer.

By Friday, David was thoroughly regretting his decision to accept the role of Head of Chambers. He had not been able to do any further reading on the Charlie Holmes' case and had felt he was spending all of his time dealing with other peoples' problems and receiving no thanks for it.

He had spoken to Julian Hawker who denied the allegation from his female client and accused David of over-reacting and wasting his time on such nonsense!

David sat in his room sipping a hot cup of coffee. He had made it himself. He looked around the room at the stacks of Chambers files which he had been given to consider. Employment files, bank statements and files on tenants and their rent payments. All needed immediate attention. He looked at them wondering where to start, and could not help but think, *I do hope that James Wontner QC makes a full recovery and wants this God-forsaken job back*!

CHAPTER 18

THE WINE FRAUD PLEA

The following Monday was the date fixed for the Wine fraud hearing. The case was originally fixed in the picturesque Sussex town of Lewes, famous for its castle, the site of a medieval battle and its real ale brewery, not necessarily in that order.

David always enjoyed a visit to Lewes, its old streets, second hand book shops, which sold first editions and books that were no longer in print, and there were good restaurants in the centre of the town. Sadly that was not to be this time as he was informed on Wednesday that the Judge would be sitting in the Court's annex, a few miles further south in Hove, near Brighton, situated by the sea like its more famous neighbour.

Although Hove was not a long journey for David, he had agreed to have a conference at 9-00am and so he decided to stay in a local hotel. He would enjoy a lie-in and a cooked breakfast. This would no doubt reduce the stress levels of a case where the client said he was guilty and wanted to plead guilty and yet the Solicitor was sending him messages instructing him that the client should plead not guilty and David should "man-up", whatever that meant.

After checking the internet David found the "Brighton Seaview Hotel" which was located on the front. He would enjoy the delights of a sea view, a spacious and clean double room and breakfast, all for the reasonable sum of £100.

He travelled on Sunday afternoon by train from London Victoria. Of course, as he should have known, the Rail company had chosen that Sunday to carry out engineering works on the Brighton line. His train took several detours and the journey took almost twice as long as normal. To make matters worse, the train was incredibly crowded with just one broken toilet and no buffet bar available.

Nevertheless, he arrived at the hotel at 4 pm and checked in within a couple of minutes. His room was on the third floor and did have a sea view, if he peered through the bird excrement that was splattered across his window and looked like it had been there since the hotel was built. *Never mind,* he thought, *they're bound to provide a good evening meal.*

At 6pm, he left his room for a stroll along the sea front, and, as he left he asked the hotel manager whether he could provide an evening meal. He was met with a stony expression by the manager, who looked at him as if he had asked for a five course gourmet meal with dancing girls and a Thai massage.

Eventually the man replied,

"We could do you a cheese toastie."

David stared at the manager thinking, *you have got to be joking!* He politely declined the offer of this culinary delight and decided to walk around the deserted streets of Hove to find a half decent meal. He passed several take-aways and was tempted by a kebab in a local Turkish restaurant, before he arrived back where he started, finding a hotel practically next door to his. There he devoured a tasty piece of Red Mullet and Crayfish risotto with a couple of glasses of Pinot Grigio. A feeling of contentment returned to him as he sat back after his meal and waited for his bill.

He returned to his room at about 8-30pm to prepare his case for the next day.

He was making progress when at 10-15pm he became aware of a dripping sound. He assumed he had left a tap on in the en-suite bathroom but after a quick check and a glance across the ceiling, he rapidly became aware that he had a much bigger problem. Looking up he saw a large wet stain, and noticed water dripping from his ceiling onto the carpet.

Great, he thought, never one to underestimate his plight, *I came all this way tonight for a stress-free evening, and now I am in a room where the ceiling is in danger of caving in on me.* A quick complaint to the manager met with a response to the effect that this always happened in that room when someone showered in the room above. The manager promised that it would stop soon, but David was in no mood to endure more dripping and insisted on being moved to another room. He was told the only other room available was in the basement where he would have to trade a sea view for a view of a brick wall. Balancing his limited options he chose a dry room rather than the indoor pool his room was beginning to resemble.

He retired to bed deciding this would be his last visit to the Brighton Seaview Hotel. In future he would stay in the Barbican and get up two hours earlier on the day of a hearing.

In the morning, he awoke early and opened his curtains to see the brick wall. He noticed that if he stood on his toes he could just catch a glimpse of the grey-blue sea through a large crack in the outside wall. He showered and dressed and hurried upstairs for breakfast. He was looking forward to a freshly cooked fry-up, but it was slightly marred by the hotel manager stating that all the fried eggs had to have hard yokes for "health regulation reasons". David decided it was not worth arguing over the intricacies of health regulations as they affect egg yokes, and opted for a coffee with brown toast and marmalade.

At 9am David arrived at Court, feeling a little tired, miserable and hungry. It did not assist his mood that the client, who lived locally, did not arrive until 9-35pm in the company of Jimmy Short.

The first twenty minutes were a repeat of the previous conference, with Jimmy insisting that Geoffrey should fight the case. The fact that Jimmy's firm would earn more money if he fought it rather than if he pleaded guilty, was of course not an issue.

However, Geoffrey Hunter would not change his mind and announced that he was pleading guilty and wanted to get it over with. With that, Jimmy Short gave an involuntary snort, looked daggers at David before walking off and out of the Court building.

David went through the written basis of plea with Geoffrey which he had negotiated with prosecuting counsel and which minimised Geoffrey's role in the fraud. They then went into Court 4 and Geoffrey pleaded guilty, and the Judge accepted the basis of plea and would sentence on that basis. Geoffrey was bailed to a date in the future, when the other Defendants were expected to be sentenced after their trials had been conducted.

David left the Court satisfied. He knew that Jimmy Short would no doubt have something to say later about the 'terrible injustice' of the day's events and David's 'poor representation of an innocent man.' *Perhaps he will report me to my*

Head of Chambers, he thought with a wide grin creeping across his face.

CHAPTER 19

THE FIREMAN'S CASE

During the following week David put aside Chambers affairs, save for seeing Wendy a couple of times!

He was concentrating now on the Charlie Holmes' case which was due to start on Monday 4th February 2013. Further evidence had been served by the Prosecution that indicated that Charlie's DNA had been found on another knife handle in the knife rack, and he needed to know if there was any explanation for this.

He arranged a visit to Belmarsh Prison through the Solicitors for the Friday before the trial was due to start. When informed about the DNA Charlie volunteered that he had been to the address a few days before the murder and could have touched the knife then though he could not remember doing so. It was clearly a possibility, so David did not pursue the matter further.

David put pressure on Charlie to tell him where he had gone the night Sheila died, but he still would not say. He said he would decide during the trial whether to give evidence or not and if he did, he would decide then whether he would answer that question.

Charlie did maintain that he was not guilty of the murder and he had not visited Sheila the day she was murdered, even though he had been on the way to see her when she cancelled the visit. David left the conference having learned little more and disappointed that Charlie would not volunteer more information. He reflected that Defendants rarely help themselves, and supposed that that must be why barristers exist.

Monday came and David arrived early at the Old Bailey to find that Jamie was already there, waiting outside the building and nervously inhaling smoke and nicotine into his eager lungs. David was much calmer and he called out, "Hello Jamie! All ready for the big day?"

Jamie gave a weak smile, "I think so Mr Brant." He took another draw on his cigarette before discarding it and added, "Anne Holmes, Charlie's mother is here, across the road in a café. As she's not allowed in the main building and has to watch the trial from the public gallery, she asked if she could have a word with you before you go into Court?"

David returned the smile with almost the same degree of enthusiasm as Jamie's. He hated meeting client's relatives. Understandably, they brought their emotions to a case. They were incapable of looking objectively at the evidence and such meetings were usually a waste of time and detracted him from his preparation. Nevertheless, he had no alternative but to meet her, he knew that in her position he would want to see her son's barrister before the trial.

He told Jamie to bring her across the road and within seconds, Anne Holmes appeared at his side.

David held out his hand, "Mrs Holmes it is nice to meet you, I just wish we could meet in better circumstances."

She looked at him strangely, "We have met before David, at your wedding to Sarah!"

"Of course we did, I'm sorry." He had completely forgotten he had met her before at the wedding, but it was over 25 years ago and he did not recognise her at all.

"Anyway David, thank you so much for taking on Charlie's case. I feel so much happier now that you are involved. I think Charlie has a real chance of getting justice now."

David nodded, "Thank you, Anne, I know how difficult this must be for you, rest assured we will do our best for Charlie."

After a few more words, David entered the Bailey with Jamie. After robing, they made their way to the cells. As was usual at the Bailey they had to book a time slot to see their client, and they had arrived early at 9am for that purpose. Nothing further was forthcoming from Charlie and so, after half an hour, David and Jamie went to the Bar Mess on the fifth floor for coffee and a cooked breakfast.

"The bloods flowing too freely in my veins at the moment, so I need an intake of cholesterol," David joked.

Jamie clearly had a limited sense of humour as he nodded as if this made perfect sense to him.

David consumed his traditional, first day of trial, Bailey breakfast including a freshly fried egg with a runny yolk (unlike in his Hove hotel) and not so freshly made cold bacon. He chose a seat on one of the benches nearest the serving area. As he ate he noted how nervous Jamie appeared. Jamie then volunteered, "I've never conducted a trial in the Bailey before."

David finished off a slice of bacon, and wondered how they always managed to serve it cold. "Don't worry Jamie, I'm not expecting to keel over yet despite eating this veritable feast, so you shouldn't be called on to do much in this trial."

Jamie smiled and said thanks and appeared visibly relieved. David was tempted to say, *I shall only want you to cross examine the first five witnesses,* but then he thought Jamie would probably have a heart attack, so he just nodded and smiled back.

"There is one subject you can help me on. The Prosecution has finally allowed us access to the unused material relating to the phone evidence in this case. As you know, up to this stage, they have claimed that it is not relevant and is not disclosable as it neither undermines their case nor assists ours. I don't have the time to go through it all, and I don't think there is any point in seeking an adjournment to look at it. Can you look through it and see if there is anything that might assist Charlie?"

"Certainly, I'd be happy to," replied Jamie, well he could hardly refuse!

David smiled and returned to the important business of finishing his breakfast. As he was popping the last morsel of bacon in his mouth, his opponents, Geoffrey Lynch QC and Stephen Davies approached him. He knew them both from other cases they had appeared in together.

Geoffrey was a particularly effective prosecutor and had the ability to charm juries. It probably helped that he was good looking, well-built and 6 feet 2 inches tall. It was well known that a few years back in a particularly notorious gangland killing trial, a female juror in the case had handed him a Valentine's Day card, proposing marriage. It had led to her being discharged from the jury, with a few strong words from the Judge. It was rumoured at the Bar that, in that particular trial, she was the juror who was least enamoured by Geoffrey's charms!

It was Geoffrey who addressed David now. "Hello David, I see you're specialising in lost causes again!"

David looked at him, he had not missed the robing room banter of the Bailey over the last few months. He smiled at Geoffrey, "Not this time Geoffrey, and I'm surprised you are wasting public funds prosecuting an obviously innocent man."

Geoffrey politely laughed as Stephen and Jamie looked at each other eyeing each other up as if they were about to have a fight. Geoffrey ignored them both.

"No, seriously David, if your client were to offer a plea to manslaughter, say by loss of control, I might be able to persuade the Crown Prosecution Service to accept it."

David had already mentioned to Charlie that the Prosecution may offer such a plea and Charlie had told him, in quite florid language, what he thought of such an offer.

"Thank you Geoffrey for your kind offer but our client is adamant that he did not kill the lady and he is not going to plead guilty to something he did not do."

Geoffrey nodded, "Pity, because it is a strong case, and your client did suffer horrendous injuries in that car crash. It is our belief he cannot perform in the bedroom department, and that's probably why he killed her when she taunted him about it."

"That's interesting Geoffrey, especially as there is no evidence of her ever taunting him. In any event, if you feel that way, you could always reduce the charge to one of manslaughter and we could have a trial on that!"

The banter was over and after discussing a few preliminary points both left to consider their respective positions.

At 10:30am they were called into court 4. It was one of the old courts in the building and one of the first to be built. David could see that Jamie was feeling over-whelmed by the experience.

Jamie looked around him and added, "This whole building is too beautiful to be a courtroom."

"I suspect Defendants see it very differently," David responded quickly.

"What strategy have you planned for the case, Mr Brant?"

David was conscious that he had not discussed the case in detail with Jamie. Jamie's clear lack of experience had not filled him with confidence that this was a case in which he could rely too heavily on his junior.

"Well Jamie, firstly call me David, I'm not that old! As far as the strategy is concerned, you have to look at this from the Juror's position. Sheila Wright was obviously murdered by someone who undoubtedly knew her. They will want to know who committed that murder. The only candidate they have at the moment is our client, Charlie. We shall have to give them someone else to think about. In this case, we have another potential candidate that we can remind them off constantly."

Jamie looked a little surprised. "Who is that Mr Br…, sorry, David?"

"Well Jamie it is clear that the murderer in this case must have known the victim. It is also clear that the husband could not have committed the murder because he was travelling to Manchester that day. If our client did not commit it, which is his case, that leaves only one candidate. We have heard that Sheila had another boyfriend. We have heard very little about him from the papers, but he is an obvious candidate, and we should remind the jury about him as often as we can."

CHAPTER 20

THE TRIAL COMMENCES

The Judge appointed to try the case was Her Honour Judge Isobel Graham. David knew her from when she practised at the Bar. She had been an excellent prosecution barrister before becoming a Judge. Many said she had become a far better prosecutor now that she sat as a judge! She was very intelligent and gave excellent judgments on the law, although, in the past, she had a reputation for engaging her mouth long before she had engaged her brain. This led to frequent rude and injudicious comments about the barristers and witnesses appearing before her. She was particularly unfair to female barristers for reasons no one could really understand.

The Bar's rumour mill said she had calmed down somewhat after some unfavourable comments from the Court of Appeal and since her move to the Bailey from Woolwich Crown Court. David was yet to find out if it was true.

David's opinion of her, based on the occasions he had appeared before her, was that she was very intelligent but that she unfortunately believed she was more intelligent than everyone who appeared in front of her. In the past, this had led to her criticising everyone around her in the belief that she could do better than both the prosecution and defence lawyers. In some cases, this was no doubt true, but not in every case and that made her a particularly irritating tribunal. He wondered how she would deal with this case.

Geoffrey Lynch QC introduced all the counsel to the Judge as was the tradition. He pointed out that there were a number of preliminary points that had to be dealt with before the jurors could be sworn in. David noticed Isobel raise an eyebrow as if to say she was surprised that there were any issues of law that she had to deal with, but she simply made a note in her red judge's notebook.

Most of the matters were dismissed within seconds of being raised by her simply stating, "Surely the prosecution are not trying to rely on that", or "what possible reason can the defence have to exclude that." As none of the matters were of real concern, the parties did not spend a great deal of time on them.

The only real issue of importance was the 999 tape. David conceded, as he had to, that the Prosecution could lead the witness on the fact that there was a 999 call and read out certain parts of the transcript which appeared relevant. However, Geoffrey was not content with this and wanted to play the whole tape to the jury to put the 999 call "in context."

David responded to this application succinctly, "My Lady, the reality is that there is no legitimate context in which to put this call. The father and children arrive home to find the victim dead. They try to revive her and then phone the ambulance and police. The tape is harrowing to listen to with the children ...."

Before he could finish his sentence Isobel felt it necessary to intervene, "Mr Brant, 999 calls are played in these Courts every day, what possible harm could there be in playing this one."

David smiled at her, hoping that might have some effect. She grimaced back. *No, that doesn't work,* he thought, *I must try something else!*

"My Lady, I accept that 999 calls are played in Court when they are relevant to an issue, for example, to learn precisely what was said and in some instances why it was said. However, in this case the tape is a traumatic recording. I suspect Your Ladyship has not had an opportunity to listen to the tape?"

He knew that would be the case. Judges were usually supplied with the papers in the case and not with tapes of 999 calls.

"May I encourage you to listen to the tape if you are minded to rule that it should be played before the jury? You will note on the transcript the reference to the children who can be heard constantly sobbing in the background and trying desperately to revive their dead mother. The only effect that playing this tape will have is to play on the emotions of the jury and of course that is not a legitimate reason to play it before them."

He knew that would be the clinching argument, not that it would play on the emotions of the jury, but she would not want to waste time hearing the tape first, before she ruled on the application. She made her ruling before Geoffrey could respond.

"Mr Lynch, I agree. I have had the opportunity of reading the transcript, having thought about the matter I can see no good reason to play the tape, at this stage. Of course, should matters develop in a particular way or Mr Brant's cross-examination makes it relevant, I will revisit the subject."

Round one to me, David thought, *a minor victory but a welcome one.*

The jury panel was then called into court. Twelve members were selected at random, and all took an oath or an affirmation to, "try the case according to the evidence."

David looked closely at the panel. He had made a note of their names as a habit, although it had never assisted him in a case to date. They were:

KEVIN HARGREAVES

PAUL HUDSON

JOSEPH WARD

VICTORIA JONES

JENNIFER TAYLOR

DEREK SMITH

ALISON PALMER

IQBAL MAHMOOD

WINSTON AMIN

ROGER LEVITT

JESSICA WALLACE

BARBARA PERCY

They were a mixed bunch. It was a typical jury selection of seven men and five women. They varied in age from about 20 to 65. They were told it was a short trial, so none of them had been able to raise any good reason not to sit. Some looked like they were positively excited by the experience.

The clerk of the court, 'put them in charge' of the case reading out the indictment, namely, that,

"Charles Holmes on the 15th day of June 2012 murdered Sheila Wright."

There were very few words on a murder indictment, not like a fraud case where the indictment could cover pages of different allegations. In many ways, it had far more impact on a jury being expressed so succinctly.

Geoffrey Lynch QC rose to his feet and now introduced the counsel to the jury. He then continued,

"Ladies and Gentlemen, at 15.48 on Friday 15th June 2012, the emergency services received a 999 call asking that the Police and an Ambulance be sent to an address in Clapham Common where a woman had been found by her husband and children.

She had been repeatedly stabbed.

We will read to you a part of the transcript of the 999 call during this case, but we will not play the tape, unless necessary, because it is far too harrowing to listen to."

The cheek of the man, that's exactly why he wanted to play it! David made a note on his computer, *'Watch this one!'* and noticed that even Isobel Graham raised an eyebrow at this opportunistic comment.

Geoffrey continued without the slightest concern, "Police Constables, Ian Battle and Jennifer Gray attended the scene at 15:59. They entered the premises together and saw that

162

Roger Wright and his two children, Susan Wright, 15, and Billy Wright, 13, were in the living room. They were all standing in front of a sofa. The children were on either side of their mother, Sheila Wright, who was collapsed on the sofa with her feet to the floor and her head to the left of the sofa. It was clear that they had unsuccessfully tried to revive her, but she was clearly dead having been stabbed many times.

The children were understandably very upset and in a state of shock and the female officer took them to the kitchen whilst the paramedic, Catherine Ford, tried to see if there was anything that could be done for Mrs Wright. Of course, there was nothing anyone could do.

You will hear that Catherine Ford is a highly experienced paramedic who has seen many dead bodies in her career. She concluded that because of the existence of Rigor Mortis, the stiffening of the body after death, Mrs Wright must have been dead for at least 2 hours by the time of her arrival. That would put Mrs Wright's death at some time before 2pm.

You will hear that Sheila Wright was last seen in her own garden at about 9:30am that morning, by a neighbour, Mrs Abigail Richards.

It follows that she must have been killed sometime between 9:30am and about 2pm. We believe that we can narrow that time down even further.

You will hear that neither Catherine Ford nor the Police Officers could see much blood at the scene.

It may seem surprising to you that despite the number of wounds sustained by Mrs Wright that, apart from some spotting on the floor in front of the sofa, there was very little blood present. This is explained by the evidence of Mr Petrov Labaski, a Forensic Pathologist. He will tell you that he examined the body on the morning of 16th June 2012. He found nine stab wounds on Mrs Wright's body. He states that, assuming a sharp knife was used, most of the injuries would have only required moderate force by the assailant.

He found that two of the stab wounds would have proved fatal, with the victim becoming incapacitated very quickly. This undoubtedly explains why he found no real defensive wounds on the body and why there was very little blood found at the scene. She probably died very quickly, cutting off the blood flow, which meant that very little blood flowed from the subsequent wounds.

Mr Labaski was asked by the police officer in charge of this case, Detective Sergeant MacDonald, to provide a drawing of what he thought the knife would look like. He did so, and you will find that it was almost exactly the same as a knife that was recovered from the scene that had been placed in a knife rack that, perhaps ironically, was shaped like a person who had been stabbed!

As I have stated, the neighbour, Mrs Richards saw Mrs Wright at 09:30am that morning. Mrs Wright told Mrs Richards that she was making a roast dinner that night for her family and asked to borrow a large carving knife as the handle of her one had broken. Mrs Richards lent her a knife.

It is believed that is the knife that was used to kill Sheila Wright.

Sheila Wright's husband, Roger, was questioned by PC Battle. You may think it was natural to question him at the home, as it appeared that she must have known her killer. After all, she was found slumped on the sofa in a position that looked as if she was just engaged in conversation.

It was soon established that Mr Wright had nothing to do with the murder. He had left the house early in the morning at about 4:30am. He had then travelled by car to a depot in Clapham where he works and then driven a lorry to Manchester arriving at about 09:30am. There he was seen by staff in Manchester. He left Manchester at about 10:30am and drove back to London arriving back at his depot at about 3pm. He was therefore nowhere near his home address when his wife was murdered.

The Police obviously had to look further afield for the murderer.

Mr Wright gave some important information to police. He believed that his wife was having an affair. He had noticed certain signs around the house and was suspicious. Their relationship was clearly not a close one and on the day of her murder, she told him she wanted him to move out of the house.

Police investigations revealed that, in fact, there were two boyfriends. The whereabouts of one has never been discovered. However, it is not believed that he had anything to do with her murder, there is certainly no evidence pointing to his involvement."

That's because you haven't looked for any, thought David.

"The other boyfriend was this Defendant. It is clear from the evidence of Mrs Richards, Mrs Wright's neighbour and a friend of the Defendants, a Mr Bevan, that Mrs Wright had a close sexual relationship with this Defendant and indeed, this Defendant appears to have become infatuated with Mrs Wright.

You will hear that the Defendant was a Fireman and no doubt had an exemplary service record. Unfortunately though, he was involved in a serious accident that crushed his right leg and caused injuries to his bladder. These injuries hospitalised him for a period of two months. They also meant that he could no longer have sex.

This affected his relationship with Mrs Wright, and you will hear that this led to a cooling of their relationship and Mrs Wright lost interest in him. Phone messages have been found that indicate that the day before her death she received a text message from someone who signed off as "C" stating he was coming round to see her the next day. She made it plain she had no interest in seeing him. We say that "C" must be the Defendant, Charlie Holmes.

The day following her murder, there were video interviews with the two children during the course of which both mentioned that they knew their mother had a boyfriend.

Young Billy Wright said he knew where his mother's boyfriend lived and gave a description of him and said that he used a walking stick to get around because he had suffered an injury in a road traffic accident. He described the walking stick as being "sick", apparently this is now teenage slang meaning "awesome" or "impressive". This was apparently because it had some image etched on it of a flame and was a copy of a walking stick used by a popular character from the television program, House.

Police took Billy in a police car to the area where he said his mother's boyfriend lived and he pointed out this Defendant's flat in Tooting. Mr Holmes was not home at the time the police arrived, and it transpired that, unusually for him, he had not returned home the night of the murder. You will hear about this from his neighbour, Mrs Betty Crawford. You will, no doubt, want to ask yourselves, why he chose that night, of all nights, not to return home.

Was it fear of being arrested after carrying out the murder?

Was it an attempt to flee the area?

Was it to dispose of clothing or any other items that might have blood on them?

It will be a matter for you to decide in due course."

David noticed a couple of female jurors sitting together on the front row, nodding in agreement.

Geoffrey continued with his beaming grin. "Whatever the reason for fleeing his home that night, he had returned by Sunday morning, for at 4:52am that day police arrived at his home address and arrested him for murdering Sheila Wright. He was cautioned on arrest, told he need not say anything but it might harm his defence if he did not mention when questioned something he might later rely on in court. He made no reply.

The police searched his flat and recovered a walking stick with the motif described by young Billy.

The Defendant was interviewed later that day over the course of a period of six hours. You will hear that he was cautioned again in similar terms to those I have already read out. He declined to answer any questions and made no comment to all the questions that were put to him.

He was charged with murder the following day, Monday 18th June 2012, at about 12pm and again he made no comment.

The Police continued with their enquiries and discovered that at 10:37am on 15th June 2012, the Defendant had purchased a top-up voucher for a 'pay as you go' phone from a local newsagent, Mr Ashiq Ali. This is captured on the shop's CCTV, and we will play that to you later.

As you will be aware Ladies and Gentlemen, London is awash with CCTV cameras although ironically none were found covering the areas of importance in this case. However, enquiries were made of London Buses, a subsidiary of Transport for London, and the company that runs all the buses in Central London. They were able to produce two CCTV clips from one of their number 155 buses. We will show you those clips now."

With that his junior, Stephen Davies, started the DVD machine to play the clips on the large TV screens situated around the court so that the judge, jurors, witnesses, counsel and the defendant could see the images. However, the screens all stayed blank.

Geoffrey gave the jury his most charming smile. "Ladies and gentlemen, this is typical, the machinery worked perfectly just before you came into court. As soon as we need it, the gremlins take over."

The jurors smiled back sympathetically.

Within a few minutes Stephen Davies and the Court Usher, Debbie, had worked out where the problem was and after reattaching a cable, the screens all lit up and the video commenced.

Geoffrey continued, "You will see that the video screen is divided into six separate segments. Each shows a view from one of the six cameras on the bus. You will note the time in the top right hand corner currently showing 10:50 am on 15th June 2013. You can see now through the first camera view that the bus is approaching a bus stop in Tooting. That is the nearest stop to the Defendant's house. You can also see as the bus approaches the stop there is a man holding a walking stick. That is the defendant. You will see that his left hand is held to his ear, and he appears to be talking on a phone.

The bus stops at 10:51am, and the Defendant boards the bus, still talking on the phone. You will see that he appears agitated as he shows his bus pass and takes a seat.

We will now fast forward as there is no need to watch the whole of the journey."

Turning to Stephen, he asked, "Can you fast forward to 11:11am, please?"

"I should add that the Defendant's phone was seized upon arrest and the phone and its SIM card were examined. The only use that day of the SIM card found was at around 8pm. It follows that the Defendant must have had another SIM card which he was using on the day of the murder and which he disposed of afterwards. Was that because he knew the SIM card linked him to the deceased?"

The video started again, and the jury could see the six camera views. Geoffrey continued, "Ladies and gentlemen, you will see that the bus is coming to a halt at Clapham Common, and you will see that the Defendant gets off, still using a walking stick. You will hear that this bus stop is the nearest to the victim's home address.

We say the inference is clear. He was clearly on the way to see her. You will note the time he got off the bus, 11:12am.

We will stop the tape there. What happened next can be pieced together from the testimony of other witnesses.

The officer in charge of this case, Detective Sergeant MacDonald, is a very experienced officer, and has walked the route from the bus stop you just saw, to the victim's address. He found that it took him some 12 minutes. Assuming a man with a walking stick may be somewhat slower, it would take something like 15 minutes or so to get to the victim's house.

That means that he arrived at something like 11:30am. Noticeably at 11:35am, Mrs Wright tops up her phone with the voucher that the Defendant had bought at 10:37am. Presumably he handed the voucher over to her when he arrived.

The next witness of importance in this case is named Bill Callaghan. He was a neighbour of the victim and his living room window overlooks the front door of the victim's home. He cannot be accurate on times …"

You have to say that as the times don't match up, thought David.

".... but he says that at some time, which he thinks was between 12-1pm he saw a man approach the victim's address. The man had a walking stick, and we say that must have been the Defendant arriving at the address.

I have mentioned that a knife was recovered from a knife rack in the house which we believe is the murder weapon. Forensic scientists examined that knife. It is right to tell you that no fingerprints were found on that knife nor was any cellular material or DNA found on it that linked the knife to this Defendant, Charles Holmes. However, small traces of blood and tissue were found on the blade of the knife nearest the handle, and this was examined by a forensic scientist, David Lawson. The blood and tissue matched Sheila Wright's DNA, and he concluded that this was the knife that was used to stab her.

It appears that there had been some unsuccessful attempt to clean the knife. No doubt the handle was cleaned well enough to remove all traces of the defendant's DNA and fingerprints, but the blade had not been subjected to the same degree of treatment.

Interestingly, one of the other knives in the same knife rack did contain DNA on the handle. It was discovered that it matched the DNA of the Defendant, Charles Holmes. You may think that the explanation for this is that he touched that knife accidentally, either when he reached for the murder weapon or when he placed the murder weapon back in the rack."

That's a bit speculative, but unfortunately quite possible, noted David.

Just half an hour after Mr Callaghan saw the man with a walking stick push the gate open, he heard a scream coming from the direction of the house. That we say must have been Mrs Wright screaming out as she was viciously attacked and killed ..."

He turned and pointed to the Defendant,

" ... by that man."

All the jurors looked towards Charlie Holmes, who avoided eye contact with them. Some jurors frowned at him.

David was impressed. It was a good opening and Geoffrey had the jury eating out of his hand. Probably one or two of the female jurors were already smitten. It looked like the prosecution had proved their case without even calling any evidence!

CHAPTER 21

THE FATHER'S EVIDENCE

Geoffrey continued with his opening, producing a Jury Bundle containing the relevant exhibits, maps, photographs and cell site information showing where Sheila's phones were when they were used and showing where Charlie's phone was when he made the calls on his phone after 8pm on 15th June 2012.

Geoffrey also played the CCTV of the bus showing Charlie catching the bus from the stop nearest Sheila's address at 2:22pm and getting off at the stop nearest his own home at 2:40pm.

Having completed his opening, Geoffrey called his first witness, Roger Wright. David had read the statements and he always spent a few moments trying to think what a witness would look like. He imagined Roger as a small, quiet, hen-pecked husband, willing to do as he was told. In fact, Roger was taller than he imagined and seemed to have an air of confidence about him that David had not foreseen.

Roger Wright was sworn and immediately looked towards the dock where Charlie was seated. He looked coldly at him for a few seconds before giving his name to the Court.

Geoffrey put on his most sympathetic look as he asked his first few questions.

"Mr Wright, I think we are all sympathetic to your loss and we will try not to keep you too long. I just want to deal with a few background matters if that is all right with you?"

Roger nodded.

"The first matter I must ask is that you answer the questions I ask as the jury must hear you and the court tape recorder will not pick up a nod."

"Oh, Sorry."

"Not at all. Now, I want to deal with June of last year, 2012. At that time you were the husband of Sheila Wright?"

"Yes."

"I understand that you had been married for fifteen years when she died?"

"Yes."

"You have two children, a girl, Susan, now aged 16, but aged 15 at the time, and a boy, Billy, now aged 14, but aged 13 at the time."

"Yes."

"Help us a little about your wife. Was she a good partner?"

"Yes, she was very good with the children and was very clean around the house. I used to joke with her that she was fanatic about cleanliness."

"Thank you, now, I don't want to be too personal, but would I be right in thinking that your marriage was not a happy one at the time of your wife's death?"

Roger looked taken aback at this question.

"Our marriage was a very happy one. We were very close, it is only when HE came on the scene that things changed."

"Who do you mean by he?"

Roger pointed at Charlie, "Him, the man that killed her!"

David was about to stand up to object when Isobel Graham decided it was time to intervene and show who was in command in the courtroom. "Mr Wright, we have certain rules of evidence. It is for the jury to decide on the evidence whether the Defendant was the murderer. It is not appropriate for you to make such comments."

She then turned to Geoffrey. "Mr Lynch, please try and control the witness. Your question was a little loose and some might think, almost invited that comment."

Geoffrey was all smiles. "Quite so, my Lady, entirely my fault. I won't be so loose with my questions in future."

David studied his opponent, *God he really is nauseating!*

Geoffrey turned to Roger, "Very well, Mr Wright, let's move on. Did you become aware that your wife was seeing another man?"

"I believed that she was, though I never saw him. If I had, things might have been different." He looked towards the dock with a murderous expression. Either the Judge did not notice or she chose to ignore it. Geoffrey hoped the jury had noticed it as he continued.

"Please tell the jury how you became aware that your wife was having an affair with another man?"

Roger Wright immediately looked down and sipped from a glass of water that the Court Usher had provided. He looked up and responded with a slight tremor in his voice. "Sheila didn't tell me but I started to see signs that someone had visited. Extra glasses and plates were out, I even found cigarette stubs on a saucer on a few occasions and as neither Sheila nor I smoked, I asked her about it, but she denied anyone had been round!"

Geoffrey nodded and looked towards the jury, a few of whom were showing obvious sympathy. David made a note on his computer, 'cigarettes?'

Geoffrey continued, "Mr Wright, let us move on to the day that your wife Sheila was brutally murdered."

David looked at him, the question although seemingly innocuous was clearly designed to elicit an emotional response from Roger. It did! Roger looked at the dock with a murderous expression and some jurors followed his stare.

Satisfied with the effect, Geoffrey moved on. "I understand that you left the house early that day."

"Yes, I had a job in Manchester that day so I got up early and left the house at about four-thirty in the morning."

"Was anybody else up at that time?"

"No."

"So was your wife asleep?"

"I assume so!"

Geoffrey had forgotten that they slept in different rooms and Roger would not know if his wife was awake or not. Not wanting to overly emphasise the lack of domestic bliss, he moved on rapidly. "I understand that your wife was planning to

179

make you and your children, a roast meal that night?"

"Yes." Roger's voice was now full of emotion and the Usher gave him a glass of water which he sipped at.

"Can you help me with this, did you have a carving knife in the home?"

"No ... ours was broken..." He decided there was no need to add that he had broken it in anger. "... Sheila said she would borrow one from a neighbour."

David looked up again, he had noticed there was no mention of how the knife had been broken.

"I understand you had to pick up a vehicle with its load at a depot near to your address. You drove to Manchester arriving at about 09:30 where you were seen by the Operations Manager and then you drove back at about 10:30 in the morning."

"Yes, that's right."

Isobel looked up to see if there was going to be any objection to leading the witness, but as these facts were not in dispute, David did not bother to object.

"Did you speak to Sheila at all that day?"

"No!"

Geoffrey looked at Roger closely. He was surprised at how adamant the answer had been.

"Let us deal with when you got back to London. I don't believe it is in dispute that you arrived back in London at about 3pm and then made your way home. Do you recall what time you arrived home?"

"Yes, I remember looking at my watch, it was 3:45pm."

"What did you see when you arrived outside the house?"

"I saw my children, Susan and Billy. I was surprised to see them as they never come home together." He smiled as he added, "In fact they never spend any time together, they fight like cats and dogs!"

Geoffrey smiled at the jurors and a few smiled back, he then asked, "What were they doing?"

"Billy had arrived home first as he usually does, but he had forgotten his key and Sheila wasn't letting him in. Susan had just arrived and was opening the door when I arrived."

"Did they go into the house before you?"

"No, I called out to them and I went in first."

"What did you see?"

"I shouted out to Sheila, I was surprised she had not let Billy in and I wondered if she was with someone. I then went into the living room and saw her. She was sitting up but with her head resting on her chest, I thought she had dozed off."

"When did you realise something was wrong?"

"She didn't say anything and I shook her and then saw blood all over my hand. I noticed she had cuts all over her body and there was blood everywhere."

David was making a note of everything that was being said. He looked at Roger. It was clear from the photographs he had seen and other eyewitness statements that there was very little blood at the scene. However, it was clear Roger believed he was telling the truth! No doubt he had relived the moment several times and actually imagined blood everywhere when he recalled the incident.

Geoffrey decided not to ask any more questions about the scene and returned to asking leading questions. "I understand that you called the police and ambulance services and within a few minutes they arrived. I want to ask you just one more question."

His junior passed him a box and he asked Debbie the Usher to show it to the witness. It had a plastic cover over the top and inside was the carving knife that the Prosecution claimed was the murder weapon. "Mr Wright, can you look closely at this exhibit. Please don't take it out of the box. It has been examined for DNA and fingerprints with the use of toxic chemicals that can harm you on touch, so it is safer to leave it in the box!"

Roger stared vacantly at the knife, "I've never seen it before. It's probably the knife Sheila borrowed from the neighbour."

Geoffrey turned to the jury and smiled. "Thank you Mr Wright, can you stay there, there will be some more questions from my learned friend."

David rose to his feet, pushing the tails of his gown behind him. He immediately noted the instinctive look of hostility on the face of Roger Wright mirrored, he felt, by one or two members of the jury. Roger had contradicted his own witness statement on a number of matters but it would not help David's client to embark on a full blown destructive cross-examination of this witness, who clearly and understandably, had the jury's sympathy.

"Mr Wright, may I echo my learned friend's comments about our sympathy for you. I have a number of questions to ask you but let me make it clear it is no part of my function or my wish to distress you and I will try and keep you here for as short a time as possible."

Roger looked at him, clearly not believing a word he said.

"You have told us that you believed that your wife was having an affair."

"Yes I did." Roger again looked pointedly at Charlie in the dock.

David looked down at a piece of paper that had just been passed to him from his junior, Jamie, who had taken further instructions from Charlie on an issue. He smiled at what he read and carried on. "There were tell-tale signs around the house, extra glasses, cups, plates and you have told us cigarette butts?"

"Yes."

"You have told us that neither you, nor your wife smoked and presumably no one else smokes in the house?"

"That's right."

"So you assumed that these cigarettes had come from Sheila's lover and this belief was fortified when Sheila lied to you about having no visitors to the house?"

"Yes," Roger confirmed. David could see that Roger was clearly angry and would no doubt lose control if he pushed too hard.

"Mr Wright, I have to ask you these questions, please bear with me.

You suspected that your wife had a lover, did she ever confirm this to you?"

"No, she didn't."

"You had confronted her about having a lover just a few days earlier hadn't you?"

"Yes."

"She denied that she had and you threw the carving knife, which is how the handle got broken?"

The expressions on the faces of a few jurors changed at this suggestion. Roger noticed it and replied, "I didn't throw it at her!"

"I'm not suggesting you did, but that is how it was broken, by you throwing it."

"Yes."

David looked at Roger's witness statement, "Sheila denied having an affair that night, but the night before she died she told you that your marriage was over and she wanted you to move out of the house?"

The jury were all looking towards Roger now wondering what his answer would be.

"She said she would make me a roast dinner with the kids and we would discuss it."

"But she had said she wanted you to move out?"

"Yes."

"Did you suspect that she wanted to move the new man in her life into your home?"

"Yes."

"You had suspected she had a lover before?"

"I've told you that."

"Yes, but did you ever suspect she had more than one lover?"

Roger looked surprised. "No," he answered indignantly.

"You had no doubt that the cigarette butts left in the house were from her lover?"

"Yes, if they were from a woman she wouldn't have lied!"

David nodded and looked at the recent written instructions, from Charlie about smoking, "Mr Wright, I will suggest that you are right, the cigarettes must have come from one of her lovers, but not my client, as he has never smoked in his life!"

CHAPTER 22

THE VIDEO AND AUDIO EVIDENCE

Isobel Graham looked up at the last comment. *Silks should know better than that, giving evidence on behalf of their clients!* She wondered whether she should say something but decided it was better to leave it, knowing this Silk he would just use it as an opportunity to repeat the point. She would leave it for now but keep an eye on him.

The rest of the day was taken up by the playing of the ABE videos of the children. David had explained to Charlie that normally these were played in the presence of the child who would then be available in the court-room for cross-examination. Although Charlie disagreed with some of the evidence of the children, David did not want them to be present in court as the videos were emotive enough and the few points he could make in cross-examining them, would be heavily outweighed by the damage that would be caused to their case from asking them questions about their dead mother.

David watched the ABE video on the screen placed in front of Counsel's row. The videos had been edited to remove repetitive questioning and other irrelevancies. They were still lengthy though and he noted the jurors intently watching the children describe how they found their mother. One lady even dabbed her eyes with a handkerchief as Susan described trying to revive her mother.

"I arrived home and saw my little brother Billy outside the address. He told me that he'd forgotten his key and Mum wasn't answering the door. Just then Dad arrived and we went to the car to see him.

He opened the front door and went in first calling for Mum. She never said anything. Then Dad went into the front room and suddenly stopped. I was a few steps behind him and I could see from behind him that Mum was on the sofa. I couldn't tell what was wrong. Dad tried to stop us going in but I went in. I could see Mum on the sofa. She was still breathing, I know she was. I could see blood on the floor in front of her and I could tell she had been stabbed. I did first aid in the Girl Guides so I tried to help her. Dad phoned the ambulance and the police and the lady on the phone kept telling him what we should do.

I tried to move her but she was too heavy. I heard her gasp at one stage. There wasn't much blood but I couldn't get her to wake up. I tried, I really tried to keep her alive, but I couldn't."

David hoped that someone had since told her that she was mistaken and that her mother had been dead for hours when she arrived at the house and there was nothing she could have done to save her. He was glad when the videos were over, although there was still a further piece of emotional evidence when Stephen Davies for the Crown, read out the transcript of the 999 call.

"Operator: Okay, are you able to move her from the sofa and lay her down on the floor?"

Caller: "My daughter is trying to move her but she can't."

Operator: "Why not?"

Caller: "She is too heavy."

Operator: "Okay, alright, do you think you might be able to move her?"

Caller: "You told me to stay on the line!"

Operator: "Okay, you're all doing really well and don't worry help is on the way, an ambulance and the police will be there very soon."

Stephen Davies then paused before turning to the jury and adding, "It is at this stage that very loud sobbing can be heard on the tape which is clearly coming from both children, who are still desperately trying to revive their murdered mother."

At 4:10pm Isobel Graham adjourned Court until 10:30am the following day. David and Jamie went down to the cells in the basement to speak to Charlie. After passing through security, David and Jamie went to cell number 4 where they both shook Charlie's hand. It was Charlie who spoke first, "I'm not happy with the way the prosecution are running this case. They're trying to get me convicted on the basis of prejudice not the evidence!"

David immediately responded as there could be a criticism of him in this statement, "Charlie, we won't allow the prosecution to prejudice the jury. I agree that they have made a few prejudicial observations today. They are allowed a certain degree of leeway in court, but don't worry, we will make the jury concentrate on the evidence. There is no doubt that they will want to hear from you. They will want to know where you went the night of the murder and why. Are you willing to tell us yet?"

Charlie hesitated before replying, "I'm going to have to think about it."

David shook his head. "Don't think about it too long Charlie, we need to know the answer in the next few days, you'll find that the decision whether to give evidence will need to be made sooner than you realise."

CHAPTER 23

THE POLICE AND THE EMERGENCY SERVICES

Tuesday began with Geoffrey calling PC Ian Battle to the witness box. He gave his evidence slowly, refreshing his memory from his notes which had been taken contemporaneously, on the day he visited Roger Wright's home. Geoffrey led him through his account, dealing with when he arrived at the house, what he saw when he entered the living room including, what he thought was a surprising lack of blood in the room and how he found what looked like the murder weapon. Having asked a few questions covering the areas he wanted to, Geoffrey sat down and David rose to his feet.

"Officer, how many years have you been in the police force?"

"Almost ten years now, sir."

"In that time, have you come across any other murder victims?"

"Yes, sir, sadly I've come across two previous murders."

"Were they similar to this one?"

"One was. That was a woman killed by her husband, although she had been strangled."

"Thank you Officer. I see that you made notes at the time you were in the house."

"Yes, sir."

"I want to ask you about a few notes you made. It's right, isn't it, that you spent some time with Mr Wright whilst your fellow officer, PC Gray took the children into the kitchen?"

"Yes sir."

"You questioned Mr Wright didn't you?"

"I did, sir."

"I note that during questioning you made two particular notes, firstly, "inconsistent answer" and secondly, you wrote that he said, "My wife was having an affair with another man and was leaving me. I suspected that another man had been round the other day and I got angry and threw the knife against the wall and the handle broke."

You then added the word "confession" by the side of the note. Why was that?"

Geoffrey quickly rose to his feet, "My Lady, I do object to this line of questioning. It can have no relevance to any issue in this case. Mr Wright is not a suspect in this case as he has an airtight alibi, consequently this questioning can only tend to confuse the issue." He smiled his most charming smile at Isobel which was promptly ignored. Nevertheless she did address David, "Mr Brant, I tend to agree with Mr Lynch, what possible relevance can this line of questioning have?"

David smiled, he always welcomed the opportunity to make a speech in front of the jury and explain the purpose of his cross examination. "My Lady, normally I would agree, but in this case Mr Holmes' defence is that the police have made a serious mistake in their investigation. They have jumped to an erroneous conclusion in bringing a case against Mr Holmes rather than fully investigating this matter. I propose to demonstrate this by showing that the investigation started in this manner. The police firstly, erroneously jumped to the conclusion that Mr Wright was the perpetrator of this murder. It was only when they discovered he had an 'airtight alibi' that they began to look to Mr Holmes. Then, because he did not have the advantage of an 'airtight alibi', rather that investigate the matter properly, they looked no further and charged him."

Isobel looked at him, regretting that she had invited this explanation in front of the jury but she realised it was too late to do anything other than say, "Very well Mr Brant, I shall allow you to ask a few more questions on this topic but it must be limited to what is strictly relevant."

David smiled again, "Thank you My Lady."

Turning back towards PC Battle, he asked, "Officer, it appears clear that, from the start, you suspected that Mr Wright had killed his wife?"

"I wouldn't say that, sir. Like anyone would be, I was interested in discovering what had occurred, so I asked him a few questions."

"A few questions, officer? Your notes make it quite clear you suspected him from the start!"

"I just asked questions that I thought were relevant."

"Officer, you questioned him about his relationship with his wife, about arguments he had with his wife, about his breaking the handle of a knife when he threw it against a wall in anger. You made notes that his answers seemed inconsistent and you even used the word 'confession' in your notes, to indicate you thought he had or was about to confess to the crime."

Ian Battle remained silent.

"Isn't that right, officer?"

"No sir, I thought he had made a few inconsistent answers but that wasn't surprising considering his state. I can't recall now what I meant by writing the word 'confession', it was probably just a reference to him admitting he had become angry."

David looked towards the jury, it was clear from their faces that he had made the point and there was no reason to continue questioning and give the Officer a chance to repair any damage, so he sat down.

Geoffrey on the other hand felt the need to try and bolster the officer's evidence, so he asked a few questions in re-examination. "Officer, do you have any reason to believe that Mr Wright was responsible for killing his wife?"

"No sir. I am aware he has an alibi and was nowhere near London when she died."

"Did you have any reason at the time to believe he may have murdered his wife?"

Ian hesitated a little before answering, "No sir."

"You are a police constable. Was it any part of your role to investigate this murder or was that the responsibility of the detectives in the case?"

"It wasn't any part of my responsibility, sir. I was there to protect the paramedics in case the murderer was still present. It was not my function to investigate the case."

Geoffrey thanked him and called his next witness, the Paramedic, Catherine Ford. She entered the witness box dressed in her freshly pressed green uniform. David noted that she was in her mid-thirties and slightly overweight, though she was quite attractive with long blonde hair which she wore down for court.

Having given her name, occupation and experience, Geoffrey moved on to deal with the main parts of her evidence.

"When you entered the living room, what did you see?"

"I saw two children standing by a dead lady on the sofa. I saw some blood on the floor in front of her and some on the sofa, although it was difficult to make out because of the colour of the sofa."

"Was there much blood present?"

"No, there seemed to be very little, more like spots of blood than pools of blood."

"What state was she in when you arrived?"

"I checked for vital signs but could not find any. I lifted the front of her tunic to check for wounds and I felt around her head and neck. I put an ECG monitor on her to check her heart. However, I noticed almost immediately that her jaw and neck were stiff. I could not move her head at all. These were clear signs of Rigor Mortis. Her pupils were fixed and dilated and there was a flat line on the ECG. It was obvious to me that she had been dead for at least a couple of hours."

"Just help us about your experience would you. I presume from your evidence that you have come across several dead bodies in your time as a paramedic?"

"Sadly, yes. I've been a Senior Emergency Medical Technician for ten years and have worked on the front line duties for most of that time. I have received training that allows me to recognize the signs of death."

"So your estimate of two hours is based upon your considerable experience as a Senior Para.. sorry, Emergency Medical Technician?"

"Yes."

"Finally, can I ask you to look at this series of photographs taken of the scene by a Scenes of Crime Officer?"

The photographs were handed to Catherine by the Court Usher. Then Geoffrey asked, "Do those photographs represent the scene as you saw it when you first arrived?"

Catherine looked at them all and then pointed to photograph 5.

"As far as I remember the photographs resemble the scene although this one shows a chair by the wall. As I recall it when I arrived at the property, the chair was nearer to the sofa, directly in front of where she was seated, as if someone had been sitting chatting to her just before she died."

Geoffrey looked at her a little surprised as she had not said this in her statement, but thinking it made no difference to his case he finished his questioning.

David was busy looking through Catherine's witness statement and a supplemental statement that she made, and which had been served by the Prosecution just before the trial.

Isobel interrupted his thought processes, "Mr Brant, have you any questions for this witness?"

David immediately got up from his seat, "I do, My Lady, I was just checking this lady's statement to see if I had missed something."

Turning towards Catherine, "Ms Ford, my apologies, I just wanted to check the statements that were taken from you by the police. I don't see any reference in those statements to this chair you've mentioned in your evidence?"

"No one asked me about it. I was only asked about the state of the body and what steps I took."

"I see, there's no criticism from me, you can only answer the questions you have been asked. You recall this chair and, as you say, it looked like someone had been seated in it just before Mrs Wright was killed, as if they were talking to her."

"Yes, that's right."

"The chair was presumably directly in front of her body, not to the right or to the left."

"As far as I remember, yes."

"Thank you. Now I just want to ask you about Rigor Mortis. You have given us the benefit of your experience although, it is fair to say you do not have any pathology training?"

"No, I do not, although I was trained to spot signs of death and my experience means that I could spot that this lady had been dead at least two hours."

"Presumably your training informed you that there are no hard and fast rules for the onset of Rigor Mortis?"

"Yes, they did."

"In fact, the onset depends upon a number of factors. For example, the temperature of the area where the body is found. The colder it is the more rapid the onset. Here of course we are dealing with inside a house in June, so the onset would probably be less rapid than outside the house?"

"Yes."

"Also the onset can be more rapid if the individual performed hard physical work just before death?"

"I believe so."

"Here of course the lady appears to have been seated on a sofa so again the onset may not have been so rapid?"

"Yes."

At this stage Geoffrey got to his feet, "My Lady, I must object to this line of questioning. Ms Ford is not an expert and it does appear that Mr Brant's questioning is treating her as one."

David immediately responded. "My Lady, my learned friend has chosen to lead evidence from this witness about Rigor Mortis. I am surely entitled to examine her particular knowledge and experience of that subject."

Isobel decided the point quickly, "This witness is not an expert pathologist as you have established Mr Brant. Nevertheless as the prosecution have relied on the evidence of Rigor Mortis I will allow you to question this witness on her knowledge."

David smiled, "Thank you, My Lady. Ms Ford I have a few more questions. In your training or experience did you discover that the onset of Rigor Mortis also varies with the individual's sex, age, physical condition, and muscular build?"

"Yes, I did".

"Thank you, finally this. You arrived at the scene at about 4pm. Presumably, you learnt that dependant on the factors I have already mentioned, Rigor Mortis begins within two to six hours of death, starting with the eyelids the neck, and the jaw?"

"I was told it was variable, at least two hours."

"The signs you saw were indicative that Rigor Mortis had recently commenced, namely the stiffness in her jaw and neck?"

"Yes."

"So, using the timescale of 2 to 6 hours, she could have died anywhere between as early as 10am and as late as 2pm?"

"Yes, I suppose so."

Achieving as wide a bracket as he could for the time of death, David thanked the witness and sat down. After all, he had established, albeit as a remote possibility only, that Sheila Wright may have died before Charlie even caught the bus in the direction of her home!

CHAPTER 24

SCENES OF CRIME

Isobel adjourned the case for lunch and in the afternoon Geoffrey called the Scenes of Crime Officer, Amanda Fry to describe what she and the officers under her control discovered at the scene of the murder.

"Ms Fry, I understand that you are a Scenes of Crimes Officer, a SOCO for short?

"My full title is actually a Principal Scenes of Crime Officer."

"Sorry, Principal Scenes of Crime Officer. Could you explain to us how long you have occupied that role, what your duties are and specifically what you did in this case?"

"Certainly. I have been a Principal SOCO for 5 years. I have been involved in this area since 2008. A SOCO is an Officer who collects forensic evidence from the scene of a crime for later analysis. We are not Police Officers as such and usually have degrees and forensic training. I have a Bachelor of Science degree in Biological Sciences from UCL, University College London.

On 15th June 2012, I arrived with my team at the deceased's house at about 6pm. I was the Senior Officer so I was the "Crime Scene Manager", I managed the crime scene, forming an appreciation of the area and deciding on the forensic strategy."

"I see, so it's not simply a case of going in and immediately looking for fingerprints?"

"Certainly not, the strategy has to be planned and roles assigned to the team." Amanda Fry looked at Geoffrey as if he was a moron.

"I'm so sorry, do carry on." Geoffrey gave his best impression of being suitably chastised.

"I assigned tasks to the officers in my command to look in various areas for possible traces of blood staining, DNA, fingerprints, fibres, or items like that. I set in place the procedures to gather all the forensic sampling and provide a checklist of things that must be done.

I then made an assessment of the scene. I noted that the door had been locked when the husband came home so I checked the lock. It was a standard Yale lock and would have locked simply on closing without the need for a key.

I went into the sitting room and saw a woman on a blood stained sofa. She was in a half sitting, half lying position when I arrived. I was conscious that there had been attempts at resuscitation so I assumed that her position had changed from when she was first found.

I took responsibility for the body. I took a number of samples including white objects taken from the inside of the mouth. I presumed these were fly eggs which I know can sometimes assist with the timing of death. Once I had taken all the samples I thought were necessary the body was moved. I did check to see if there were any wounds in the back but could not find any. Also, I could not find any trace of a potential murder weapon at the scene, although I understood that a police constable had found a knife in a knife rack which he had removed."

It was obvious to the Court by the way she spoke that she disapproved of any police officer moving anything before she arrived.

Geoffrey took her through a number of specific exhibits that were recovered from the house by her team, pointing out that 129 items had been recovered in all. He then took her through a number of photographs that were taken at the scene. He sat down, waiting for David to deal with this witness, and privately hoping that he gave her a hard time!

David assumed a serious expression. He had concluded that smiling at this witness would be treated with contempt. "Ms Fry, as you told us, you arrived at the scene at about 6pm, so that was about two hours after the husband, children, police and paramedics had arrived."

"Yes, I understand that police officers arrived at different times."

"Do you know how many people had attended the house before you arrived?"

"No, I was not told how many."

"Of course, the more people that go into a property, the more likely it is that the crime scene will be contaminated?"

"Of course."

"Which is why you were no doubt concerned that a knife had been moved by a police officer from a knife wrack, before you arrived?"

"Yes, that's right."

"One matter you may have wanted to discover is whether there were any traces of any footsteps in the house that might belong to the murderer?"

"It was one consideration."

"Were any footprints discovered?"

"The hallway and the living room were carpeted so there were no obvious signs of footprints."

"Yes, but the kitchen was not carpeted and you will be aware that it is feasible that the murderer may have stepped in blood and a trace of a footprint could then be left behind on the kitchen floor or indeed on a carpeted area?"

"As far as I recall, no footprints were recovered and in any event by the time my team arrived a number of police officers and others had been walking through the house."

"Isn't it standard practice to take elimination prints, namely to take everyone's footwear who has been in the house to eliminate them as the possible causes of any prints?"

"Not in every case."

"Was it done here?"

"No, I do not believe it was."

"So it is possible that the murderer left bloodied footprints in the house and no one checked to see that, for example, they could have been left by someone with a different size shoe to those worn by my client?"

"I suppose that is possible but I do not believe any such prints were found."

"Or perhaps no one looked for them?" He then added before she answered, "thank you, I have no further questions."

Geoffrey decided not to ask any questions in re-examination in case this witness made the situation any worse by trying to blame the police for ruining the crime scene.

As it was just after 4pm, Isobel decided that was enough for one day and adjourned the case until Wednesday morning. David was happy with the points he had been able to make but knew that they were minor and probably unimportant victories in the long run. Tomorrow was going to be the important day because Sheila Wright's neighbours were going to be called and David knew, in many ways, the case relied upon their evidence.

Will I be able to make any headway with them, he wondered.

David and Jamie visited Charlie in the cells again at the end of the day. Charlie was looking a little happier than the day before.

"Mr Brant, thanks for today. I think you've definitely shown the police didn't make any attempt to find out who killed Sheila. They just chose to say it was the first person that came along!"

David looked at him closely and explained, "Charlie, today has gone reasonably well, but we have a long way to go. The Prosecution are going to call some important evidence tomorrow. They have lined up Mrs Wright's neighbours and your neighbour, Mrs Crawford. You still haven't told us why you left your flat that night, or where you went?"

Charlie looked down at his nails which David noted had been bitten and torn by him, no doubt in frustration. Charlie chewed on the remains of one nail before speaking, "I told you Mr Brant I don't want to say."

David looked around the cell. "I suppose your cell in the prison is a little bigger than this?"

"It's a little bigger but not much."

"Have you got used to it?"

"Not really."

"That's a pity Charlie because you could be spending the best part of 25 years in that cell. The jury will want to know where you went the night of the murder and why. If you don't tell us they will probably convict you and you will spend up to 25 years in a small cell before you can apply for parole."

Charlie looked at him dumbstruck. He thought for a few moments as everyone around him was silent and then he added, "Alright Mr Brant, I will tell you."

CHAPTER 25

CHAMBERS

David returned to his Chambers that night and went into the Clerks' room where he took some papers from his pigeonhole. He was looking at them as John Winston, his Senior Clerk, approached him.

"How's the trial going sir?"

"Well at least it's started John, though we haven't had to deal with any of the important witnesses yet."

"Oh well sir, we know you are the man to get him off, if anyone can."

David stopped looking at the papers he had picked up and looked at John suspiciously, he was not used to this behaviour, and normally John was too busy to get involved in idle chat with him.

"Is there anything wrong John?"

"No sir, not that I'm aware of. I do know Mr Martin did ask if you could speak to him."

David inwardly groaned, Graham Martin would only want to talk to him about some problem in

Chambers. The last thing he wanted to deal with after a long day in court was a Chambers' squabble.

"And you have no idea what it is about?"

"No sir."

Half an hour later David was in his room, seated in his large red swivel chair behind his red leather topped desk. In front of him, on the other side of the desk, was Graham Martin. He had still not fully forgiven Graham for suggesting he become Head of Chambers so he was not feeling that approachable, but nevertheless, he made an effort, "Graham, what can I do for you?"

Graham took a seat opposite David, "David, I'm sorry to trouble you with personal problems, so soon after you've taken on the role of Head of Chambers, but I thought I needed to raise the question of my practice with you. I wouldn't bother you with it, if it wasn't for the fact that, as you know, under the Bar Code of Conduct, Heads of Chambers are responsible for ensuring that everyone is fairly treated in Chambers."

David stared at him, *why is he quoting the Bar Code of Conduct at me?*

"Graham, I am fully aware of my responsibilities under the Code of Conduct and I am surprised you feel the need to mention it to me. I should hope that you and I are old enough friends that we don't need to make implied threats to each other?"

Graham looked hurt, "David, I am sorry, I didn't mean to make any implied or express threat. I just wanted to raise an issue with you about my practice. Basically, the Clerks haven't provided me with any decent work for weeks now and I think they are favouring that youngster, Julian Hawker."

David inwardly groaned again. Throughout his career he had heard allegations of favouritism of one tenant or another, by the clerks, indeed he had felt that the former Head had been favourably clerked over and above other Silks. However, it was one thing complaining about it to a fellow tenant over a glass of wine and another thing to have to deal with it as a formal complaint in the role of Head of Chambers. He also knew that Graham was no fan of John Winston and might be starting another campaign to try and remove him.

"Graham, I think we all know that Julian is a very successful Barrister with an excellent personal practice. Are you sure the clerks are favourably clerking him, or is it possible he is simply doing his own work that he has brought with him?"

"David, I have been in Chambers virtually every work day recently and have heard the Clerks on the phone. Sometimes it seems to me the only two words that John Winston knows are 'Julian' and 'Hawker'."

David looked at him quizzically. Graham continued, "Those are the only words he uses when a Solicitor phones up asking them who they should send a brief to!"

David smiled at him. *I am in the middle of a difficult murder case and I have to deal with this nonsense.*

"Graham, I promise you I will look into this. I appreciate that I am duty bound to ensure that there is a fair distribution of work in Chambers and I will find out what is happening."

After Graham left his room David walked back into the clerks' room to hear John Winston on the phone to a Solicitor.

"Yes, well Julian Hawker's the man for that sort of case."

Great, there probably is something in this complaint so I have to investigate yet another matter.

An hour later David and John were in El Vinos sharing a bottle of house claret in a corner of the wine Bar under a Victorian portrait of a once famous Barrister. David looked at it and thought, *I wonder who he was?* He wondered for a moment if anyone would hang a portrait of him in a wine bar and a hundred years from now someone would look up and equally have no idea who he was. He immediately dismissed the silly notion and turned to John, "Only one bottle tonight John, I have rather a lot of work to do and my days of sharing four bottles with you are long gone."

"Yes, I know sir, the results of that liver function test couldn't have helped."

How does he know about that?

"Yes, well the reason I've invited you out for a drink tonight is to deal with a concern that has been raised in Chambers."

"Oh is that what Mr Martin wanted to discuss with you?"

David tried to think of a suitable answer. "Mr Martin has mentioned a concern. Is it right that he has not been in court for a number of weeks now?"

"Not quite, he has had a few half day mentions in the Crown Court, but he's not had a trial for a couple of weeks."

"John, I'm not going to mention any names, but concerns have been expressed in Chambers that you are showing favouritism to one of our new tenants, Julian Hawker, at the expense of other tenants."

John immediately sat up, "That's nonsense sir, I treat all my Governors equally. The problem is, as you well know, it's like selling any product, it's easier to sell some tenants than others. As clerks we find that Mr Hawker has, certainly in the past, been accepted by a wide range of solicitors whereas, I'm sorry to say, Mr Martin is not acceptable to many. It's a case of 'horses for courses'."

David had a sudden mental image of his members of chambers in an animal pen, wearing saddles, with John Winston trying to sell them. He sipped at his wine and quickly came back to reality, he really must stop day dreaming, he seemed to be doing more of it since he became Head of Chambers.

"John, as I recall, Mr Martin had a reasonable practice until quite recently, can't you help revive it a little?" David asked.

John laughed, "Not to put too fine a point on it sir, I'd find it easier to revive the ham in a ham sandwich, than Mr Martin's practice!"

David could not help himself as a smile crossed his face. *Now I remember why I didn't want to be Head of Chambers dealing with this. How could he ever discover whether his Clerks were telling the truth. Oh well, one last try.*

"Nevertheless, John, I want you to try and find work for Mr Martin. He has been a loyal member of chambers and we don't want to lose him."

"Well sir, it's like this, Mr Martin is a good advocate, he gets the results but Solicitors complain that he is too pessimistic. He meets a client and gives them all doom and gloom, telling them they have little chance of success. They are not best pleased and they report that to the solicitors. The irony is that if he is still instructed, he goes on to win the case. The problem isn't his ability in Court, it's ensuring that he gets to Court in the first place!"

"I understand all that but I still want you to try and resurrect his practice."

"Very well sir, it will mean probably having to show favouritism to him at the expense of someone else, but if that is what you want."

"No John that is not what I want, I do not want someone to lose out, nor do I expect ANYONE to be shown favouritism by the clerks' room, all I am asking is that you try to get Mr Martin some trial work."

John smiled, particularly at the word 'ANYONE'.

Their conversation continued onto other matters before David decided that he really must go and do some more work on his case. After paying the bill, David left the Wine Bar and caught a taxi to his flat in the Barbican. He was not surprised that they had not limited themselves to just one bottle of claret and another had mysteriously appeared and been quickly consumed. *Old habits die hard,* he thought.

CHAPTER 26

THE NEIGHBOUR

David arrived at the Old Bailey early on Wednesday morning and ordered a cooked breakfast, consisting of the usual freshly fried egg and cold bacon. He had not slept well. He had returned to his flat by about 9pm and then worked until 2am before going to bed. In the past he had discovered that his steady intake of House Claret and Rioja had helped him sleep, but he had cut down recently and he found that he was staying awake as a result.

He was also thinking of many different issues; his relationship with Wendy, whether it had any future, Chambers business, did he really have the time to deal with all the issues his clerks and colleagues kept raising, and, of course, the trial. Charlie had revealed where he had actually gone the night Sheila had been murdered and that he had gone to the same place the previous two Fridays. He had already asked the solicitors to obtain a witness statement from the person that Charlie had mentioned.

This was only the third day of the trial but he really felt like he needed a break. Murder trials always exhausted him. It was not so much the intricacies of the trial, murder trials were usually simple affairs on the facts, it was the stress of representing someone who might be innocent and yet might receive a life sentence if David made a slight mistake.

The trial started later this day because the judge had to deal with a number of other cases, bail applications and short hearings to set trial dates and deal with disclosure and other pre-trial matters in other cases. Charlie's trial began at 11:30am.

Once all the parties had assembled, Geoffrey called his next witness, Abigail Richards, Sheila's next door neighbour. David watched her walk into Court and noticed she was wearing a peacock blue skirt suit (Wendy had a similarly coloured dress which he had learnt recently was called 'peacock blue'.) She wore a large brooch on the left lapel of her jacket, shaped like a large lizard. She carried a black patent handbag (also a concept he had learnt from Wendy) with shoes to match. As she took the oath and held up the New Testament, he noted her bright red nail varnish. She had clearly made considerable efforts for her big day in court.

Having given her name and the fact she was Sheila's neighbour, Geoffrey began to question her about the important details of her evidence.

"Mrs Richards, you were a neighbour of and a friend to Sheila Wright, the victim in this case?"

"That's right, I'd known Sheila for about eight years and I think I was probably her closest friend." She smiled sweetly at the jury to convey the genuineness of her belief.

Geoffrey lowered his hands which were holding her witness statement and looked over the top of his reading glasses at her. "Quite so, I'm sure that was the case and as her closest friend, you no doubt had many personal conversations?"

"What do you mean?"

She looked concerned, as if he was asking her about matters personal to herself.

"I'm sorry, I just wanted you to tell the jury about any personal conversations you had with Mrs Wright before her death, which might be relevant to this case."

"Oh, I see," she said smiling at Geoffrey and fluttering her eyelids at him. *She's clearly loving this attention,* thought David. He had explained to Jamie that there was an argument for excluding this evidence as hearsay but as she was one of the few witnesses to refer to the second boyfriend, he was not going to argue the point.

"Well, as best friends do, we did discuss personal matters. I knew for some time she wasn't happy in her marriage because she told me so. It had started off alright, but after a few

219

years she found her life and, I'm sorry to say, her husband Roger, boring."

She did not notice, because she could not see from her position, that Roger Wright was in the public gallery above, looking down on the court and as a result she gave her evidence without a hint of embarrassment.

"Do you remember when this conversation took place?"

"Not exactly, no, but it was probably about a year before she was killed."

"Thank you, did she tell you whether she had done anything to ease her boredom?"

"She told me that she had met other men and had affairs with them."

"Did she mention anything in particular about these other men?"

"She told me about two men. She said that both were younger than her and both were her lovers."

Geoffrey looked at his copy of Abigail's witness statement, "Can you recall any particular phrase she used?"

Abigail smiled nervously, "She said they were both, 'virile and exciting lovers'."

"Did she tell you anything about their occupations?"

"She told me that one was a Fireman. He was her favourite. The other worked on a meat counter in a Supermarket, I think."

David looked up from his copy of the witness statement. There was no reference to the other boyfriend working in a Supermarket in her witness statement. She had said nothing about his occupation.

Geoffrey had also noticed this added information. "You recall her saying the second boyfriend worked in a Supermarket?"

"I'm not sure now, she said he had something to do with the meat counter."

"Very well, did she say much about this Supermarket worker?

"No, I got the impression that he wasn't that important to her and she didn't see him that often."

"Now, it is an agreed fact, between the Prosecution and the Defence, that the fireman was the Defendant in this trial, Charlie Holmes."

He turned briefly and looked at Charlie as did the jury and Abigail.

"Now, what did she say about Mr Holmes, the Fireman?"

"She said she really liked him. I remember her describing him as tall with blond hair and blue eyes and he was very strong. She said they met up twice a week and had sex at her house. That is until he had his accident!"

David again noticed a change from her witness statement. There she had said she had never seen either man visit the house, and had not mentioned Sheila saying anything about Charlie coming to the house to have sex.

"What did she tell you about the accident?"

"She didn't say a great deal. She said he was on an emergency call when he was involved in a serious accident. She said she visited him at hospital as much as she could."

She laughed, "She told the nurses, she was his sister."

"Did she say what happened when he came out of hospital?"

"Yes, she told me he was in hospital for two months. He'd been crushed 'down below' and when he came out of hospital, he had to use crutches at first and then a walking stick."

"Did she say what her relationship was like with Mr Holmes after the accident?"

"Yes, she said he couldn't perform."

"I assume you mean, he could not have sex."

She looked at him as if he was an idiot, she was sure everyone knew what she meant. Geoffrey noticed the look and smiled at her, "I'm sorry Mrs Richards, we have to be precise in Court."

"Oh, yes then, he could not have sex."

"Did she say what effect that had on their relationship?"

"She said she still loved him, but she had sex with the other man 'to fulfil her needs'."

"When was the last time she discussed these men with you?"

"It was a couple of weeks before she was killed. I think she'd gone off them both."

"Why do you say that?"

"She always used to mention them and then she suddenly stopped. Also, the day before she died I heard her talking in the garden on her phone to one of the men."

"Do you remember what time this was?"

"It was about 3:30pm, I remember that her children hadn't come home from school yet."

"What was she saying?"

"She was telling the man she had had enough and she didn't want to see him again."

"How do you know it was a man she was talking to?"

"She said a name, I can't remember what it was, now, I think it might be Chris."

Geoffrey quickly reacted, "Mrs Richards you made a witness statement much closer to the time of the incident recording this name. Do you think your recollection was 'significantly better at that time' than it is now?

"Yes, it must have been."

"Then My Lady I ask that the witness refresh her memory from her witness statement in accordance with the provisions of section 139 of the Criminal Justice Act 2003."

Isobel turned to David, "Any objection Mr Brant?"

David rose to his feet, knowing there was no objection he could realistically make in the circumstances, section 139 permitted such applications, "No My Lady, I have no objection whatsoever to this evidence."

He tried to make it look like he welcomed this evidence, even though that was far from the case.

Abigail was shown her witness statement by the Usher and then Geoffrey asked her, "Do you see what name you put there just a few days after the event?"

"Yes, it says 'Chas' in the statement."

"Yes, thank you, now I would like to move onto the day of the murder. Did you speak to Mrs Wright that day?"

"Yes, I saw her in the morning. We were in our gardens."

"What did you talk about?"

"She told me she was going to cook a roast meal that night and needed to borrow a carving knife. Roger had broken the handle of hers. So I lent her a carving knife. That was the last time I saw her..," she paused,

" …. or the knife," she added.

Geoffrey had one last question for her. He asked the Usher to show her the knife recovered in this case, still in its presentation box and now labelled Exhibit One. "Mrs Richards, do you recognise this knife?"

Abigail looked closely at the box and then looked quizzically at Geoffrey, "No, I don't, I've never seen it before!"

CHAPTER 27

THE OTHER BOYFRIEND

Geoffrey was clearly surprised by the answer just as everyone else was in court.

"Mrs Richards, please look closely at the knife again, are you sure you have never seen it before?"

Abigail looked at it once more, "I know it's not mine. It's longer than my knife and the handle is shaped differently."

Geoffrey knew he was defeated on this point so he gave his thanks to Abigail and sat down and whispered something to his junior, the jury could not hear it but David who was closer just made out the words, "Where did that bloody knife come from?"

David stood up and asked the judge if he might see the knife for a moment. The Usher handed the box to him and he spent a few seconds looking closely at it. He had of course seen it before but had no reason to examine it then in any detail, now he looked closely at the handle. There was something different about the shape but he could not think why it was important. He returned the knife to the usher and turned towards Abigail, smiling.

"Mrs Richards, forgive me, I just wanted to check the knife myself."

She smiled back at him.

"Mrs Richards, you are sure this is not your knife?"

"I'm sure it's not."

"The knife you have been shown is probably the murder weapon so you are probably relieved to hear it was not your knife that killed Mrs Wright?"

"Yes," she replied. In reality she was thinking that she could no longer tell her friends how 'horrified' she was to discover that it was her own knife that had killed her friend Sheila.

David wondered for a moment if he should show her photographs of other knives found in the house, but decided against it. She might identify the knife that had Charlie's DNA on it as her knife and that would definitely suggest to the jury that he did enter the house that day. *No, better to move on.*

"Mrs Richards, you have told us you were a very good friend of Mrs Wright?"

"Yes, I was, I still miss her."

David nodded, "That's perfectly understandable. You have told us she confided in you?"

"Yes."

"And she even told you she had two lovers?"

"Yes."

"Did she ever tell you their names?"

"I don't think so."

"You recall that last phone call you heard her make to a man. You told us originally you thought his name was, 'Chris'?"

Geoffrey quickly rose to his feet and interjected, "This witness has been shown her witness statement and corrected that answer to "Chas". It is common knowledge that is short for Charles or Charlie."

David remained standing, even though it was customary to sit when an opponent made a submission, but he was annoyed with what he saw as an unnecessary interruption. He addressed the judge. "I'm grateful to my learned friend for pointing out the obvious. He is quite right that this lady used the name 'Cha' in her witness statement, but what my learned friend did not read out from this lady's statement was that this witness said, 'I believe she used the name "Chas" but I'm not sure.'

I merely want to investigate whether the name actually might have been 'Chris', which ..." He turned to Geoffrey," ...is usually short for Christopher or Christian."

Isobel considered the point for a few seconds. "I will let you explore this for a short time, Mr Brant."

"Thank you My Lady". Geoffrey quickly took his seat. Turning back to Abigail David continued his questioning, "Mrs Richards, can you remember now what name Mrs Wright gave over the phone?"

"No, no not really."

"So it may have been Chris, which was your first thought today?"

"It might have been, I can't remember after this length of time."

"I'll move on then. She referred to the two men, one was the Fireman and there is no dispute, that is my client, Charlie Holmes. The other was somebody who worked on the meat counter at a Supermarket?"

"Yes."

"A place where no doubt there was easy access to sharp knives!"

"Sorry?"

"My apologies, it was more of an obvious statement than a question.

It was clear to you from your conversations that she liked the Fireman best?"

"Yes."

"Indeed, she said she was in love with him?"

"Yes."

"She invited him back to her home where they made love?"

"So she told me."

"And you had no reason to doubt her word?"

"No."

"After the accident, she showed how much she loved the Fireman by visiting him in the hospital and inviting him to her home when he was allowed to leave the hospital?"

"So she told me."

"Now, you told the jury you thought she may have, 'gone off' both of these men."

"Yes."

"But she never said that to you?"

"No she didn't."

"You assumed that this was the case because she no longer spoke to you about either of the men."

"I suppose so."

"So in fact she could have still been very much in love with the Fireman?"

"I don't know."

"Also, it could have been the other man, Chris, or whatever he was called, who she was telling not to come round on the day she was murdered?"

"I don't know, it might have been."

"Yes, thank you, you've been very helpful, I've no further questions."

Geoffrey decided not to re-examine the witness. As far as he was concerned she had caused enough damage to the Prosecution case and he did not want to risk her causing any more. He also wanted to discover from the Senior Officer in the case, why no Police Officer had ever shown the murder weapon to Abigail.

As it was now close to lunchtime, Isobel adjourned the case until 2-05pm.

After the jurors left Court, David and Jamie travelled by lift to the Bar Mess. They sat together and discussed the case between

231

mouthfuls of today's speciality, chicken curry, steamed rice and a rather damp looking poppadum.

"It never ceases to surprise me, even after over 30 years in the job that the witnesses that you expect to be irrelevant can often derail a good Defence case whereas the witness you expect to have that effect actually help you. Mrs Richards was very useful to us. She has raised the existence of another boyfriend before the jury, she has even given him a name and has caused the prosecution problems with their theory about where the knife came from and when."

He bit into the poppadum, grimaced and then stared at his own knife before adding, "You know Jamie, there is something strange about the murder weapon. The handle looks strange to me but I can't think why. It's probably nothing but it's worth having a look at it again."

CHAPTER 28

THE EYEWITNESS

The Court assembled at 2:10pm after Isobel and her fellow judges had finished lunch in their own dining room. Geoffrey was not really concerned about Abigail's evidence. It was not fatal to his case and he was now calling a witness who should give the strongest evidence that Charlie Holmes visited Sheila's house the day of the murder. He called his next witness, Bill Callaghan.

After a number of preliminaries, including taking Bill through a map and pictures of the area and then establishing where Bill lived, Geoffrey moved on to deal with the day of the murder.

"Mr Callaghan, I want to move on to the 15th June of last year, the day Sheila Wright was murdered. Can you recall where you were that day?"

"Oh yes, I was at home, I usually am at that time in the day."

"We can see from the map of the area and the photographs that your house is almost directly opposite that of Mrs Wright?"

"Yes, that's right."

"The road is quite wide in this particular area. We can see from the dimensions on the map that the distance from your front room window to the gate of her property is approximately sixty feet?"

Isobel quickly commented, "Mr Lynch, we are supposed to use metres in court these days."

Geoffrey gave her his best smile and turning to the jury, he said, "I do apologise, I've never really got past feet and inches."

A few older members of the jury smiled at him, the younger ones just looked blank. Geoffrey turned back to face the witness. "My apologies, Mr Callaghan, the distance was something like 18-20 metres?"

"Yes, something like that."

"Tell us what you saw that day that may have some relevance to this case?"

"Yes, well I was in my sitting room reading the Newspaper when I saw a man on the opposite side of the road just outside Mrs Wright's house."

"Did you know Mrs Wright?"

"I'd seen her around, although I didn't know her name until the police told me."

"Very well, can you remember what time of day it was when you saw this man?"

"I wasn't really paying that much attention. I think it was sometime between 12-1pm. I hadn't had lunch yet. I usually have it around 2pm as I'm now 'unemployed', I don't get up until about 10am and after a late breakfast I don't feel like eating before 2pm."

There wasn't a person in court who had missed his emphasis on the word unemployed. He clearly still resented the circumstances of his redundancy.

"Can you be certain about the time?"

Bill took off his NHS spectacles and gave them a wipe. It was noticeable to those closest to him that there was adhesive tape wrapped around the nosepiece holding the frame together. "No, I wasn't looking at my clock or my watch."

"What did this man do?"

"He opened the gate to Mrs Wright's garden, using a walking stick to push it open."

"Had you seen the walking stick before he used it in this fashion?"

"Yes I'd seen him use it as he approached the house, I'm sure I noticed him limp."

"Did you notice anything in particular about the walking stick?"

"What do you mean?"

"Well, can you tell us the colour?"

"It was dark, I think it was black in colour."

"Did you notice anything else about it, any markings for example?"

"No, it was too far away."

"Did you see whether the man went into the house or not?"

"No, I was distracted at that time by the whistle on my kettle. I'd just put it on to make a cup of tea, so I got up and went into my kitchen. When I came back the man was no longer there."

"Did you see him leave the property?"

"No, I didn't see him again."

"Can you describe the man?"

"Not really, I didn't take a great deal of notice. He didn't seem particularly tall or small."

Geoffrey looked down at the description Bill had given in his witness statement that had described the man as 'average height, average to muscular build with brown hair'.

"Did you notice the colour of his hair?"

"I think it was light brown, but I can't be certain."

Geoffrey smiled, that was near enough to the colour of Charlie's fair hair. He noted a few members of the jury looking towards Charlie in the dock.

"Can you help us as to what the lighting was like when you saw this man?"

"It was a bright sunny June day, there had been some drizzle earlier on but it was bright sunshine at this time."

Geoffrey smiled, "Did you notice anything else that day?"

"Yes, it was about half an hour later, I can't be precise on times, but I heard a scream coming from the direction of the house."

"Could you tell whether it was a male or female scream?"

"I was sure it was a female scream."

"Yes, thank you. Will you wait there please, there will be some more questions for you."

David put down Bill's statement, rose and smiled at the witness.

"Mr Callaghan, I take it from reading your statement, that you had never seen this man before?"

"No, I don't think so, but I can't be sure."

"You don't have any recollection of him visiting Mrs Wright's house before?"

"No I don't."

"To be fair, you never gave a very detailed description of the man you saw?"

"I didn't see him for very long."

"Nor were you asked to attend an identification parade in this case?"

"No."

"So it's fair to suggest, you could not identify this man if you saw him again?"

"No, I don't think so."

"Very well, presumably you have your own regime in your house, getting up at 10:00am, then sitting and reading in your lounge until lunch?"

"I'm sorry, I'm not sure what you mean by 'regime'."

"A daily regime, presumably you sit reading in your living room quite frequently?"

"Since I was made redundant from the local library I have."

"When were you made redundant?"

"Just over two years ago," he said bitterly.

"Mr Callaghan, I mean no criticism in what I'm saying, but is it fair to say that for about a year before Mrs Wright was murdered, you would frequently be seated in your living room by the window?"

"Yes, because the light is good there for reading," he said defensively.

"You would be facing Mrs Wright's property?"

"Yes, but not deliberately, it was just a good place to read."

"There is no suggestion otherwise Mr Callaghan, I just want to establish the facts. You never saw this man approach her property before the day of her death?"

"No I never did. I didn't sit by the window every day, I did go out you know."

"Yes, I am sure you did, but you frequently sat in a position where you could see her house and you never saw this particular man visit her house before that day?"

"No, I didn't."

David smiled, it had taken a while but he had got there.

"Now on the 15th June 2012, where was this man when you first saw him?"

"He was just outside the gate."

"So you hadn't seen him walk up to the house?"

"No."

"You didn't see him approaching the gate then?"

"Not really, no."

"Did you see him go through the gate?"

"No, I saw him push the gate open and assumed he went inside, but then I was distracted by my kettle whistling."

"When did you see him limp then?"

Bill paused and thought before responding, "I can't remember now. I thought it was as he approached the gate."

"But you told us a second ago that you did not see him approach the gate. From what you have told us there was no opportunity for you to see him limp."

"I'm sure I did, but I can't remember when."

"You would accept that you only saw this man for, at most, a matter of seconds, maybe even a second or less?"

"Yes, it was a very short time."

"A fleeting glimpse."

"Yes I suppose so."

"You were not really concentrating on him?"

"No."

"Can you really recall the colour of his hair?"

"I'm sure it was light brown hair."

"Might it have been darker, say dark brown?"

"I don't think so."

"But you only had a fleeting glimpse?"

"Yes."

"You saw the man push the gate open?"

"Yes, as I've said."

"You only had a fleeting glimpse of the man so presumably you only had a fleeting glimpse of him pushing the gate open?"

"Yes, that's right."

"In those circumstances, can you be sure it was a dark walking stick that he used to push the gate open. Might it have been something else?"

"I thought it was a walking stick."

"Could it be something like a black furled umbrella?"

Bill looked confused, "I'm not sure, now. I think I might have mentioned an umbrella to the police."

"Sorry?"

"I think I wasn't sure when the police asked me whether it was an umbrella or a walking stick."

David now paused, "That does not appear in your witness statement."

"No, I'm not sure why, I'm sure I mentioned it to the police?"

"Which officer?"

"I don't know his full name, he's called Duncan something."

"Duncan MacDonald? The Officer in Charge of this case?"

"Yes that's his name."

David looked towards Duncan MacDonald who was seated in Court behind Geoffrey. Duncan looked away. David pointed at Duncan and asked, "That officer, Mr Callaghan?"

Bill smiled at Duncan, "Yes, that's him."

David addressed the judge in order to make the point in front of the jury. "I had agreed that the officer could stay in Court and assist my learned friends with the presentation of the evidence as I considered his evidence to be uncontentious at that time. However, in the light of this evidence, I submit it is appropriate that the officer immediately leave Court and remain outside."

Isobel looked towards Geoffrey, "Mr Lynch?"

"Yes My Lady, I agree, I shall ask the officer to leave the courtroom immediately."

Geoffrey turned to Duncan who rose from his seat and left Court. After he had left, David turned to the witness again, "Mr Callaghan, can you recall now what you said to the officer?"

Bill paused, he was a bit embarrassed for Duncan who had been nice to him. "I think I said to him it could be either a walking stick or an umbrella, but I wasn't sure."

"Did the officer say anything to you about seeing the man limp?"

"I don't remember."

"Or about the man having light brown hair?"

"I don't think so."

"Did he put words in your mouth?"

"I don't think so."

"Let's move on then. You have told us you heard a female scream coming from the direction of the house?"

"Yes."

"Did this alarm you?"

"What do you mean?"

"Well you heard a female scream, but you did not contact the police at that stage. Why was that?"

"Well, as I told the police, there's a girls' school in that direction and around lunchtime you frequently hear female screams."

"Did this one sound any different to the screams you usually hear?"

"No not really."

"So the scream you heard that day could have come from the school, not the house?"

"I suppose so."

"Is that what you thought at the time when you heard the scream that day and that's why you did not contact the police there and then?"

"Probably."

David thanked him and sat down. Geoffrey decided he had to ask some questions in re-examination, otherwise the jury might think he was giving up.

"Mr Callaghan it was put to you by my learned friend, that you only had a fleeting glimpse of the man outside Mrs Wright's house. How long do you think it was now?"

"It's difficult but it must have been a few seconds."

"Do you have any doubt that the man you saw has light brown hair?"

"No I'm sure he did."

"You mentioned a limp. Do you think you saw a limp?"

"I believe I did."

"Let me ask you about the walking stick/umbrella. You saw this man walk with a limp, thinking back now, do you think it was an umbrella or a walking stick he had on that bright sunny day?

"I think it was a walking stick."

"Thank you."

CHAPTER 29

CHARLIE'S NEIGHBOUR

The rest of the afternoon was taken up with the prosecution's junior counsel reading out witness statements in court. These witnesses had not been required to attend court by the Prosecution or the Defence because neither wanted to ask them any questions about their statements.

David went straight to his flat in the Barbican rather than into Chambers. He did not want to deal with any more of Chambers' problems. He wanted a night off and soon he had opened a bottle of Rioja Reserva and was sitting in his comfy old armchair. He decided to call Wendy. She was staying in Leeds in a small and shabby hotel, whilst she conducted a trial in the Leeds Crown Court.

They chatted about their cases and a few chambers matters, but nothing serious. He enjoyed having someone to re-cap his day with and was sorry when she rung off to prepare her case for the next day. But he looked forward to Saturday when Wendy promised to make him his favourite meal of Beef Stroganoff. She said she would make it from prime beef fillet and they would wash it down with a bottle of decent claret.

He smiled as he put the phone down noticing that he had only consumed half of the bottle of the Rioja. That was progress he thought, normally he would have finished it by now and probably be starting the second. He put the cork back into the bottle, another wholly unusual act for him. Corks usually had a one way trip from the bottle to the waste bin. Feeling suitably chaste, he settled down to look at the papers in the Holmes' case, in order to prepare cross examination of tomorrow's prosecution witnesses.

On Thursday morning, the case commenced punctually at 10:30am and the prosecution called a number of witnesses to give evidence. They were mainly unimportant witnesses dealing with the taking of photographs, the production of maps and charts and certain background information. David simply asked a few perfunctory questions to establish distances and times.

In the afternoon, the prosecution called Betty Crawford, Charlie's neighbour, to give evidence. She came into court slowly and was helped into the witness box by the court usher. Isobel told her she could stand or sit in the witness box as she pleased and Betty gave her a large smile in return and elected to give her evidence seated.

Geoffrey took her through some background details including where she lived and how long she had lived there.

"Oh, it's close to twenty years now. I moved there with my late husband after our children had grown up and left home. We only needed a two bedroomed flat by then."

"May I ask you your age?"

"Yes, I was 77 on my last birthday in November last year."

"Thank you, now I want to move on to ask you about your neighbour, Charlie Holmes, the defendant in this case."

Betty's expression immediately changed at the reference to Charlie, the smile disappeared and was replaced by a grimace.

Geoffrey was delighted by the change of expression and what it might convey to the jury, "You know Mr Holmes?"

"Yes I do."

The grimace became a frown.

"How do you know him?"

"He moved in next door about two years ago."

"We have heard he was a Fireman at that stage?"

"Yes, he was a very nice man when he moved in, very helpful, but that all changed after his accident."

"You were aware he had an accident?"

"Oh yes, I was very concerned for him when I heard he was in hospital."

"I don't think there is any challenge to this, I believe he came out of hospital after about two months?"

"Yes, I remember him coming home using two crutches at first, but within a couple of weeks he was using a walking stick. I wondered just how serious the accident was!"

Geoffrey decided to ignore this gratuitous comment, "Did you notice anything in particular about the walking stick?

"No, I think it was a dark one, dark brown or even black."

"Thank you. How in your opinion did he change after the accident?"

David immediately objected, "With respect My Lady, how can this witnesses' lay opinion of my client's demeanour, after he had a terribly serious accident, have any relevance to any issue in this case?"

Isobel immediately responded, "I can see how his demeanour is very relevant, but, Mr Lynch, the witness should not be asked to give her personal opinion on matters about which she has no expertise."

Geoffrey smiled, "Of course, My Lady."

Turning back to Betty he said, "Mrs Crawford, let me rephrase the question, did you notice any change in Mr Holmes after the accident?"

"Oh yes, he was much less friendly. He seemed depressed and he made a lot more noise in his flat. Frequently shouting and throwing things. It was very annoying.

I remember once he brought a hulking great man to the house, he was carrying a chair for him. I went outside, just to say hello, and he was very rude to me. Before I could say anything he told me he wouldn't be long and I didn't need to complain about the noise!"

Geoffrey again gave her his best beaming smile. "You will be aware that this is a murder trial, the victim was a Mrs Sheila Wright. Did you ever meet her?"

"Oh yes, she frequently visited his flat. She looked a little older than him. She was very quiet and never really wanted to speak."

"Did she ever visit his flat after the accident?"

"Oh yes, I saw her a few times."

"Do you remember now the last time you saw her visit his flat?"

"I'm not sure, it might have been about a week before she was killed."

"I want to deal with the day she was killed. We know it was Friday, 15th June 2012. Do you remember seeing Mr Holmes that day?"

"Yes, I remember that day very well, my daughter was supposed to come and visit me but she cancelled in the early morning."

She gave a look as though this was a regular occurrence.

"I saw him leave his house at about 10:30 in the morning, I remember the time because I was listening to Woman's Hour on Radio 4."

"Do you recall how he was dressed or if he was carrying anything?"

"Not really, he had his walking stick but that is all I recall."

"Did you see him again that day?"

"Yes, it was about 3pm. He didn't stay long, about half an hour later he left and he didn't come back that night, which was strange."

"How do you know he didn't come back that night?"

"You can always hear him when he comes back, he makes such a noise. His front door is a heavy one and it doesn't matter what time he comes home, I always hear the door banging. "

"Why do you say it was strange that he did not come back?"

"Because, since his accident, he has come back every night."

"Did you notice when he did return?"

"Yes, he made his usual loud noises when he returned at about 5pm on Saturday."

Geoffrey finished his questioning there, satisfied with the answers.

David smiled at her as he began questioning. He had assumed she was a lonely woman and this was one of the most exciting times in her life. She obviously would not want to admit that she spent all her time looking through a gap in the curtain of her living room and he wanted to build on that.

"Mrs Crawford, in your witness statement you state the walls between your flats are very thin?"

"That's right."

"And that is presumably why you can hear so much noise from your neighbour's flat."

"Yes."

"And how you can tell when he is coming and going from the flat. Obviously, you don't spend your day constantly looking out from behind the curtains?"

"No, of course not, I'm not a busybody."

David smiled, "I'm sure no one is suggesting that. The truth is, because you are not constantly looking out for Mr Holmes, you may miss occasions when he does stay away for the odd night, here and there."

"I don't think so."

"You see, I'm going to suggest it wasn't that strange or unusual for him to stay away from his flat at night. In the last couple of weeks before 15th June 212, he did leave the flat and stayed away every Friday night."

"I don't think so, I'm sure I would have noticed."

"I'm suggesting that on three separate Fridays in a row he stayed away from his flat and you never noticed."

"No." She hesitated before adding, "I'm sure he didn't."

David was in the process of sitting when Geoffrey turned to his junior counsel, Stephen, and asked in a voice loud enough for David to hear, "Is there any reference to these regular Friday nights away in the Defence Case Statement?"

Stephen replied in a similarly loud voice, "No, none whatsoever."

"I thought not."

CHAPTER 30

THE NEWSAGENT AND THE BUS DRIVER

The rest of Thursday was taken up with Stephen reading out statements from further witnesses who were not required by either side. As no further witnesses had been warned to attend court for that day, Isobel adjourned the trial early at 3:55pm.

David again avoided Chambers and went back to his flat. The prosecution only had a few witnesses lined up for Friday. The expert witnesses; namely the Pathologist, the Blood expert and the Cell site expert dealing with the mobile phone evidence, could not make it until Monday morning.

Geoffrey began by calling Ashiq Ali, a newsagent, to give evidence. David watched him as he walked into Court. He was about fifty and clearly did not want to be there, no doubt he would have preferred to be back at his shop.

"Mr Ali, you are the owner of the AA Newsagents in Clapham?"

"Yes sir."

"Obviously you sell newspapers and basic provisions in the store?"

"Yes sir."

"I understand that you also sell top up vouchers for phones?"

"Yes sir."

"How does that work?"

"People come into the shop and purchase a voucher for their phone." He answered quizzically.

"Yes, I'm sure it's my fault, I wanted to know what actually happens? Does the person have to have the phone with them for example?"

"No sir. A person comes into the shop, he asks for a top up voucher for a phone company and we provide him with one. It has either a 14 digit or 16 digit code number which the customer can then use to top up their phone."

"How does a person actually top up their phone?"

"Well, you phone the number on the receipt or text it, and provide the 14 or 16 digit number."

"Now I want to ask you about a specific voucher you sold that day."

Geoffrey produced a voucher for the witness that Mr Ali had earlier provided to the police.

"Yes sir, that is the voucher I gave the officer."

"We see that it's dated 15th June 2012 and timed at 10:37am?

"Yes sir."

"Were those times accurate?"

"Yes sir, the machine accurately records the time."

"You have also produced a clip from your shop's CCTV?"

"Yes sir."

The clip was played to the jury. It showed Charlie Holmes entering the newsagents and purchasing the voucher. Geoffrey explained that the times on the video were slightly different because the camera was out by a few minutes. Everyone watched as Charlie entered the shop and went up to the counter, purchasing the voucher. It was noticeable from the CCTV that he had a pronounced limp.

"You also provided a copy of a credit card slip for this transaction?"

"Yes could you just look at the slip and tell us the name of the purchaser?"

257

Mr Ali looked closely at the credit card slip, "Yes sir, it was purchased by Mr Charles Holmes."

Geoffrey thanked Mr Ali and David began to question him.

"Had you seen this customer before?"

"Yes sir, on many occasions, I believe he lives locally."

"I think you had seen him come into the store with a young lady in the past?"

"Yes sir."

"Do you know who the lady was?"

"I do not know her name sir. I recognised her from her picture in the newspaper. She is the lady who was killed."

"Yes, Sheila Wright was her name. Do you have any CCTV clips of the two of them coming into the shop?"

"No sir, we only keep our video for one week and then we record over it."

"You saw my client, Mr Holmes, come into your shop on a few occasions with this lady?"

"Yes sir."

"Whenever they came in, did they look happy together?"

"Yes sir, they were always very affectionate towards each other."

"You never saw them argue or have any problems?"

"No sir."

"Just one final matter, about the voucher you supplied. In fact two vouchers are produced by the machine, one for the customer and one for the shop?"

"That's right sir."

"We shall hear that the other voucher was never found. The one you produce is the one from the shop?"

"Yes sir, the voucher I gave the officer is from my shop records."

"In order to top up a phone you don't actually need the physical voucher. This was a 16 digit code. All you need is the 16 digit code, for example Mr Holmes could have bought the voucher and read the digits out over the phone to Mrs Wright, who could then have written them down and then phoned her provider and given the number?"

"Yes sir."

David sat down as that was all he could achieve from this witness. At least he had given the jury the image of Charlie and Sheila being close with no suggestion of any problem in their relationship and he had shown that Charlie did not need to be in her house to provide her with the top up voucher.

Geoffrey called his next witness, John Richardson, a bus driver. He was a stocky man and, in contrast to Mr Ali, seemed happy to be in court taking a day off from work.

"Mr Richardson, in June of last year you were the driver of a number 155 bus which travelled between Tooting and Clapham junction?"

"That's right."

"The police have obtained a clip from the bus CCTV cameras for a journey that was undertaken on 15th June 2012, just before 10:50am. I want you to watch it with us."

The CCTV clip was shown again to the jury. David noticed how closely they watched it and that two women sitting together in the front row were scribbling notes and nudging each other at certain parts of the video. He wondered what interested them so much as there was nothing he noticed on the CCTV.

After the video was played Geoffrey asked a few further questions.

"Do you recognise the man with the walking stick who got on the bus at 10:51am that day?"

"Yes I do. He travels on the bus most days during the week. He used to have crutches and was much slower getting on and off, but by this time he was quite nippy."

"Nippy?"

"Quick, he's a lot quicker getting on and off."

"Did you notice anything about him this particular day?"

"Yes, normally he's quite polite, just says hello and shows his bus pass, but on this occasion he was on the phone. He seemed annoyed about something and I remember him swearing when he got on the bus."

"Do you remember what he said? Don't worry about the words he may have used, we've heard them all before in court."

"Yeah he said something like, "fucking cow", something like that."

"We see him getting off the bus at 11:12am. We know that is the stop nearest to Sheila Wright's address."

John Richardson looked at him blankly, "I've no idea."

Geoffrey smiled, "No, that was for the benefit of the court Mr Richardson. Later we see him get back on your bus again at 2-22pm. That is at the stop across the road from where he got off?"

"Yeah, that's right."

"We then see him get off the bus at the stop nearest his flat at 2:40pm?"

Again John looked quizzical, "I don't know where he lives."

Geoffrey smiled again, "Yes, thank you Mr Richardson."

David asked that the start of the video clip be shown again.

"Mr Richardson, we see Mr Holmes getting on your bus. There are a large number of other people as well?"

"Yeah."

"As we see you are separated from passengers by security glass, no doubt to protect you from attack?"

"The screen must reduce your ability to hear what is being said by a passenger?"

"Yes a little, but there are holes in the screen so you can hear if they ask any questions."

"Yes, but that is when they stand right next to you?"

"Yes."

"The screen must interfere with your hearing and with large numbers of passengers getting on the bus at the same time, some talking, it must have been difficult to hear what my client said?"

"Yeah, well, as I said, I thought he said something like "fucking cow.""

"Yes, but you are not certain that he said that?"

"No, but it was something like that."

"Might you have missed the first part of what he said, might it have been something like, "You tell me fucking now".

"I thought he said "fucking cow".

"You had seen him travel on the bus on a number of occasions?"

"Yeah, as I said."

"Do you remember him ever being in the company of a lady?"

"Yeah, a few times."

"Do you know who the lady is?"

"No."

"You've not seen her picture in the papers, the victim in this case?"

"No,"

"Anyway when he was with this lady, how did they behave?"

"What do you mean?"

"Were they affectionate to each other?"

"I was driving the bus I didn't really see."

"No, but you would have seen if they were arguing, causing a scene on the bus. That never happened did it?"

"No."

"They presumably seemed like a normal couple when you saw them?"

"Yeah, I suppose so."

"Thank you."

The rest of the morning was spent with the reading of further witness statements and, at 1pm, Isobel adjourned the case for lunch. David and Jamie took the opportunity to go upstairs to the Bar Mess to discover what culinary delights were on offer today. Having selected the breaded fish and chips, both sat at their usual table.

Having consumed the meal silently, David noticed that Jamie was deep in thought and enquired, "What's the matter with you today Jamie?"

Jamie looked up as if he had been suddenly awakened, "Sorry, I was just thinking about the evidence. You're doing a great job but the timings really do add up in this case. Charlie just happens to be in the right place at the right time, or the wrong time depending upon how you look at it!"

David looked at him closely, surprised that Jamie was only just realising this. "I agree, circumstantially it's a strong case. A lot will depend on how the jury view Charlie which is why he's going to have to give evidence. I just hope he will be ready by early next week. He's got one shot at this and so far he has shown little to no interest in helping himself."

CHAPTER 31

THE FIREMAN AND THE NURSE

At 2:10pm the Court sat again and the prosecution junior, Stephen took the next witness, Mary Young, who was a nurse at the hospital where Charlie was taken after his accident. Stephen appeared a little nervous in comparison with the experienced advocacy of Geoffrey.

"Ms Young, its right that you are a Nurse and in March 2012 you were working at the St. Joseph's hospital in Clapham, London?"

"Yes that's right."

"Did you get to know a patient by the name of Charlie Holmes?"

"Yes, I did, he was a Fireman who was seriously injured in a road traffic accident."

"We understand that he received a severe injury to his leg and an injury to his bladder and he was in hospital for two months?"

"Yes that's right, as far as I can recall. We do have a lot of patients in the hospital."

"I want to ask you about visitors he had to the hospital during that period. Do you recall any particular visitors he had?"

"He had the usual visitors, relatives and friends. I remember a lot of firemen visited him."

She smiled at the memory of seeing these strapping young men in the ward.

"Do you recall any female visitors?"

"Yes I remember one in particular. She said she was his sister, but I doubted that."

"Why was that?"

"They were too affectionate to be brother and sister. She was always kissing him."

"Did she give a name?"

"Yes, it's in my statement, Sheila Wright was the name she gave."

Stephen thanked her and sat down. David rose slowly to his feet, "Mr Holmes suffered serious injuries in the accident?"

"Yes he did."

"They were life threatening?"

"When he first came into hospital yes, I think his bladder had torn."

"He was very weak for quite some time?"

"Yes, but he was strong, probably because of his occupation. He recovered much more quickly than expected."

"The lady you mentioned, she was a frequent visitor to the hospital?"

"Yes, she visited him every other day except at weekends."

"During this time, Mr Holmes was probably subject to mood swings, happy one day, depressed the next?"

"Yes, he had suffered serious injuries, that wasn't surprising."

"Mrs Wright kept on visiting though?"

"Yes."

"Her attitude, her affection towards him did not change during this period?"

"No, she was always the same, always very affectionate."

"It was obvious to you Mrs Wright was not his sister. Throughout the period he spent in hospital these two acted like a couple who were very much in love?"

"That's what I thought."

David thanked her and sat down.

Stephen called the final witness for the day, James Bevan, a friend of Charlie's, who had worked with him as a fireman.

"Mr Bevan, do you know the Defendant in this case?"

"Yes, I know Charlie."

He smiled at Charlie in the dock who smiled back.

"How long have you known him?"

"Since I first started working as a fireman in Clapham, so probably, four years now."

"So you knew him before his accident?"

"Yes."

"Did you see him after his accident?"

"Oh yes, I visited him in hospital a few times and then saw him once at his flat, when I moved some furniture in for him."

"We have heard in this case that he had a relationship with Sheila Wright, the victim in this case. Did you ever meet her?"

"I saw her once at the Fire station, before Charlie had his accident. She was meeting Charlie."

"Did you see how they were together?"

"They were very affectionate."

"Did you ever see her with him after the accident?"

"No, I only saw her the one time, at the Fire station."

"Did the Defendant ever talk to you about her?"

"Yes he spoke to me about her before I met her. It must have been shortly after they met because he said he had met a married woman and he was having a sexual relationship with her."

"Did he put it like that, 'a sexual relationship'?"

James Bevan smiled, "Not quite those words, but that was what he meant."

"Did he discuss her again with you?"

"Yeah, just before the accident he said how much he loved her, how he wanted her to get a divorce so he could marry her."

"Did he speak to you about her after the accident?"

"Not really, he was obviously depressed. The accident really affected him."

Stephen looked down at his copy of James Bevan's witness statement and looked coldly at James, as if he was trying to hide something.

"Did he say anything about their relationship at that stage?"

"He did say something the day I delivered the chair for him. He just said that he thought she was getting a bit cold towards him, mainly because he couldn't have sex with her anymore."

Stephen smiled, "Thank you, would you wait there."

David looked at James Bevan closely, "Mr Bevan I'm going to ask you a few questions on behalf of Charlie Holmes."

It helps to tell him I'm on the side of his friend.

"As you have told us, you worked with Mr Holmes when he was a Fireman. What was he like at his job?"

James smiled, "He was one of the best. He always had your back. He was very brave and wouldn't think of the risk to himself if someone needed saving. He received an award for saving children during a fire."

"Can you tell us what happened?"

"It was a house fire and four children were trapped. The floors were in danger of collapsing at any time, but Charlie kept going back in and rescued the children one at a time until he had rescued all four."

"Thank you. You have known Charlie for about four years now?"

"Yes."

"In that time, have you formed an impression about his character?"

"Yes."

"How would you assess his character?"

"He's a good man, a true friend. As I said he is brave and would help anyone."

"Have you been able to assess whether he is honest or not?"

"Yes, in my opinion he is very honest and completely trustworthy."

"Is he a violent man?"

"No, certainly not."

"Thank you, I just wanted to ask you about his relationship with Sheila Wright. He told you they were very close, he told you he wanted to marry her?"

"Yes."

"He also told you she felt the same way about him?"

"Yes."

"Obviously after the accident he did feel low, depressed as you put it?"

"Yes."

"He told you that he thought she was cooling a little bit in the relationship, because of his problems with sex?"

"Yes."

"But he never said anything about their relationship ending?"

"No."

"In fact, there was nothing in what he said to suggest that they did not love each other."

"No."

"And there was nothing to suggest that their plans had changed. They still wanted to be together despite the problems with sexual function?"

"I suppose so."

David sat down and Stephen immediately rose to his feet.

"Mr Bevan, your friend..." He paused for full effect, "....told you the day you delivered a chair to his flat, that she was cooling in their relationship?"

"Yes."

"From what you have told us, there was no discussion about them having a future together?"

"No, that's true."

"So how can you say to my learned friend, that they still wanted to be together?"

James paused before answering, "Well he had told me they both wanted to be together and nothing he said to me suggested that they didn't."

David turned to Jamie with a smile, "that's a prime example of the prosecution asking one question too many. You should learn from that Jamie. Always stop when you have the answer you want."

CHAPTER 32

THE JUNIOR TENANT

David returned to Chambers, feeling satisfied with the week. The case was not over and there was still a large amount of circumstantial evidence to counter, but he felt he had made significant headway. He deserved a restful weekend. He would pick up any papers, say 'Hello' to the clerks and make his way home.

As he arrived at the door of the clerks room and noticed that they seemed their usual busy selves, he thought he would just give them a cheery greeting and then leave. However, as he walked in, John put the phone down and greeted him, "Good evening sir, how's the case going?"

"Well, its early days yet but I think it's going as well as it can."

"Excellent sir. When you're settled in your room, can we have a word?"

Oh no, what is it now, wondered David.

"Of course, just give me a couple of minutes."

"Okay sir, I'll get Ryan to make you a cup of tea."

My God it must be serious, thought David.

He went to his room clutching a number of letters and documents from his pigeon hole. Most were junk mail, offers of loans to Barristers, letters from accountants offering services 'specially tailored' for QCs, offers to test drive cars which were completely outside his income bracket, the usual rubbish. There were a few circulars from the Bar Council and the Inns of Court offering free lectures to barristers so they could complete their required 12 hours annual Continuing Professional Development (CPD). He filed most of the letters in what he called his 'spherical filing cabinet' known to most people as a waste paper bin. The Bar Council and Inn circulars would make it to the Chambers Notice board in the Clerks' room, where, no doubt they would be ignored by everyone in Chambers.

A few minutes later, Ryan brought him a cup of tea, and John joined him, carrying a cup of tea in one hand and a letter in the other.

David sipped at his tea looking ominously at the letter. John sat down facing David and reported, "Sir, there's been an official complaint to Chambers."

David put his tea down, his mind racing. Had he said or done something after too many bottles of red? It would not be the first time, *I'm giving up drinking forever.*

John looked at him quizzically, "It's about Mr Hawker sir."

Thank God, you know I really do fancy a glass of Claret right now.

John continued, "We've had a complaint from the Head of Number One Queen Catherine's Chambers, Richard Lafferty QC, you know sir, the commercial set."

David nodded.

"The Senior Clerk there, Martin, told me that Mr Lafferty would be writing to you. It appears Mr Hawker has taken a shine to a female pupil in that set, called Natasha Bloomfield."

"I wasn't aware that was either a criminal offence or a breach of professional conduct."

"I agree sir. The problem appears to be that Mr Hawker has become a bit of a nuisance. He apparently sits outside the Chambers for hours with chocolates and flowers waiting for her to leave. She apparently isn't interested in him and has asked him to stop, but he won't.

Indeed, it's got to the stage that she has obtained a Court Order against him to stop him harassing her."

"You're joking, how long have you known about this?"

"Only the last week or so. I didn't want to trouble you as I know you are busy. I'd hoped the Court Order would stop him, but it hasn't."

"Why what's happened?"

"Well it appears he has continued to wait outside her Chambers and now she is thinking of taking Committal Proceedings against him, you know sir, to commit him to prison for breaching the Court's Order."

"Thank you John, I do have some distant recollection of such cases."

"Of course I know that sir. Anyway their Head of Chambers has asked the pupil not to start Committal Proceedings until you have had a chance to, well, hopefully, talk some sense to him. That's the reason he has written this letter."

"I thought Julian Hawker was a busy tenant, how does he have the time to spend hours sitting outside a Chambers waiting for a female pupil to leave?"

"Well, he's not been so busy recently. To be frank sir, he has annoyed a few of chambers' solicitors, particularly female ones."

"I thought you told me just a few days ago that he was easy to sell to solicitors, 'horses for courses' you told me."

"True sir, as I told you at the time, the clerks room has found him easy to sell in the past and we expect he will be easy to sell in the future. He is an exceptional barrister. The problem is he has reached a low point and we thought it might help if you could have a word with him. I've asked Mr Hawker to stay behind tonight for that purpose. I also ought to mention that there is another issue, he's not paid his chamber's rent or clerks' fees for two months, ever since he bought his Ferrari."

David had heard about the Ferrari. He had been told that Julian had purchased a second hand Ferrari for £40,000. Julian had returned to chambers from court the day after he purchased the car and had gone to his room which he shared with Graham Martin and others. With a remarkable disregard for the other tenants in the room, most of whom were struggling to pay their mortgages, he threw his new car keys on Graham's desk and announced, "I've just bought a £40,000 Ferrari."

Graham had not even bothered to look up when he responded, "You need one." Julian had apparently looked surprised at the comment and then picked up his car keys and left without a further word.

The story had amused David at the time but the fact Julian was not paying his rent did not.

"How much does he owe?" he asked.

"I don't know the exact amount but I know he has received some large fees recently. I believe he owes about £10,000 in rent and clerks' fees."

John then handed over the letter and left the room. David read the letter and a few minutes later, Julian appeared.

"Hello David, how's the murder trial going?"

David looked at him with a frown, "It's going very well, thank you, but you know we're not here to exchange pleasantries."

"Yes, I'm sorry, I've heard there's been a complaint from Natasha. It's all very silly, we had a quick fling, she's a gorgeous filly but a bit thick. She phoned me up, asked me to come round to her chambers and then accused me of harassing her! I think she found out I was seeing somebody else and just wanted to embarrass me."

"Really Julian? Do you think it appropriate in this day and age to refer to a female barrister as a 'gorgeous filly'?

"I suspect that's what you used to call them in your day."

David was beginning to see red. "May I remind you Julian, this is still 'my day'. In any event, you were seen by her clerks hanging around outside her chambers with flowers and chocolates for hours. She has even obtained a Court Order against you."

"Yes I know, she's taken it a little too far."

"A little too far?" repeated David loudly. "If the Court Order was improperly obtained you should have challenged it."

"I thought about it, but decided it was a waste of my time," said Julian.

"She is thinking of bringing committal proceedings, alleging you are still visiting her chambers."

"I assure you David I am not. I may pass those chambers on the way home, but that's all."

"Well I suggest you find another way home and don't go anywhere near her or her Chambers again."

Julian paused as if in deep thought, "Very well David, I promise I will find another way home and will not go near her Chambers again."

"Good, because whatever the truth or otherwise of the allegation, the last thing we want is the Press getting hold of a story that a barrister from these chambers is harassing a young female pupil! It's totally unacceptable behaviour."

"Understood, is that it David?"

"No, there is the issue about your rent and clerks fees. I understand you haven't paid them for two months."

"Yes, sorry about that, it's only a temporary thing. I've had a few large expenses recently."

"Julian, we all know you've paid £40,000 for a Ferrari. What you spend your money on is up to you, but you must pay your chambers' rent and clerks' fees when they fall due. There are no exceptions. I expect you to pay the full arrears by the end of next week even if you have to take out a loan to do it."

"Ok David, fair enough. Actually it was £36,000 and worth every penny, but you have a point. I'll get the money to you by the end of next week."

David watched as Julian left the room. He had not believed a single word Julian had said.

God he's going to be a problem, I wish I had voted 'No' to taking on that little creep.

CHAPTER 33

DINNER WITH WENDY

"He said what?"

"He referred to her as a 'gorgeous filly'."

It was Saturday. David was in the living room of Wendy's rented flat which she shared with two female friends. Both were staying with their boyfriends tonight so she could entertain David.

David was telling the story of his encounter with Julian the night before.

Wendy volunteered, "I'm surprised a young man uses the term 'filly'. It's more a term you would hear from someone ...."

"Don't say my age!" David quickly added.

"I wasn't going to." Wendy added, a little too quickly for David's liking.

Wendy continued, "He is a creep though. I don't know a single woman in chambers who likes him or wants to be in his company alone. I had to warn off our female pupil, Jemma Leadbetter the other day. She'd offered to do some work for him and he said he'd repay her with dinner. I advised her not to go."

"Did she go?"

"No. She told him she was seeing her father that night. She said she was very proud of her father because he got a boxing blue at Cambridge and that he was still very fit. She apparently added that the only annoying trait her father had, was he took too much interest in her love life! Clever girl."

"How did this chap get into Chambers?"

"Senior people like you didn't put your foot down."

"I didn't know anything about him."

"Well now you do."

Wendy finished her glass of Claret and walked towards the kitchen. "Come on, you can help me prepare dinner."

David smiled, finished his glass and followed her into the kitchen dutifully.

Wendy took the fillet steak that she had left out for a short time and then took a carving knife and started to cut small thin strips for the Beef Stroganoff.

He poured them both another glass of Claret and put on an apron containing a picture of a half-naked man, which he tied round himself. If he was going to be domesticated, it was only right that he looked the part.

He watched as Wendy sliced the steak, cutting it into small pieces. He noticed how she held the fillet down with her right hand as she cut with her left. He was enjoying the feeling of domestic bliss, so far removed from his own empty flat in the Barbican. He then noticed the carving knife that Wendy was using. It looked strangely familiar.

"That's an unusual handle."

She stopped, put the knife down and showed it to him, "Not if you're left-handed it's not."

"What?"

"It's a present from my mother, she bought it in a shop in Central London that sells items designed for left-handed people. This is a special Chef's knife. It gives me an excellent grip, ideal for work like this."

David picked the knife up and looked at it closely. He remembered immediately where he had seen a similar one and a large smile suddenly appeared across his face.

CHAPTER 34

THE PATHOLOGIST

It was soon Monday and after a very pleasant weekend with Wendy, the realities of life at the Bar came back with a vengeance. Today, David had to deal with three expert witnesses. All of whom were very experienced in their fields and all of whom had given evidence in court in many cases. Each of them would undoubtedly prove challenging.

Petrov Labaski, the Forensic Pathologist, was the first to give evidence that day. David had never come across him in court before, but had heard that he was fair and would consider any reasonable scenario put to him.

Mr Labaski began his evidence by detailing his impressive CV and array of qualifications which began to sound like alphabet soup. He gained a BSC in Neuroscience from Imperial College London in 1986 and obtained a MBBS in 1999. In 1996 he gained the Diploma of Medical Jurisprudence in Pathology; he became a member of the Royal College of Pathologists in 1997 and in 1998 became a Fellow (FRCPath). Having held surgical posts in various hospitals in London he had spent five years training in general histopathology and then two years subspecialist training in forensic pathology. He had been a registered and practising pathologist since 2000.

David had no intention of suggesting he was not a suitably qualified expert to give this evidence.

Geoffrey moved on to deal with the autopsy, establishing the date and time first, then moving to the detail, "Mr Labaski, can you tell us what your findings were?"

"Yes, the body was of a white female, medium build, 168 cm (5 feet 6 inches) and 70 kgs (154 pounds). There was no Rigor Mortis in the arms or the legs."

"Could I just stop you there? Mr Labaski, we have heard a little evidence about Rigor Mortis in this case, but could we benefit from your expertise. When does Rigor Mortis start?"

"Rigor Mortis is dependent on many variables and once a body has been refrigerated it also alters the affects. There are differing medical opinions about when it starts. Usually it comes on between 6-12 hours after death and is complete by about 24 hours and then ceases by 36 hours."

"Could the signs commence before 6 hours?"

"Yes, it begins in the smaller muscle groups, so it could be seen in the jaw earlier than 6 hours."

"Thank you. Could you tell us please about the rest of your findings?"

"Certainly, I noted that in the right side of the mouth there were unhatched fly eggs. However, flies are quickly able to find a corpse, sometimes within seconds or minutes of somebody dying, so I did not find this of any importance.

Having checked all the organs and other parts of the body I was able to conclude that there were no signs of natural disease that may have caused or contributed to the death. The toxicology reports indicate that she was not under the influence of drugs or alcohol at the time of her death and there was no evidence of a blunt force trauma, such as a beating. There was also no evidence of sexual assault.

I then moved on to consider the wounds seen on the body."

Geoffrey turned to the jury, "Ladies and gentlemen, there are some computer-generated pictures showing a computer model of the deceased indicating where the wounds were inflicted. You will find them in your jury bundle. I am happy to say that we will not need to trouble you with any gruesome photographs in this case."

He would show them if he could, thought David, *it's only because the rules effectively prevent showing such photographs these days that he isn't troubling them!*

Geoffrey continued, "Mr Labaski, can you assist us with the wounds that you saw, and perhaps point them out on the computer image that the jury have?"

"Yes, certainly. There were nine wounds in all. Some were superficial injuries, others were more serious, two would have been fatal on their own, and one more would have led to death without medical intervention. All the wounds were inflicted from the right to the left, most were angled downwards, although two were upwards in direction."

Geoffrey then took him through all the wounds individually, pointing to them on the computer image of the victim's body. He pointed out the six that he said were 'insignificant' in that they would not have caused death. He described the three major injuries,

"Major injury number one was located just below her jaw line. It was close to the midline and internally left a hole in the front of the windpipe measuring 1cm. It is not possible to be certain, but if this was the first wound inflicted it would have gone through the muscles and small vessels, it would have bled and the blood would have entered the airways. This injury was fatal.

The second major injury was in the same area and caused a V-shaped defect in the windpipe, this would have had the same effect as the first injury and would have been fatal.

The third significant injury penetrated the chest cavity between the right 2nd and 3rd ribs and into the pericardium."

"I'm sorry, what is the pericardium?"

"It is the sack that the heart sits in. An injury here will usually quickly fill the sack with blood and cause a tamponade," replied the doctor.

"Again, Mr Labaski, I am sorry, I'm afraid I tend to suffer from an ailment known as hippopotomonstrosequippedaliophobia."

Mr Labaski looked at him quizzically, "I'm sorry what does that mean?"

Geoffrey smiled, "A fear of long words!"

There were a few polite laughs around the Courtroom, including a number from the jury, others gave him a look as though he was completely idiotic, including Mr Labaski. Geoffrey was completely oblivious and moved on, pleased that he had won a bet with his junior that he would get the ridiculous word into his examination!

"Mr Labaski, can you assist us, what is a tamponade?"

"It is pressure in the Peri .... the sack around the heart, which increases as the blood flows into the sack. This puts great pressure on the heart and can lead to death unless the patient is operated upon quickly, by opening the chest and relieving the pressure."

Geoffrey thanked him and then asked, "Can you tell us what force was used to cause these wounds?"

"A sharp knife using only moderate force was required for each of these wounds. Once a knife has penetrated the skin there is nothing to stop it until it hits bone. That did not occur here."

"Are you able to assist us as to what type of knife was used?"

"Yes, the wounds all appeared to be squared-off on one edge. This suggested that the knife only had one cutting edge. I drew a picture for the officer indicating what I thought the blade would look like, and its dimensions."

"Yes, the jury have a copy of that drawing. I would like to show you the knife that was recovered in this case."

The boxed knife was shown to Mr Labaski.

"In your opinion, could this knife have caused the wounds you saw?"

Mr Labaski looked carefully at the knife through the clear cellophane on the top of box. "Yes, it has one cutting edge and the width and length are of the right dimension."

"Thank you, can you assist as to the sequence the wounds were inflicted in this case?"

"It is difficult to give an exact sequence of events in a dynamic situation involving a multiple stabbing incident. However, it does appear from the lack of defensive injuries that the lady was incapacitated quickly. In my opinion, it is likely that the first injuries were the injuries to the airways. The airways would have quickly filled with blood, coupled probably with the injury to the pericardium; there would have been a rapid loss of blood pressure, respiration and a rapid loss of consciousness."

"Can you explain why there was so little blood at the scene?"

"Most, if not all, of the injuries here would have bled into her clothing. Also she was seated on the sofa and if the attack was sudden, she would have become rapidly incapacitated without any chance to move, hence there would have been little blood flowing from her body or deposited around the scene."

"Can you assist with where the parties were seated when she was attacked?"

"Having looked at the angle of the injuries, the photographs of the scene, and the position of her body on the sofa, it is my opinion that the assailant was seated on the sofa to her right and that he was right-handed."

"Why right-handed?"

"It would be almost impossible for a left-handed person to have inflicted these injuries if he was seated to her right. The knife would probably have hit the settee."

Geoffrey gave one of his usual smiles, thanked the doctor and sat down.

David got up and gave a much smaller smile to the doctor. "Mr Labaski, as you have told us, you have considerable experience in the world of forensic medicine."

"Yes, I do, I have carried out a large number of autopsies and I have given evidence on many occasions."

"I do not dispute either fact. In this case, you have used your experience to give an opinion as to the likely position of the assailant and which wounds were caused when?"

"Yes, although there are, of course, limitations. I cannot be certain of the position of the assailant nor the sequence of infliction of the wounds."

"No, as you have said, you are giving your opinion based on your experience, but it is impossible to be certain about these matters."

"That's right."

"I want you to help with the Rigor Mortis issue. You have stated it 'comes on between 6-12 hours.' In this case, we have heard that paramedics state that they saw signs of Rigor Mortis when they attended at about 4pm, that would mean death occurred before 10am?"

"No, Rigor Mortis does set in but I can't say exactly when. It depends on a number of factors including the environment, such as the building and temperature around the body. Six to twelve hours is a broad parameter. It is right that you witness it first in the smaller muscle groups, the largest last, it also fades in reverse order."

"I want to ask you about the position of the assailant in this case. You have told us you think it likely that he was right-handed and seated on the right of the victim?"

"Yes, I think that is the most likely positioning."

"Of course, you did not hear the evidence of the Catherine Ford, the Paramedic who attended the scene?"

"No, I did not, though I believe her statement was provided to me by the Crown Prosecution Service."

"She gave evidence that wasn't in her statement and it was to the effect that when she arrived there was a chair in front of the victim, in a position as if they had been in conversation just before she was killed."

"I wasn't aware of that."

"Might that change your opinion?"

"No, I still believe the most likely scenario is that the assailant was seated to her right at the time of the murder. They may well have been seated differently beforehand."

"Let me ask you to consider these different scenarios. Imagine the assailant was seated in the chair directly in front of her when he attacked her. These injuries could have been caused by him if he was left-handed, but not if he was right-handed, correct?"

Mr Labaski thought for a few moments.

"Yes, that is possible."

"Likewise, if the assailant was standing to her left, he could have caused these injuries if he was left handed?"

Mr Labaski paused for thought again.

"That is possible, but he would have to stoop down to cause the injuries as they were inflicted in an upwards direction."

"Thank you, so the assailant in this case could have been left-handed?"

"Yes, although it would have been almost impossible for him to cause these injuries if he was seated on her right side if he were left-handed."

"Is it fair to say from your experience and expertise, you cannot say whether the assailant was seated on her right, or directly in front of her or whether he was standing and stooping to her left as he stabbed her?"

"That is right. I cannot say categorically where the assailant actually was at the time, as I said initially."

"Or, indeed, whether he was right or left handed?"

"No, I cannot say for certain, there are many different possible scenarios."

"Thank you, Mr Labaski. May I just deal with just one final matter to see if the assailant was right or left handed? Could you look at the knife in the box again?

The usher showed him the knife again.

"Mr Labaski, would you look carefully at that knife. You have examined the blade but not the handle. If you look closely, can you see the handle has a specific design? In fact, you can see from the handle that it is specially designed for those who are left handed!"

CHAPTER 35

THE BLOOD EXPERT

David sat down and looked at Geoffrey, who immediately asked if he could look at the knife again. After a few moments, he turned to Mr Labaski. "Mr Labaski, please look at this knife one more time."

The knife was again shown to him. Geoffrey continued, "Although it appears this knife was designed for left-handed people, would that preclude a right-handed person using it to cause these injuries with his right hand?"

Again Mr Labaski paused before answering, "This is not really within my expertise, but common sense dictates that this knife is designed to make it easier to be used by left-handed people. Of course that could not stop a right-handed person from using it."

"You have told us there are a few possible scenarios here as to how Mrs Wright was killed. Using your experience and expertise, is there a scenario you consider to be the MOST likely in all the circumstances of the case?"

"It is right there are a number of possible scenarios but the one I prefer is that the assailant was sitting on the right of the victim.

That position accounts for all the wounds seen, although it is possible the assailant was left-handed and sitting in front of her or standing or stooping to her left, although in this scenario it it would have been more difficult to cause some of the injuries we have seen, though not impossible."

Geoffrey thanked him and called his next witness, David Lawson, a Forensic Scientist specialising in blood and DNA matters.

Geoffrey took him through his professional background, covering his qualifications, his expertise, the items in the case that he examined and some basic background information about DNA and blood stains. He had been a forensic scientist for about 10 years and had dealt with hundreds of cases involving the interpretation of body fluid evidence and DNA profiling.

He had received a large number of items in this case, which he examined in his laboratory, including tissue samples, swabs, clothing and footwear items taken from Charlie when he was arrested and clothing and footwear taken from his flat which matched the clothing that he was seen wearing on the bus's CCTV. He had also examined Charlie's walking stick, recovered from his flat and the knives recovered from Sheila's address.

Geoffrey moved on to question him about specific matters, "Firstly, what was the purpose of your examination?"

"The purpose of the examination was to determine if there was any blood or other cellular material or body fluids on the footwear, clothing or other items, from which a DNA sample could be obtained. This might in turn link the items recovered to the murder and assist the police in finding the murderer."

"Why is such evidence relevant?"

"During an assault, blood from the victim may be transferred onto the clothing or shoes of the assailant, or any weapon used. The distribution of the blood transferred depends on many factors, including; the proximity of the parties to each other, the movement of the victim and the assailant, the type of weapon used, the nature of the injuries, the volume of the blood present at the scene, the force of any impact and whether or not the impact is into an area of wet blood. The distribution of blood on the assailant's clothing or on a weapon may assist in determining how that occurred."

"We have heard that there was very little blood staining at the scene, can you assist the jury on the relevance if any of that?"

"Yes, I have examined the photographs taken at the scene, as well as the Pathologists' report, the post mortem photographs of the body, photographs of the scene and various witness statements from the Scene of Crimes Officers and those who attended the property. I noted that there was very little blood staining on the floor and none at all on the walls of the living room or in any other room. However, I understand that most of the blood soaked into the deceased's clothes and there was a large amount of blood that soaked into the sofa and was not immediately discernible because of the colour of the sofa."

"In relation to the floor of the living room, can you help us as to the bloodstaining found?"

"The majority of blood found is in spots and drips so it has fallen downwards onto the floor. I could see no examples of projected blood or blood splatter. Projected blood moves under a force in a particular direction, droplets of blood move away from the point of impact and when they land on a surface they form an elliptical stain which can determine the point of origin. Here the blood stains were circular which suggests that there was no particular angle and therefore it was not possible to discover the direction they came from. They could have been shed when the body was moved after the incident."

"Did the Defendant's clothing, footwear or walking stick have any trace of the victim's blood on them?"

"No, no trace of blood was found on any item."

"Can a violent assault occur without any transfer of blood?"

"Yes, it is possible for a serious assault to occur without blood transferring to the assailant's clothing. As there was no evidence of any projected blood here, it is quite feasible that no blood would be found on items worn by the assailant. In any event, as I understand it, the clothing here was not recovered immediately."

"Why is that relevant?"

"The clothing could have been washed in the intervening period."

"So, does the absence of any bloodstaining on the Defendant's clothes or on other items, preclude him from being the assailant?"

"Certainly not," said Mr Lawson.

"I would like you to look at the knife now if you would please Mr Lawson, which we have exhibited in this case. Did you examine that knife?"

"Yes, I looked at the kitchen knife and noted that it has a non-serrated blade. I found a small amount of blood and body tissue on the blade of the knife."

"Is there any significance in the fact that it was a small amount?"

"Not really, it may be because there was an attempt to wash the knife."

"What did you do with the blood and body tissue that you discovered?"

"The body tissue and the blood were submitted for examination and DNA profiling. Full DNA profiles matching the victim were found from both. It was estimated that the probability of obtaining matching profiles, if the blood and body tissue came from another individual, other than the victim, was in the region of one in a billion. If it is accepted that the blood and tissue came from the victim, the nature and distribution on the knife indicates that the knife was used to stab her."

David looked up from his papers towards the jury to see how they received this evidence. He knew that, for legal reasons, forensic scientists had to give DNA evidence in this formulistic style. In simple terms, Mr Lawson was stating that this was her blood on the knife.

Geoffrey gave his usual smile, "Thank you Mr Lawson, now I want to ask you about another knife that was discovered at the property which was seized and exhibited by the Scenes of Crime Officer. As the jury has heard, this was discovered next to the knife we have been discussing in the peculiarly shaped knife rack. Did you discover any traces of the victim's blood or DNA on that knife?"

"Both sides of the blade and the handle were swabbed and tested for blood and submitted for DNA profiling. No traces of blood were found on any part of the knife. No DNA profiles were discovered on the blade but the handle revealed a mixed profile from three separate people. The major forms provided a full profile matching the Defendant. The probability of obtaining a match if unrelated is in the region of one in a billion. Minor parts of profile were unsuitable for comparison and therefore it is not possible to demonstrate who they belonged to."

"What do these findings indicate?"

"The usual explanation is that three separate people handled the knife."

"Is it possible to say when they might have handled the knife?"

"No, it is not possible to date DNA so I cannot determine when the knife was handled."

"Does the absence of the victim's blood or bodily tissue on this knife lead you to any conclusions?"

"Only that the absence on the second knife of any blood or body tissue means that there is no evidence to suggest that it was used to stab the victim."

With that, Geoffrey sat down, satisfied with the way the evidence had come out in court. It covered the essential gaps in his case he thought.

David rose to cross-examine. He could see that Mr Lawson was a 'no nonsense' type of witness who would probably be dogmatic in his answers, it was time for a bit of the Locard principle. "Mr Lawson, what is Locard's Exchange principle?"

"I'm sorry?"

"Locard's Exchange principle, it's a principle of fundamental importance in your line of work. You have heard of it, haven't you?"

Lawson looked at him with clear umbrage, "Of course I've heard of it. It comes from a French pathologist. He stated that if two bodies are in contact, each would receive some evidence of that contact."

"Often summarised as, 'every contact leaves a trace'?"

"Yes."

"He was known as the 'Sherlock Holmes of France' and was a very able scientist?"

"I believe I have heard that expression before."

"According to his proposition, 'every contact leaves a trace' yet here we have an allegation from the prosecution that Mr Holmes repeatedly stabbed Mrs Wright and yet there is no evidence of any blood, bodily fluids, fibres or other trace of contact on his clothes or any items associated with him."

"As I have stated, it is possible for a violent assault to take place without such transference."

"Yes, but is it likely?"

"I cannot say what the probability is, it depends on many factors."

"Presumably, there would have been many opportunities for transfer. For example if they embraced upon meeting, fibres, hairs, bodily fluids like sweat or saliva from a kiss?"

"Yes, if they did those things."

"Equally, it is possible in a violent assault that some blood could have got onto the assailant or his clothing or shoes?"

"It is possible, but not necessarily the case."

"If blood had got onto his hand and he had touched his walking stick, blood could have transferred to that item?"

"That is possible."

"But there was no such blood."

"It could have been washed or wiped off."

"Is there any evidence of that?"

"There is no evidence either way."

"Let's look at the clothing. Is there any evidence it was washed?"

"I presume the clothing must have been washed at some stage!"

David was beginning to dislike this witness. "Quite right of course, but was there any evidence of recent washing, were the clothes wet for example?"

"I don't believe so, but they could have dried by that stage."

This is proving a little difficult, was David's only thought.

"Put simply, there is no scientific evidence of any contact between Mr Holmes and Mrs Wright that day?"

"That is right."

"Let me ask you about the only DNA trace found in the flat that could be associated with Mr Holmes. Namely, the DNA on the other knife's handle. This was discovered in the knife rack?"

"Yes."

"As I understand your evidence, the knife had a mixture of three people's DNA on its handle?"

"Yes."

"Looking at your notes, it appears you were only able to find a match for one of those profiles?"

"I wouldn't put it in those terms, but essentially, yes."

"From your notes, it appears that one of those profiles could have come from Mrs Wright?"

"There was insufficient material to provide an adequate profile, but from what I saw there were some elements that could have come from Mrs Wright. Certainly she cannot be excluded as a potential source of the DNA."

"Can you assist on a number of matters, firstly, you cannot tell from what Mr Holmes' DNA came, whether it was his sweat or saliva or cellular tissue from his hand. What you can say is that it was not from blood?"

"That is right, there is a separate test for blood and that proved negative."

"The same applies to the material found from the other two sources of DNA, they could not have been blood, but other than that you cannot tell us what it was?"

"That is right."

"Secondly, you have told us that the manner in which these profiles would have been deposited on the knife handle, would usually be by touching the knife?"

"Yes."

"So, Mr Holmes could have used the knife to cut bread for a sandwich and his DNA be deposited on the knife handle?"

"Yes, that's feasible."

"But that is not the only way, is it?"

"No, that would be the usual way, by direct transfer from the hand to the handle."

"True but it is possible to have secondary transfer?"

"Studies have shown that is possible."

"Yes, secondary transfer could occur, for example, by my shaking hands with you and then you touching the handle of the knife. The knife handle could then have a mixed profile of my DNA and yours?"

"That is feasible."

"So, assuming for the moment that it was Mr Holmes' DNA found on the knife handle, it could have got there without him even touching the knife?"

"Yes that's possible."

"As an example, Mrs Wright could have touched his cheek, then immediately afterwards, have touched the knife?"

"That is possible, as are a number of other possibilities."

"Finally, you have told us you cannot date DNA?"

"That is right."

"So you cannot say when this DNA got on the knife. It could have been days or even weeks before Mrs Wright was murdered?"

"That is right."

David sat down content that he had managed to make some real headway with this evidence. Geoffrey obviously felt the same way as he rose to re-examine his witness. "Mr Lawson, there is just one matter I want to ask you about. It relates to the DNA on the knife handle that matches Mr Holmes's DNA. You have told us that it is impossible to date DNA?"

"Yes, that is right."

"However, this was a knife in a kitchen. If it was in regular use, would you expect to find Mr

Holmes' DNA on there, for weeks or even for days?"

"No, if it was in regular use, I would expect it to be regularly washed and the DNA would be washed off it. Consequently his DNA would not be on it for weeks or even days."

"Is there anything to indicate that it wasn't deposited the day Mrs Wright died?"

"No nothing whatsoever!"

CHAPTER 36

THE PHONE EVIDENCE

The case was adjourned and David and Jamie 'enjoyed' another Bailey lunch. Jamie received a call that the solicitors had obtained a witness statement from, Helen Rogers, who would give evidence of where Charlie had stayed on the night Sheila had been killed.

The statement was sent through by email and David checked the contents. "Excellent, Jamie, this fills an important gap in the case. Under the rules we will have to provide the prosecution with her name, address and date of birth. It will give them a little time to dig, but there is nothing we can do about that. Can you draft the notice Jamie?"

"Certainly David, is there anything else you want me to do?"

"Yes, how is your research into the telephone evidence going?"

"There's a large amount of unused material to look through but I've managed to look through most of it. I'm hoping to finish it by the end of tonight."

"Good, because I need it before Duncan MacDonald, the Officer in the case gives evidence. Have you found anything of any interest yet?"

"Not really, Mrs Wright did make a lot of phone calls to one number, but that's the 3317 number with the texts to and from 'C' which the prosecution say is our client."

"OK, well if you do find anything important, send me an email saying what and where it is please Jamie."

In the afternoon, the prosecution called George Rollins, an expert on telephones and cell site evidence, to deal with the location of certain phones when calls were made. Most of his evidence was uncontroversial, covering the two phones that Sheila Wright used.

Mr Rollins provided a breakdown of the limitations of cell site evidence, how the exact location of a phone could not be discovered but that he could determine which phone mast or cell the phone was using when a call was made. He explained how a phone would not necessarily use the nearest mast geographically due to a number of reasons. For example, one mast may be used by too many phones at the time and a phone would have to use another mast, or reception may be blocked by high buildings. Geoffrey established that there was little in issue here. Sheila Wright did use one of her mobile phones on the day that she died. Her last call was at 11:35am when she topped up her Pay As You Go phone with the credit that Charlie had purchased. When she used her mobile phone that day, she used one of two masts. These were the geographically nearest to her home address and Mr Rollins established by further tests that these were the phone mast that would almost invariably be used by anyone at her home address, using the same network as hers. The suggestion was clear - she had not left the vicinity of her home address on the day of her murder.

Geoffrey then moved on to Charlie's phone, "Mr Rollins, you have also conducted a similar test for a phone that was found at the Defendant's address when he was arrested?"

"Yes, I did."

"What were your findings?"

"This was somewhat different. There was no evidence that the particular phone number was used that day before approximately 8pm. Then there were a series of phone calls between 8 and 9pm, mainly to the same phone number."

"Were you able to discover where his phone was at the time those calls were made?"

"Yes, they were all in the same area of London, around Pimlico in South West London."

"Are you able to narrow the area down any further?"

"No, three different cell site masts were used, so the area could easily cover as much as a square kilometre."

"One further matter, a phone was recovered from the Defendant and the SIM card that you have dealt with, was found in that phone. However, if we look at still photographs taken from a bus CCTV, we see Mr Holmes boarding the bus that day at about 10:51am and using what looks like the same phone. You have not referred to any calls made by that phone at that time. Can you explain that?"

"The only possible explanation is that there was another SIM card being used in that phone. A different one to the one used after 8pm."

Geoffrey thanked him and sat down. David noticed his Junior, Stephen, nod to him and then after bowing Stephen left the Court.

I wonder what that is all about, thought David.

David ignored the thought and began asking some general questions, "Mr Rollins, you have told us something about the limitations of cell site evidence. Am I right that the problems can become more acute in a city where there are a greater number of masts?"

"The ranges of the masts are different and it is right that in a city several masts can serve the same area, but the general principles still apply."

"Thank you. Now it appears from the evidence that Mrs Wright was in the area of her home when she made phone calls that day from her mobile phone?"

"Yes."

"In fact, we can see from your report on the evidence, that you have produced that although she was probably at home, probably in the house, her phone used two different cell site masts?"

"Yes."

"There is nothing unusual in this, she could activate a different mast simply by moving between rooms or going into her garden, or indeed, as you have told us, one of the masts had too much phone traffic when she made a call."

"That is right."

"Let's move onto Mr Holmes' phone. The same applies to the calls made after 8pm. He could have been moving around, or there may have been too much phone traffic on one mast?"

"That's correct, as I've said."

"Yes, I want to put a proposition to you. You have produced a map showing the different cell sites that Mr Holmes' phone used. Could you look at that map now? You will see a road on that map, Belgrave Gardens. Could these phone calls that you have listed, have originated from around that area?"

Mr Rollins looked carefully at the map. "Yes, all the calls could have been made from that area."

David smiled and swiftly moved on before Geoffrey's team spent any time checking Belgrave Gardens with the defence witness's address.

"Mr Rollins, you have been asked why Mr Holmes' earlier call is not listed on your chart. On behalf of Charlie Holmes, we accept that he used a different SIM card in his phone during that part of the day."

Geoffrey looked up and smiled towards the jury before David continued.

"However, Mr Rollins I trust you can assist on this point. In order to encourage use of their own networks as opposed to others, some mobile phone operators offer incentives, such as, making calls to the same network, cheaper than calls to rival networks?"

"Yes. I have come across that practice."

"So people can have two different phones and use them to call different numbers depending on the network a person is using?"

"Yes."

"Or if a person does not possess two phones, he can simply change the SIM cards in one phone when he wishes to?"

"Yes, I am aware of that, provided the phone is 'unlocked' and can accept cards from different networks."

"And that could easily be the explanation in this case?"

"Well, I don't know the specifics in this case."

"No, but you will have noticed that all the calls made between 8pm and 9pm were made using the same network, even though different numbers were called?"

Mr Rollins looked at his data again before answering, "Yes, I see that."

David could not resist adding for Geoffrey's sake, "Thank you Mr Rollins you have been very helpful."

CHAPTER 37

A LATE APPLICATION

The case was going very well. The prosecution case was coming to an end and so far, he had been able to provide an explanation for the most challenging pieces of evidence. He smiled at Geoffrey who, for once, did not seem as happy as usual.

David noticed Geoffrey turn as his junior Stephen returned to Court and began speaking to him in a hurried fashion. Geoffrey then addressed Isobel and asked the jury to leave Court.

What's this all about? wondered David.

Once the jury had left, Geoffrey addressed Isobel.

"My Lady, there has been a development in this case. The defence during this trial has made frequent references to a second boyfriend. It is clear that suggestions have been made to witnesses in court positively suggesting that this second boyfriend may have been responsible for this murder. Your Ladyship will recall the many references to a left-handed person, cigarette stubs and the like."

Isobel nodded in agreement and Geoffrey carried on.

"I have been informed that another boyfriend has made himself known to the police this morning and is willing to give evidence in this case and openly state that he had nothing to do with the murder. Clearly this is unusual and the defence have had no prior indication that we propose to call this witness, but in view of the suggestions made by them, I seek leave to call him. Obviously, I concede that this is a very late application made at the 'eleventh hour' but this was unavoidable."

Isobel looked a little lost at this suggestion. She had dealt with many cases where late witnesses were called, but not those who the defence suggested actually committed the murder! She decided to take the safe course. She turned to David, "Mr Brant, do you have any observations?"

David was taken aback. He had heard nothing about the other boyfriend being willing to give evidence. This was the last person he wanted to appear in court. At the moment the boyfriend, was just a shadowy figure and with just a little assistance from him, the jury could conjure up their own dark image of a potential murderer. The real man would probably not look the part. In David's experience, even supposedly vicious murderers rarely look the part when they were

320

in a court room setting. Even if this was the murderer, why should he be any different? He had to put a stop to this if he could.

"My Lady, as the prosecution concede, this is a very late application, it comes literally at the end of the prosecution case, not the 'eleventh hour' but the twelfth. The defence are, I hesitate to use the word but it's the most appropriate one, 'ambushed' by this development. I'm not suggesting it was intentional, but nevertheless we are completely surprised and unprepared for this development. With all the investigatory powers the police and prosecution possess, one would expect that they would have discovered his whereabouts long before now. Calling this witness now will potentially derail this trial. We have conducted the defence in a certain way, having pursued a particular strategy. If we had known that the prosecution were going to call this witness, we may have conducted the case in a wholly different way.

Further, if we had known they were going to call him, we would have wanted to conduct our own investigations into his past, his occupation and probably his whereabouts when the murder took place. We have been denied that opportunity now and are unable to conduct any meaningful investigations at this late stage. The effect of allowing such a witness to give evidence now is that the defence is severely prejudiced and there is a lack of fairness. We object strongly to the very late application to admit this evidence."

Isobel thought deeply for a few moments before deciding the point. "Mr Brant, you make an excellent point and I am fully aware of the potential for prejudice and unfairness. However, I have to think of both parties. Unfairness and prejudice can work both ways. You on behalf of your client have made suggestions that someone else committed this murder and there is a clear suggestion, or there will be in your speech, that the murder was committed by the other boyfriend. That is your client's defence and I make no criticism of your conduct of his defence in this way. However, I accept, as I must, that the prosecution has not deliberately ambushed the defence.

The prosecution is now in a position, albeit at a very late stage, to deal with the suggestion that the other boyfriend was the murderer. The jury is entitled to hear this evidence and assess it for themselves. I am going to allow this evidence to be called but, because I do not want your client to be unfairly prejudiced, I will give you an option. If you wish, I will stop this case now and discharge the jury and I will order a retrial in a few months' time which will give you more than adequate time to investigate the matters you refer to.

Alternatively, if you request, I will carry on with this trial and this jury, but adjourn for two days, so that you can consider this evidence and prepare cross examination of this witness. I will adjourn now for you to take instructions from your client as to which course you prefer."

"They can't do this can they?" asked Charlie desperately.

David, Jamie and Charlie were in the cells below the Court discussing their options. Charlie was clearly worried. David spoke to try and calm him, "Charlie, they can do this. Frequently witnesses are called in a trial about whom the defence have been totally unaware. Although I confess, I've never come across this situation before, calling a witness who we say is probably the murderer."

Charlie did not seem to be listening. "This cannot be right, it's unfair, we've had no chance to investigate the matter."

David looked serious, "That is why the judge is being very clever. She has given us an option. We can adjourn for a few months and conduct some investigations, which may assist us. However, she knows we have made some headway in the case. We have made many good points and significant in-roads into the prosecution case and I am sure we have all noticed how the jury is listening intently to the points that are being made. They appear to be looking upon you Charlie, far more favourably than they were at the beginning of this trial.

Unfortunately, the prosecution know almost every point we are going to make and if we adjourn for two or three months, they will do everything they can to deal with those points. They will not make the same mistakes again, such as where the murder knife come from. We have been given the option to continue, even though it gives us no real opportunity to carry out any investigation. The judge has put the onus on us so we cannot complain later. It means in reality there will be no appeal whichever course we choose."

"It's just not right Mr Brant. What can we do?" asked Charlie.

David thought for a few seconds before answering, "It has to be your decision Charlie, we can only advise you, but the actual decision has to be yours. My opinion is we should continue. It has its risks, but the reality is legal aid won't provide enough funding to do a proper investigation in any event. We probably won't be in any better position in two or three months' time. However, we could be in a far worse position. The prosecution will not have any funding difficulties with their further investigations, they might even find that their new witness has a cast-iron alibi. We don't have any other suspects we can suggest as being the murderer and the jury would then be left with nobody but you to blame. I suggest we continue, even though we know it is risky, the alternative is undoubtedly worse. But as I said, it's you who must decide."

CHAPTER 38

THE OTHER BOYFRIEND

David looked up as the next witness was called. It was Thursday morning and the jury returned to Court after a two day break without any idea why the case had been adjourned for 48 hours.

Geoffrey announced that he was calling Nicholas Andrews to give evidence. Charlie had accepted David's advice and not requested a discharge of the jury. As he watched the witness walk into court, David wondered whether he had given the right advice. Nicholas Andrews walked slowly into court and looked around nervously. As David had predicted, he did not look like the stereo type view of a murderer. He was about the same height as Charlie, but thinner and more timid by comparison. He looked like he could be the victim in a murder trial, not the perpetrator.

Nevertheless, David asked Isobel to warn the witness that he did not have to answer any questions if they might incriminate him which Isobel did in front of the jury. In his opinion, it always helped to have the jury listen to such a warning from the judge as they might begin to think that the witness might be concealing something. Nicholas nodded as the warning was given but rather annoyingly added, "I have nothing to hide."

Geoffrey's beam could not be bigger. He watched the jury as they looked towards Nicholas. He was very satisfied with their apparently favourable response to this answer.

"Can you give your full name to the Court please?"

"Yes, Nicholas Andrews."

"Thank you, Mr Andrews."

Geoffrey looked towards the jury hoping they had noticed that there was no 'C' in his name, just in case they had not, he decided he would push it a little, "Have you ever been called by any other name?"

Nicholas paused for a few seconds before announcing, "No" in a loud voice.

Geoffrey quickly moved on. "Mr Andrews, as I understand it, you contacted the police about this case on Monday this week. Why did you do that?"

"The local paper, 'The Clapham Echo' comes out on Saturday. There was a report about the case which referred to it being about Sheila's murder. I noticed that the article referred to, 'another boyfriend' and that there was a suggestion that the defence was alleging that the other boyfriend was the murderer. I am the other boyfriend, I was horrified when I heard what was being said. I wanted to clear my name, I didn't murder Sheila, I loved her!"

"Can you tell the jury how you met?"

"Yes, I was working in Clapham, near to where I live. I was working at the time in a supermarket. Sheila came in and we started chatting. She was very attractive and very friendly. I saw her a few times, just when she came into the shop, and we became friends."

"When was this?"

"Sometime around the summer of 2011."

"Did your relationship progress?" asked Geoffrey.

"A few weeks after we met, I had a day off work. At lunchtime I went to Clapham Common, just to relax and I met Sheila there, purely by accident. She was on her own. We started chatting, she was her usual friendly self and we went for a coffee together and then back to my place. We made love and that's how our relationship started."

"How often did you meet?"

"We met at least once a week, usually at my flat."

"Did you ever visit her house?"

"I did a couple of times but most of the time she would visit me."

"How did you arrange to meet?"

"I would phone her and she would phone me."

"Did you have a mobile phone?"

Nicholas put on a quizzical expression, "Of course I did."

"What was the number of your phone?"

"I don't recall, I got another one recently."

"Can you recall now if the number ended 3317?"

"I don't think so, "I'm sure it ended in a 2."

"Did you phone her often?"

"A couple of times a week. She didn't want me to phone more in case her husband found out about us."

"Do you smoke cigarettes?"

"I do smoke occasionally."

"Did you ever smoke at her house?"

"I may have done, I can't recall."

"Were you aware she was married?"

"Yes, she told me."

"Were you aware that she had children?"

"Yes, though I never met them."

"Did your relationship change in any way?"

"What do you mean?"

"Did your relationship become cooler or end altogether?"

"No, we loved each other. She often talked about leaving her husband to be with me."

"Were you aware of her having any other boyfriends?"

"No, not till I read about her murder."

"How did you find that out?"

"I didn't hear from her for a few days. She never wanted me to phone at the weekends because her husband and children would be there. I saw a local news programme on the Monday following her murder. It was about her and said a boyfriend had been arrested for her murder. I was shocked, I couldn't believe she had been murdered and I didn't know that she had another boyfriend."

"Did you contact the police when you found out that she was murdered?"

"No, I was scared that they might think I had something to do with it."

"Why?"

"They usually suspect the husband or boyfriend, don't they?"

"But they had arrested someone else."

"Yes, but that did not mean that they wouldn't suspect me."

"Can you tell us where you were on the day Sheila was killed?"

"I was not in London. I had gone to the Midlands to visit my sister, Lucy, she can confirm that I was there with her."

"Can you tell us, are you right or left handed?"

"I'm right-handed."

"Have you ever worked as a chef?"

"No."

Geoffrey asked for the left-handed chef's knife to be shown to the witness. "Is this your knife?" he asked.

"No, I have never seen it before."

"I have to ask you this. Did you kill Sheila Wright?"

"I resent that, no I did not, I loved her and I would never hurt her never mind kill her."

Geoffrey turned to the jury and smiled and then sat down. David rose to his feet slowly and paused before asking any questions. The two days had revealed nothing about this witness save for what the prosecution had told them. Nicholas Andrews had no criminal convictions and appeared to be a perfectly respectable man. Jamie had found one text message in the unused material that might assist, but other than that, they had found nothing. David had thought long and hard about how to handle this witness, and even now he was not sure of the best way to start.

"How old are you Mr Andrews?"

Nicholas looked taken aback. He could not see the relevance of such a question. Neither could David, but he had to start somewhere.

"I'm 36."

"Can you tell us a little about yourself, what jobs you have had for example?"

"I left school with a few GCSEs and have worked almost constantly since. I have done some building work but I have mainly worked in stores and supermarkets."

"What part of the stores have you worked in?"

"I don't understand."

"You've worked in supermarkets, they have the general store and often have specific counters like ..." he paused before continuing, 'meat counters'. Have you ever worked behind the meat counter?"

Nicholas looked suspiciously at David, "Yes, I have."

"Were you working behind the meat counter when you met Sheila Wright?"

"I may have been."

"Can't you recall?"

"I believe I was."

"No doubt you were still working there when she died?"

"Yes."

"Now as part of your duties you no doubt have to cut up large pieces of meat .." He paused, "...with sharp knives?"

"Yes."

David could see some members of the jury involuntarily leaning forward as the answers were given.

"Did you ever eat together at Sheila's house?"

"Sometimes."

"Presumably you did not rely upon her to provide the food each time?"

"No, I took food there on occasions for her to cook."

"Did you take cuts of meat?"

"Sometimes."

"You and Sheila Wright would often text each other on your mobile phones, wouldn't you?"

"We contacted each other a couple of times a week."

"I want to read two text messages to you." David then turned to Isobel, "My Lady, these come from the unused material and were discovered by my learned friend, Mr Wilson, in his searches of that material."

He turned to acknowledge Jamie, "We will provide copies in due course." Turning back to Nicholas he read out the text, "This first one is from Sheila's phone and reads, 'Hi darling, can you bring a good cut of steak tomorrow, I'll cook it for you. S'. The reply states, 'I'll bring the best piece of fillet I can find.' Did you send that text?"

"I might have, it's possible, I don't recall."

"It seems to be suggesting that you were working behind the meat counter and were going to take Sheila a good piece of fillet steak?"

"I never stole any meat. I would have bought it, but I really don't recall that particular occasion."

"I'm not suggesting that you stole any. You could have purchased it and it follows from what you have just said that this text may have been from you?"

"As I've said, it may be, I don't recall."

"Let me help you, I'll supply copies now."

David had his junior Jamie hand sufficient copies of the text message to the usher who gave a copy to Isobel, Geoffrey, the jury and the witness. He then carried on with his questioning. "I'm sorry, I missed out one part of the message. The second text was signed 'C'!"

Nicholas' expression visibly changed and from a timid-looking man he suddenly assumed an angry look of hate for David. David smiled and continued. "I also forgot to mention that the first text message was to and the second text message was from, a mobile phone number ending 3317.

Was that your phone?"

"I told you, it's not my number."

"Did you often use the initial 'C' or the name Chris' in your relationship with Sheila?"

"No I never use my middle name."

"I'm sorry, your middle name? Are you telling us your middle name is Chris?"

"It's Christopher, but I never use it."

"Did Sheila call you Christopher or 'C'?"

"No."

"Are you sure?"

"Yes."

"It's just a coincidence that you have a middle name with the initial 'C'?"

"I don't understand."

"Some people prefer to use their middle names than their Christian or forenames, are you the same?"

"No, I've told you, I never use my middle name and nor does anyone else."

"Let's move on shall we. You have told us that Sheila would come to your flat and sometimes you would go to her house. I'm going to ask you to draw a plan of her house showing the position of the front door, the living room and the kitchen."

Geoffrey immediately got to his feet, "My Lady, the jury has such a plan in their jury bundle at page ...."

David interrupted, "I am aware of that, I want this witness to draw a plan from memory to see how much he recalls of the property."

Geoffrey shrugged to try and indicate to the jury that David was wasting time and then sat down. Nicholas was handed a piece of paper and a pen and began to draw. After a few seconds, David stopped him, "Thank you, Mr Andrews, I see you have just drawn that plan with your left hand!"

Nicholas looked shocked and suddenly realised why he had been asked to draw a plan, as did Geoffrey who, for a moment forgot to smile at the jury.

Nicholas recovered as quickly as he could and swopped hands and continued drawing, "Actually, I'm ambidextrous, I prefer to write and draw with my left hand but for virtually everything else I use my right hand."

David smiled, "Really, then why did you just tell my learned friend, Mr Lynch, you were right-handed?"

"Because that's the hand I use most."

"Or is it because you know the murderer was left-handed?"

Geoffrey rose quickly to his feet, "My Lady, I must object, we don't know the murderer was left-handed, the pathologist's evidence is that the murderer was more likely to be right-handed."

David tried to copy Geoffrey's smile, "I'll rephrase my question. Mr Andrews, you used to chop meat at the meat counter in your supermarket?"

"Yes."

"No doubt you used special knives, like butcher's or chef's knives?"

"Butcher's knives."

"With special grips for both right and left-handed people?"

"I don't recall."

"Did you use your left-hand for chopping meat?"

"No, I used my right hand."

"If you were ambidextrous, you could have used either hand?"

"I could, but I used my right hand for cutting meat."

"You have told us you did not kill Sheila Wright."

"I didn't, I loved her."

"You were with your sister at the time of her killing, in the Midlands?"

"Yes."

"Do you know if she has been contacted by the police?"

"No, she's on holiday in Spain with her family at the moment. She's not contactable."

"Really, not even by mobile phone?"

"No."

"Or have you made that up to avoid anyone checking your alibi?"

"No, I haven't."

"Isn't it right that Sheila told you she was in love with someone else?"

"No, she never mentioned anyone else to me."

"She told you she didn't want to see you anymore."

"No, she loved me."

"At 4:12pm on 14th June 2012, it was you who used your mobile phone ending 3317, to send Sheila the text message, 'See you tomorrow at 12 noon, C', wasn't it?"

"No, it wasn't me."

"At 4:13pm, Sheila replied by sending a text message, 'I told you I don't want to see you any more, please stop pestering me'. You received that text didn't you?"

"No, she didn't send that message to me."

"You couldn't take no for an answer, could you?"

"That's not true."

"You pestered her and then on 15th June 2012 you went to her address with a knife you had taken from work and you repeatedly stabbed her?"

"No, that's not true, it never happened like that. I didn't kill her. I would never have come to this court to give evidence if I had killed her."

"You say that, but of course you discovered that she had another boyfriend. You resent that don't you?"

"No." It was clear to David that Nicholas was becoming agitated.

"You knew about it and you resented it at the time?"

"No."

"That's why you lost it and killed her, out of jealous rage?"

Nicholas hammered his fist down on the side of the witness box, "No, I didn't, I didn't."

"I have just one further question. At the time of her murder did you possess a long black umbrella?"

"Doesn't everyone?"

"We have heard that there was some rain on 15th June 2012 in London. Did you carry a long black umbrella with you?"

"I don't know, I probably did if it was raining."

"So you were in fact in London that day?" stated David.

Nicholas looked uncomfortable and after a pause he replied, "No, I was in the Midlands."

David sat down, as far as he was concerned he had gone as far as he could, pushing the witness any further might only make him more adamant and convincing in his denials. The only issue for him was whether he gone far enough, at least to raise a reasonable doubt in the jury's minds. *Have I done enough this time?* wondered David.

CHAPTER 39

THE OFFICER IN THE CASE

Duncan MacDonald stepped into the witness box knowing he was the final prosecution witness and that there would be some criticism thrown his way from the defence, about his conduct of the case. He was not concerned though. It was not the first time he had faced criticism from a defence barrister, and it would not be the last. He was confident he could handle any allegation that was thrown at him.

Geoffrey took him through some background details about the case; his first involvement, speaking to Roger Wright, arranging the video interviews of the children and taking the witness statements. He then moved onto the subject of Nicholas Andrews.

"Mr MacDonald, were you aware of Mr Andrews before he attended the police station on Monday of this week?"

"I was aware that another boyfriend existed but was not aware of his identity."

"What enquiries had you made to discover Mr Andrews' name and whereabouts?"

"Quite a number. We asked questions of all the neighbours and friends of the victim, I sent police officers out in the area to ask questions to see if anyone knew him. No one did. We put up notices in the area and in a local newspaper to see if there would be any response, but there was none."

"Did you ever consider that he might be a suspect in the case?"

"Oh yes, anyone who was close to the victim was a potential suspect, but we found no evidence to suggest that he might be the murderer."

"We have heard that he has a middle name, 'Christopher', When did you first become aware of that?"

"Only after he gave evidence. He gave me only two names, Nicholas and Andrews."

"Have you any reason to believe that he uses the name 'Christopher' in his dealings with people?"

"No sir, I've no reason to doubt that he uses the name Nicholas in his dealings with others."

"He has told us he has an alibi for the time of the murder, have you been able to check that out?"

"No sir, I have no reason to doubt that he was in the Midlands, but I have been unable to contact his sister. I understand that she's on a camping holiday in Spain at the moment. I have made enquiries through Interpol to see if she and her family can be contacted but we have had no response to date."

Geoffrey took the officer through some further witness statements he had made covering the continuity of the evidence obtained and then asked him to wait as David 'may' have some questions.

David stood and looked at a witness statement before asking his first question. "Officer, you have told us you took witness statements in this case?"

"Yes sir, not everyone's, but I did take several."

"Now, it's no secret that when you take a statement you are not just supposed to record evidence that helps the Prosecution but it is your duty to write down matters that might assist the defence as well?"

"Yes sir, and I pride myself in doing exactly that."

"Really, let's take the statement of Mr Callaghan as an example. He gave important evidence didn't he?"

"Yes sir, he was the only one to see your client actually enter the gate of the victim's house on the day of her death."

David glared at him. "Officer you know full well his evidence did not go that far. He stated in his evidence as he stated in his witness statement that he saw someone open the gate that day at sometime between 12 and 1pm?"

"Yes sir, using a walking stick!"

"Well, let us just think about that for a moment. You were in court when he gave his evidence that he did not know whether it was a walking stick or a furled umbrella."

"Yes sir, I remember him saying that to you, when you questioned him."

"He also said that he had told you about the umbrella when you questioned him."

"He did not sir, I think he is mistaken, probably confused by the questions. He never mentioned an umbrella to me. As far as I recall, he only mentioned a walking stick."

"I suggest that's not true Officer. The reference to an umbrella did not fit the prosecution case, so you left it out of the statement?"

"No sir, I did not. He never mentioned an umbrella."

"No doubt as part of your investigation you checked the weather in London on that day?"

"I did, sir."

"There were light showers in the morning."

"There were, sir."

"So it would not be surprising to see people carrying umbrellas at 12:00pm?"

"No sir, it would not."

"Also, you have checked the times that my client, Charlie Holmes, caught the bus and arrived in the area of Mrs Wright's house that day?"

"I have, sir."

"He would not have arrived between 12-1pm unless he walked very slowly from the bus stop?"

"I agree, sir, that's why we think Mr Callaghan has made a mistake about the time."

"Officer, the reason you think Mr Callaghan has made a mistake about the time is because his times do not fit your theories that Mr Holmes was the murderer."

"That is partly right."

"Which part?"

"I'm sorry?"

"You said partly right, what else makes you think he has his times wrong?"

"I can't think at the moment, sir."

"Do you want some time to think?"

"No sir, that will not be necessary."

"Of course, arriving at 12pm fits the text sent the day before where 'C' said he would be visiting at 12pm?"

"Yes sir, and we believe 'C' is your client."

"Because that fits your theory officer, not because it's the only possible inference."

"I don't agree, sir."

"Let us look at this investigation for a moment. You discovered the whereabouts of Mr Holmes very quickly?"

"Yes sir, it was good police work."

"You then made an arrest very quickly?"

"Yes sir."

"You then charged him very quickly."

"Only after we had the evidence, sir."

"You never looked for any evidence that might demonstrate his innocence?"

"That's not correct, sir."

"Let's look at Mr Andrews for a moment. You never investigated whether he might be the murderer?"

"We checked everything we could. There was no evidence to suggest he was the murderer."

"And no evidence to suggest that he wasn't!"

"I'm not sure what you mean sir?"

"Come now officer, you did not even know his name until he walked into a police station. You have not checked out whether he is right or left handed, what his occupation was, which involved, as it turns out, cutting up meat with sharp chef knives, nor have you been able to check out his so-called alibi?"

"I don't accept that, we have done what we could in this investigation."

"No officer, you have only looked for evidence that might support a case against Charlie Holmes, you have ignored any evidence that might suggest someone else committed the murder!"

CHAPTER 40

THE FINAL CONFERENCE

The prosecution case ended after a few questions in re-examination by Geoffrey. It was now time for the Defence case to be presented. David asked for an adjournment until the following day for him to have a final conference with his client and Isobel agreed.

David and Jamie made their way to the cells where Charlie was waiting eagerly, and drinking a cup of tea. He was very pleased with David's cross-examination but nervous about giving evidence himself. Charlie began the conversation, "Do I have to give evidence Mr Brant? I've seen what you have done to the prosecution witnesses, twisting their words. I'm worried that might happen to me."

"Charlie, I haven't been 'twisting' anyone's words, I've been trying to put the most favourable light on the evidence from your point of view. It is right that you should not underestimate Mr Lynch. He is a very able advocate but if you tell the truth, he will not be able to make any in-roads into your evidence.

Admittedly, it is no easy thing giving evidence in. It's also true that no one can force you to give evidence. You can choose not to. However, in my opinion you should do so in this case. The jury has heard from Nicholas Andrews. They have heard him answer questions under cross-examination and called a murderer and seen his denials. They will expect you to give evidence and if you don't, they will probably hold it against you and they may convict you of murder.

We have made in-roads into this case, but I can't guarantee you an acquittal. The last thing you want to do is be found guilty of murder and spend years in prison, and regret that you never gave evidence."

Charlie turned to Jamie, "What do you think Jamie?"

Jamie cleared his throat, "I think Mr Brant is right. He is a very experienced advocate and has done a superb job, but the jury will want to hear from you and if you don't give evidence they might convict you simply because you didn't."

David smiled and added, "Of course, we cannot guarantee an acquittal if you give evidence, but both of us believe that your chances are far better if you do."

CHAPTER 41

THE DEFENCE CASE

It was Friday morning and David decided that it was time for another high cholesterol in-take before Court started. As usual, the bacon was cold. *Why do I still order this rubbish? he asked himself.* He had managed a few bites when Geoffrey approached him.

"Hello David, is your little hero going to give evidence then?"

David put down his fork, "What do you think Geoff?"

"Well, if you don't mind me saying, I think you've done an excellent job. But I doubt it's enough. Having mercilessly attacked that poor man, Nicholas Andrews, the jury will want to hear your chap's denials, so I assume I will be given an opportunity to ask him a question or two!"

"Well, there's your answer Geoff."

Geoffrey smiled, "Enjoy your breakfast David, I don't know how you manage to eat that stuff. I have to contend with a bowl of muesli these days, otherwise my wife is straight on the phone to the Doctors."

David smiled and continued eating. At least Geoff agreed with his advice even if he had managed to ruin his breakfast with the last reference. *Perhaps I ought to have another check-up after this case?* he thought.

Half an hour later, he was standing in court, calling his client Charlie Holmes to the witness box."

Charlie walked to the witness box from the dock, followed by a prison officer, who would sit behind him whilst he gave evidence, to make sure he didn't make a run for it. Charlie took the oath, swearing to tell the truth and then gripped the edge of the witness box with his hands, before slowly assuming a more relaxed position.

David took him through; his background, his date of birth, where he was born, the fact that he was right-handed, his schooling, his early occupations and his dream to be a Fireman.

"Why did you choose that occupation?"

"I always wanted to be a fireman. I thought it would be exciting and I wanted to save lives."

David looked towards the jury to see how they were reacting to this evidence, hoping they would get the point. Here was a man who wanted to dedicate his life to saving lives, not taking them. He was encouraged when he saw how intently most of them were listening to the evidence. A couple looked completely uninterested though, particularly an older woman who would not even look at Charlie, but that was not unusual in David's experience.

"Did you receive any awards in the Fire service?"

"Yes, I was awarded a 'Spirit of Fire Award' for my part in rescuing four children trapped in a fire in a house in Tooting, South London."

"Perhaps you could tell the court what happened?"

"It was in April 2010, we were called out to a serious fire in a semi-detached house in Tooting. It was a suspected arson. The mother was already dead when we arrived. She was in an upstairs bedroom. There were flames coming out of the front door and on the stairway. We discovered that there were four young children upstairs in two bedrooms. They couldn't get downstairs because of the flames and they were in danger of suffocating because of the smoke. We used the ladder to get up to a front bedroom and I went in and passed the children out of the window, one by one, to my colleagues."

"It must have been a terrifying experience?"

"It was, the children had all succumbed to smoke inhalation and I had to carry them. The fire was penetrating the floor of their bedrooms and it was touch and go whether I would be able to rescue them all before the floor collapsed. Fortunately, it didn't and I was able to save them all."

"And you received a prestigious award for your efforts?"

"Yes, but I thought my colleagues deserved awards just as much for taking the children down the ladders through the smoke and flames and staying long enough so that I wasn't trapped by the fire."

David looked towards the jury to see how this was being received. He did not want to overdo it, but it was important that the jury saw this side of Charlie. From what he could see, it appeared to be working. It was time to move on.

"Mr Holmes, I want to ask you now about Sheila Wright. When did you first meet?"

"In the summer of 2010."

"Where did you meet?"

"On Clapham Common. I had a day off and I went out for fresh air and to relax a little. I was reading a book I'd bought about travelling in Mexico, when Sheila came up to me. She pointed at the book and asked if I'd ever been to Mexico. I told her I hadn't but I was interested in it. She told me it was her childhood dream to visit Mexico but she never thought she would make it."

"What happened then?"

"We chatted together for about an hour. We found we had quite a lot in common. We arranged to meet the same time the next day and our relationship began from there."

"You had a sexual relationship with her?"

"Yes, but not at first, I guess we were both lonely. I didn't get to meet many women working the shifts I worked at the fire station and she told me she was in a loveless marriage and wished she could escape."

"Did you visit her house?"

"Quite a few times, on my days off I would go to see her before lunch and leave before her children came back from school."

"Did you ever meet the children?"

"I did later on, when we started to talk about being together."

"Did she ever visit your flat?"

"Yes, several times."

"Did you love each other?"

"Yes. We talked about her getting a divorce and us getting married."

"Did you know she had another boyfriend?"

"No, not until this case. She never told me and I thought she loved me, and only me."

"We know you had a serious accident. Tell us about that?"

"We were on an emergency call. A fire had started in a furniture warehouse. I was driving the fire tender with lights flashing and sirens on full blast, when a tanker hit me from my right. It crushed the side of the cab, crushing my right leg and causing a tear in my bladder. I was in hospital for two months."

"We have heard that Sheila visited you there, claiming to be your sister?"

"Yes, it was a local hospital and she was worried people would recognise her so she claimed she was my sister. I guess it's obvious now that it didn't fool anyone!"

"After the accident, were you able to have sexual relations?"

"No, the injury and the drugs made that impossible, so my sexual relationship with Sheila ended."

"Did that affect your relationship together?"

"Not as far as I was concerned. She still said she loved me and wanted to be with me. She said she would wait for my injuries to heal."

"How did you feel about your injuries and the fact that your sex life with Sheila had ended?"

"Frustrated, there is no other word for it."

David noticed Geoffrey, who was taking a note of the evidence, underlining something furiously, no doubt the word 'frustrated'.

"Did you do anything about it?"

David noticed Geoffrey now look up and stare at Charlie.

"Yes, a couple of weeks before Sheila died I contacted a Sex Therapist to see if she could help with my problem."

"Who was that?"

"Her name is Helen Rogers, she lives in Belgrave Mansions, in Pimlico."

"What service does she provide?"

"She counsels you about your problems and helps to 'physically alleviate' them."

"How does she do that?"

"I don't really like to say."

David had been expecting this.

"Mr Holmes, we are all adults in this courtroom, please answer the question."

Charlie looked down. Then he looked up and smiled, "I suppose you could say she adopts a 'hands-on' approach!"

A few male members of the jury smiled, but none of the female ones did.

David tried not to react, wondering why witnesses always feel the need to overcompensate when they're embarrassed.

"Did you have sex with her?"

"No, I couldn't but I spent three nights with her and she massaged me and tried to help me with my problem."

"Did you feel you were making progress?"

"Yes, I couldn't manage an erection but I certainly began to have feelings in that area, which I had not had for some time. I thought, given time, I would be able to have sexual intercourse with Sheila again."

"Did your relationship with Sheila grow colder because you did not have sexual intercourse?"

"No, she was very attentive and helpful."

"Did you tell your colleague, Mr Bevan, that you thought Sheila was becoming colder because you were not having sex?"

"I was depressed because of the accident and I did have mood swings. I doubt Sheila found it easy to be with me at times. I did tell James it was because I wasn't able to have sex, but in reality she never complained about that."

"What was your relationship like in the last few weeks before her death?"

"It was good. We were very close, we never argued."

"Did you see each other?"

"Yes, we met up virtually every day, except weekends. Her husband was at home from Friday evening until Monday morning so I never saw her at the weekends."

"When was the last time you saw her?"

"I saw her on the Thursday. I went to her house for lunch."

"Who made the lunch?"

"She did, but I did help."

"What did you do?"

"I remember offering to chop up some vegetables for her."

"Did you chop any?"

"No, I picked up a knife to chop them and she told me the knife was too good for that, so I put it away."

"Can you remember where you got the knife from?"

"Not really, it might have been from that strange knife stand but, I have to be honest, I just can't remember now."

"Can you remember if it was the same knife that has been exhibited in this case, taken from the knife stand?"

"I can't, I'm sorry."

"Let us deal with the afternoon of Thursday, 14th June 2012. We have heard that someone sent a text from a mobile phone ending 3317, trying to arrange to meet Sheila and she sent a text back saying she did not want to meet them. Did you send that first text and/or receive the second?"

"No, I didn't send or receive those texts."

"Did you arrange to meet Sheila on the Friday?"

"Yes we did arrange to meet up."

There was more frantic underlining from Geoffrey.

"What time did you arrange to meet?"

"When I left her house on the Thursday, we agreed to meet at about 11:30am the following day. Sheila asked me to get her a top-up card for her phone as she wasn't planning on going out, so I said I would get one for her."

"Did you get one?"

"Yes, the next day I got one for her from my local newsagent."

"What did you do with it?"

"I went to the bus stop to catch the bus to her place and just as I was getting on the bus she phoned me. She told me not to come that day as she had to see someone else at noon."

"How did you feel about that?"

"I was annoyed as I was just getting on the bus. That's why you see me the way I was on the CCTV."

"What did you do with the Phone Top-up voucher?"

"She asked me to give her the number on the voucher, which I did."

"Where did you go?"

"I got off at the normal stop and just spent my time around Clapham Junction."

"Did anyone see you?"

"No one I knew. I did get a coffee from a street vendor but I wouldn't recognise him again, so I doubt he would recognise me."

"We can see from the CCTV that you caught the bus back home a few hours later. Did you meet anyone you knew, make any phone calls, or buy anything with a credit card or obtain a timed receipt from anywhere that might place you in the area during that period?"

"No, I'm sorry to say I didn't, believe me I wish I had."

"We have seen that you were on the phone when you got on the bus. You told us you were speaking to Sheila. However, there is no trace of that call on the SIM card that was recovered in your phone, why is that?"

"I had two SIM cards at the time. One, from the company Nimbus, which I used to phone my family, my mother and friends who had the same network, because the calls were cheaper. That was the one in the phone when the police arrested me. I had another Pay As You Go SIM, I can't remember the exact number now, but I remember it ended in 83. I remember that because that was the year I was born. That's the one I used to phone other mobiles, like Sheila's."

"Where is that SIM now?"

"I don't know. When I took it out of my phone I placed it in my wallet, like I always did. I presumed it was still there when the police arrested me. Though I know my lawyers have checked the wallet and it's not there now."

"We have heard from your neighbour that you arrived home and then left a short time afterwards. Where did you go?"

"To see Helen in Pimlico."

"Do you recall when you met her that night?"

"I had a 6pm appointment. She let me stay there that night as she had on the previous two Fridays. She said it would help me to progress, staying in the same bed as her. I came back on Saturday and stayed in my flat that night and I was arrested just before 5am."

"Did you know why the police were there?"

"No. I had no idea. I was shocked and speechless when they said Sheila was dead."

"You were taken to a police station and then interviewed. You made no comment to any of the questions asked and just presented a written statement. Why was that?"

"I was told I could see a solicitor so I contacted my Union and they arranged for a solicitor to come and advise me. He advised that I should not answer any questions and just put in a short written statement. I had never been in that position before so I took his advice."

"Mr Holmes, there is just one further question I want to ask you. The prosecution say you murdered Sheila Wright, for reasons unknown, with the knife that has been exhibited in court. Did you kill her?"

"Certainly not. I wanted to make my life with her, I would never have harmed her. I loved her more than I have loved anyone in my life, more than I will ever love anyone again!"

CHAPTER 42

CROSS EXAMINATION

Geoffrey slowly rose to his feet, glancing at his notes before putting them down slowly and putting his hands behind the tails of his Silk gown, gripping them firmly. He then turned and faced Charlie, with his chin tucked into his neck.

"Mr Holmes, in this Court you have given us a detailed account of your defence. You have told us about your relationship with Mrs Wright. You have told us you were not the one who spoke to her on the phone on 14th June 2012 at 3:30pm or sent and received texts at 4:12 and 4:13pm. You have told us that you were on the way to her house on the day of her death. You also told us that you did not actually go there. You received a call from Sheila just as you were getting on the bus, cancelling your visit. You gave her the number of the top-up voucher when you were on the bus. You then spent time around Clapham Junction and finally returned home. Then you spent that Friday evening with a Sex Therapist. In addition, you have given us a potential reason for why your DNA would appear on the handle of the other knife. In fact, you have given us a complete answer to all the allegations made against you, haven't you?"

"I believe so."

"Have you had any difficulty in giving this account to the jury?"

"No."

"No lapse of memory?"

"No."

"No difficulty in recalling the sequence of events?"

"No."

"You have had no difficulty in expressing yourself?"

"No."

"So tell the jury why you did not give this version to the police when they first questioned you?"

"I told you, I was advised not to answer any questions by my solicitor and I gave them a brief statement."

"It was certainly a brief statement, Mr Holmes."

Geoffrey turned to the statement in the jury bundle.

"You stated,

"I knew Sheila Wright and I had a relationship with her. We were both in love. I did not see her on the day she was murdered. I did not kill her."

"Yes," confirmed Charlie, "that's the truth."

"There is very little detail though."

"I was advised by my solicitor."

"But Mr Holmes, you are an intelligent man. Your solicitor advised you, but you knew it was your decision whether to answer questions or not?"

"Yes, but I relied on the advice,"

"Even though you were told by the officers that it might harm your defence if you did not mention when questioned something you might later rely on in court?"

"Yes."

"So, even though you knew it could harm your defence, you, an intelligent, articulate man, deliberately chose not to answer any questions?"

"Yes."

"Or is it, you could not answer questions at that stage and had to wait until the prosecution had served all its evidence, so you could make up an account that would provide an answer to the prosecution case?"

"No, that's not true."

"I suggest that is true, that is the only possible reason you did not answer any questions, you had no answer at that stage. You had not had enough time to think up this detailed account."

"No, I told you, I relied on my solicitor's advice."

"Very well, let's look at your evidence then. You were a member of the Fire Service, a fit and clearly, brave, fire fighter?"

"I did my duty."

"Don't be modest Mr Holmes. You were brave, strong and ... virile?"

"Sorry?"

"Well, you started a sexual relationship with a married woman and had a regular sexual relationship with her. Did you have sex every time you met?"

"Not every time."

"But frequently?"

"When we went to each other's addresses we usually did."

"You had sexual intercourse at her home?"

"Yes."

"In her bed."

"Yes."

"The one she shared with her husband, the father of her children?"

"Yes."

"All that came to a sudden end though, with your terrible accident?"

"Yes."

"As you told us, understandably, that made you feel frustrated?"

"Yes."

"So much so, that you tried to remedy it by visiting a Sex Therapist?"

"Yes."

"Did you pay her for this therapy, the 'hands-on' approach, as you called it?"

"Yes."

"How much would you pay for this ... service?"

"She charged £100 per session."

"You would spend the night with her for that small amount?"

"Yes."

"Yet, despite all her ministrations, you still could not manage to get an erection?"

"No."

Geoffrey nodded, assuming an air of apparent sympathy.

"That must have been devastating for you."

"It was."

"As you say, frustrating?"

"Yes."

"It must have caused problems between you and Mrs Wright?"

"I don't know what you mean."

"Oh come now, Mr Holmes. Mrs Wright was clearly a highly-sexed woman?"

David turned towards the jury to see how they reacted to terminology that seemed distinctly outdated and sexist, but none of them responded, no doubt interested more in the answer than the question.

Geoffrey continued, "After all, she was sharing a bed with her husband, with you and with Mr Andrews."

"Not at the same time," Charlie answered facetiously.

Charlie's attempt at humour fell flat with the jury. Geoffrey took immediate advantage of this.

"This is a serious allegation, Mr Holmes. An innocent woman, a mother of two, has lost her life."

"I'm aware of that."

"Do you find this funny?"

"No."

"You told your friend, Mr Bevan, that Sheila started to become cold towards you."

"As I've said, it was because I was depressed, not because I wasn't able to have sex."

"Really, Mr Holmes, then why not say that to Mr Bevan?"

"I don't know."

"I suggest that the answer is simple, it is because you told Mr Bevan the truth."

"No."

"She was becoming colder towards you because you could not perform the service she expected from you?"

"No, that's not true, that's not the way it was."

"Do you usually lie to friends?"

"No."

"Are you lying to this jury?"

"No, I'm not!"

"Did Mrs Wright ever complain to you about the lack of sex?"

"No, she didn't."

"Did she taunt you with your inability to perform?"

It was clear to everyone in court that Charlie was becoming annoyed with the questioning, he raised his voice and shouted, "No!"

"Is this a sore point Mr Holmes?"

"No."

"Did you fall out with Mrs Wright sometimes?"

"Yes, doesn't everyone fall out now and again with someone they love?"

"What I am suggesting is that you fell out with Mrs Wright because you were not able to satisfy all her needs."

"No, that's not true."

"Did she taunt you with the fact you could not perform in bed?"

"No, she did not."

"Is that why you killed her, in frustration?"

"I never killed her."

"Let us look closely at what happened over the last 24 hours of her life. You have told us you saw her on Thursday, 14th June?"

"Yes."

"Did you fall out?"

"No."

"Did she refer to you as 'Chas' when she spoke to you?"

"No, everyone calls me Charlie."

"Really?"

"Yes."

"Did you phone her at about 3-30pm asking her if you could meet the next day?"

"No, I'd only left at about 3pm and we'd arranged to meet on Friday, there was no need to phone her."

"I suggest she said she didn't want to meet you. Is that why you sent her a text just after 4pm again trying to arrange a meeting?"

"No. I didn't, that was not my phone."

"So you say, but of course we only have your word for that. What happened to your SIM card that you say you put in your wallet?"

"I don't know, I must have lost it."

"That's quite a coincidence isn't it?"

"I don't understand?"

"The SIM card that could prove whether your phone number was 3317 just happens to get lost the day Sheila Wright was murdered?"

"It was lost, the police might have lost it when they took my wallet."

"That's the first time we have heard that alleged. Are you making your story up as you go along?"

"No, I don't know what happened to the SIM card."

"Did you throw it away after the murder because you knew it connected you to Mrs Wright?"

"No."

"Now, you tell us you were on the phone to Mrs Wright just when you got on the bus at about 10:50 that morning?"

"Yes that's right."

"You have seen the telephone evidence in this case?"

"Yes , I have."

"Now, in fairness to you, there is no phone call to or from her phones to the number 3317 that morning. However, there is also no call to or from any of her phones at 10:50am, when you are seen on the phone getting on the bus. Can you explain that?"

"No, my barrister did point that out to me in conference. I don't know why that is. Maybe it did not register for some reason or she was using another phone?"

"Hardly likely Mr Holmes, isn't it more likely that you were on the phone to someone else. You didn't phone her because you wanted to surprise her and surprise her you did!"

"That's not true."

David wore his poker face during this cross-examination, so that the jury did not detect any concern on his part. He had pointed this same issue out to Charlie in conference, but Charlie was adamant that he had received the call from Sheila when he was on the bus. He had decided not to deal with it when he asked Charlie questions, hoping, though not expecting, that Geoffrey might miss the point.

Geoffrey carried on, sensing he was making some headway.

375

"Mr Holmes, you tell us that the SIM card with which you used to contact Mrs Wright had a phone number that ended '83'?"

"Yes."

"We have checked the phone records for Mrs Wright and can see no phone contact at all with a number ending 83. Is that another invention by you?"

"No, that is definitely the number I used. I think she had another phone that you have not found."

"How convenient!"

"I can assure you it does not feel convenient for me."

"Very well, let's move on. Mr Holmes, you have told us you arranged to meet Mrs Wright that Friday, the day of her death?"

"Yes."

"You were on the bus when you received a call from her, the call that never registered to any of her phones?"

"Yes."

"Nevertheless, you carried on travelling on the bus to your usual stop, the one nearest her house?"

"Yes."

"You got off the bus there and stayed in that area for three hours and ten minutes before catching the bus back?"

"Yes."

"Why did you spend so long in that area?"

"I just walked around."

"Come now Mr Holmes, Clapham Common may be a pretty park but it's not that interesting, not for over three hours!"

There were a few smiles on the faces of some jury members who knew the area reasonably well.

Charlie scowled, "I walked around, got some coffee and then went home. It didn't seem that long at the time."

"Of course, that time would have allowed you to go to Mrs Wright's house; to give her the top up voucher for her phone, allow her to make the call to activate that voucher, then for you to get the knife, kill her, wash the handle of the murder knife, then leave to catch the bus home."

Charlie paused, "No, I've told you, I never visited her that day."

"You were still using your black walking stick at that time?"

"Yes."

"The one Mr Callaghan saw you use to open the gate to Mrs Wright's home?"

"He said that may have been an umbrella!"

Geoffrey shrugged as if it was unimportant. "It could look like that but I suggest it was your black walking stick."

"No, I never visited her that day,"

"You knew Mrs Wright very well, was she a fanatical about cleanliness, like her husband suggested?"

"She was clean."

"She was not the type to leave a dirty knife lying around for a day or two, she would clean it?"

"Yes, I suppose so."

"So she would have cleaned the knife that did have your DNA on it."

"I suppose so."

"And if she was a fanatic for cleanliness, she would have cleaned it thoroughly and there would be no trace of your DNA a day or so later?"

"Well there was."

"I'm suggesting that what you have told us is a pack of lies."

"No, I've told the truth."

"What I suggest is that you were deeply frustrated by your condition and during an argument, she tormented you about the fact you could not get an erection?"

"No, that never happened. She would not do that to me."

"In anger, you went to the kitchen, touched the knife rack, touching the handle of one knife, depositing your DNA on the handle?"

"No, I didn't."

"You then picked up the other knife from the kitchen. You returned to the living room hiding the knife from her, sat next to her on the sofa, on her right side, and repeatedly plunged the knife into her?"

"No, I never. I would never hurt her, I loved her."

"You then returned to the kitchen, washing the knife, cleaning the handle thoroughly and the blade less so and then you put it in the knife rack, where it did not belong?"

"No, that never happened."

"You then caught the bus and went home. Worried that you might be caught, you almost immediately left your flat."

"No, I went to Helen's where I went every Friday."

"But your 'treatment', wasn't working was it?"

"It was, I was beginning to get some feeling."

"What time were meetings arranged for?"

"About 6 pm."

"Mr Holmes, you will be aware that defendants have to serve a Defence Case Statement well in advance of a trial?"

"Yes, I know."

"That document outlines important parts of your defence."

"Yes."

"Would you agree that where you went after the murder is an important issue?"

"I don't know."

"Come now Mr Holmes. You were aware from the prosecution papers served long ago, that your neighbour, Betty Crawford, gave a statement saying that you never left your flat in the evenings. She found it unusual that you left the flat the night of the murder."

"I'd been doing that every Friday for three weeks."

"Then why not put that in your Defence Statement?"

"Sorry."

"Nowhere in your Defence Statement do you say where you went that Friday night and that you had gone to the same place every Friday for three weeks running."

Charlie looked down as he mumbled an answer.

"Sorry Mr Holmes, I did not hear that and I suspect the jury did not either."

Charlie looked up and spoke loudly, "I was too embarrassed."

"Really, Mr Holmes? You didn't seem too embarrassed when you joked about your Sex Therapist being 'hands-on'. Or is it that when your Defence Statement was drafted, you had no explanation for leaving your flat that night and had yet to arrange for someone to support your account?"

"No, that's not true."

"Mr Holmes, I suggest that your whole account is a lie. You arranged for you alibi later and you brutally murdered that poor woman and will not admit the truth."

Charlie Holmes looked down, "That's not true, I didn't kill her."

Geoffrey turned to the jury and smiled, "I have no further questions for this ..." he paused as if finding a suitable word, but with apparent reluctance he settled for, "...witness."

CHAPTER 43

THE WEEKEND WITH WENDY

David's re-examination of Charlie did not take long and established nothing new. David could see that Charlie was nervous and exhausted by his ordeal. Here was a man who would willingly throw himself into a fire to rescue others without any thought for himself yet he had clearly found the experience of being questioned in the witness box to be far more frightening and exhausting.

The next witness could not make it until Monday and the case was adjourned until then. David and Jamie made a trip to the cells to discuss Charlie's evidence with him and for David to give him some encouragement, "One thing Charlie is that ordeal is over now. You did your best out there and the jury appeared to follow your evidence closely."

"I was useless Mr Brant, I've probably blown it. I lost my temper with the prosecutor. The jury will probably convict me now!"

"Charlie, you don't know that. The case is far from over and it's impossible to predict what juries will do."

"Some of the women looked at me as if I was an animal."

"Charlie you cannot read too much into people's looks. Remember you answered every question, you were not caught out in a lie. I think you did very well, don't you think so Jamie."

Jamie nodded in agreement and added a few words of his own to encourage Charlie. However, both knew it was hopeless, Charlie was clearly depressed and in fact both thought his performance in the witness box was not great. He hadn't seemed to communicate well with the jury, but there was no point in telling him that now and making him feel worse.

The weekend was over almost as soon as it started. David spent all of Saturday with Wendy. He had gone on a shopping trip to Oxford Street whilst Wendy tried on numerous dresses, an activity that he had not been involved in for years and one which he had not missed. Wendy had tried on four dresses in one shop all of which he thought fitted her perfectly but she had not been satisfied and had announced, "There's a bloody obesity epidemic in this country, why can't I find one large enough to fit me?"

David decided to try some encouragement hoping he would achieve more than he had with Charlie. He looked at her, "You're not large, you've got a fantastic figure. Your curves are all in the right places!"

Wendy smiled at the compliment, "Isn't that sexist, coming from my Head of Chambers?"

"If it came from me as your Head of Chambers it would be, but it doesn't, it comes from me as a man who loves you."

She looked at him surprised at this display of softness from an otherwise guarded man. He had certainly never said that before! He was also surprised by his comment, worried that in the words of the old Nancy Sinatra song, he had said 'somethin' stupid', but Wendy appeared happy. She smiled, walked across the room and planted a kiss on his cheek, "I love you too!"

CHAPTER 44

THE THERAPIST

Wendy left David's flat before lunch on Sunday. He was sorry to see her go, but he had to work on Charlie's case, preparing questions for the Sex Therapist and putting the finishing touches to his final speech.

At 10:30am Monday morning he rose from counsel's bench in court and announced he was calling Helen Rogers as his final witness.

Helen Rogers strolled in with an air of supreme confidence about her. She was about five feet seven inches tall, but was wearing black high heels which added at least two further inches to her height. She was dressed in a black business suit with an open red frilly blouse. She had clearly been to the hair dressers recently because hair was perfectly set. She was wearing it up when she came into Court but once she was in the witness box she let it down. With a shake of her head it fell effortlessly around her shoulders and framed her attractive face. Her make-up was immaculate.

David had not seen her before and he felt a little stunned by her appearance. It was obvious to everyone that she had made a real effort for her moment in court.

As David asked her name, he noticed Geoffrey and Stephan talking to each other and pointing to some document. He ignored them, he would not be distracted.

"Can you tell the jury what your occupation and qualifications are?"

Helen turned towards the jurors without prompting and spoke in a clear articulate voice, "Of course, I am an Experienced Sex Therapist and Relationship Counsellor. I have a First Class Honours degree in Hospitality and Psychology from the London Campus of the American, Hoplin University."

David nodded sagely, as though he had heard of the particular University, in fact he had not and doubted its existence or at least its legitimacy. He rapidly moved on, "Please tell the Court what service an 'Experienced Sex Therapist and Relationship Counsellor', provides?"

David noticed a couple of male members of the jury involuntarily move forward in their seats, whilst an equal number of female jurors appeared to shift uncomfortably backwards.

"The main part of my work involves dealing with problems that couples have in their sexual relationships. Most of my work involves discussing their issues and suggesting potential solutions."

David knew he had to handle the next topic carefully if Geoffrey was not to make a meal of it.

"Does your work have a physical aspect?"

Helen smiled, "Yes, but that is not the most important part of my treatment. Sometimes couples have problems with areas of their sex lives and I do assist by showing them techniques where necessary, such as how to perform oral sex on a man ... or a woman."

Some of the male jurors were looking intently at Helen now, whereas an older female looked at the grey-haired male next to her and they exchanged glances that suggested someone from Sodom and Gomorrah had visited the courtroom. David moved rapidly on.

"Ms Rogers, you mentioned couples. Do you ever work with single individuals?"

"Oh yes, obviously it's not just couples who have problems with sexual matters. Sometimes I will help a man who has for example, problems of confidence or in extreme case, problems such as impotency. In that case, I will teach exercises and assist him with his problem."

The grey-haired male juror now moved slightly forward in his seat.

"Do you know Charlie Holmes, the Defendant in this case, who sits behind me in the dock?"

Helen looked behind David and smiled at Charlie who smiled back.

"Yes, I know Charlie."

"How do you know Mr Holmes?"

"In the summer of 2012, Charlie answered one of my adverts that was in a local newspaper." She looked towards the grey haired man on the jury, "I advertise in quite a few local newspapers in South London."

"Can you recall exactly when this was?"

"Yes, I have brought my accounts to court."

She turned to Isobel, "I keep full records for Inland Revenue purposes."

Isobel did not look up from writing her notes. After a pause, Helen looked away and began turning the pages of her accounts.

"Oh yes, here it is. David Beckhan (CH) attended weekly sessions on Friday 1st, 8th and 15th June."

"David Beckham?"

"Well my clients do like some anonymity so I give them the names of famous sportspeople and then list their initials in brackets behind."

"What time were these sessions?"

"They were all at 6pm, for two hours. I find two hour sessions are essential. It takes some people the first hour to relax. I usually give my clients a drink in order to help them feel at ease. Then we move on to the therapy."

"How long did he stay?"

"As I said, the sessions are for two hours and Charlie went home after the first one finished, but the second two he stayed with me over night."

David noticed the inconsistency with Charlie's account but rapidly moved on. "Why was that?"

"The first session had not gone well. Poor Charlie was seriously injured in a road traffic accident. He could not obtain, never mind, maintain an erection. I felt sorry for him and when the same thing happened on the next occasion I told him he could stay the night with me. His were the last sessions I had booked on those days, so I gave him extra-long sessions in order to try and stimulate him a little bit more."

"Can you recall what time he left on these last two occasions?"

"Not exactly, I wasn't keeping an accurate time as I wasn't charging him ....". She again looked at Isobel and noticed she was again ignored, she continued, "but it would be around 1pm on both occasions."

"Did he respond to your ... therapy?"

"Not at first, but I thought we were making some progress on the last occasion. Although he was not able to maintain an erection, I did notice some hardness, a slight stiffening in his penis, which was definite progress."

That was all David wanted from the witness, so he asked her to remain in court while the prosecution asked her some questions.

Geoffrey rose to his feet and ignoring Helen he addressed Isobel, "My Lady, there is a matter of law that arises from this evidence. It won't trouble the jury and I ask that they and the witness leave court for a short while please. There will probably be sufficient time for them to have a coffee."

Isobel agreed with the request and the jury were sent for a coffee in their canteen. Helen was asked to remain outside court. Once they had all left, Geoffrey addressed the Court.

"My Lady, you will recall that this witness was not referred to in the Defence Statement served on behalf of Mr Holmes before the trial."

Isobel nodded in agreement, "I do recall."

Geoffrey continued, "Indeed, no amended Defence Statement has been served referring to this witness. It was only last week that the defence gave us the name, date of birth and address of this witness. Details which of course should have been supplied before trial. Consequently we were given very little notice. The officer in the case was busy last week but over the weekend he did the necessary checks and discovered that this witness has a large number of previous convictions, most of which we say are relevant to issues in this case."

David looked at her witness statement, it clearly stated she had no previous convictions so she had lied to his solicitors about that, *what else has she lied about?*

Meanwhile, Geoffrey continued, "My learned junior, Mr Davies, has been drafting a written application to adduce evidence of this witness's bad character pursuant to section 100(1)(a) and (b) of the Criminal Justice Act 2003 as it is important explanatory evidence and it has substantial probative value in relation to a matter that is in issue in the proceedings and is of substantial importance in the context of the case as a whole.

We have not been able to serve the application on my learned friends yet and I anticipate they will want a few minutes to read it and possibly take instructions?"

Isobel turned to David, "Is that right Mr Brant?"

David stood up, "Until this moment I was not aware that this witness had any criminal convictions, I was certainly not aware that any application was going to be made to adduce them. Indeed, I am surprised that the prosecution is seeking to ambush the defence in this way. My learned friend should at least have done me the courtesy of telling me what previous convictions the witness has, before I called her. I may have wanted to deal with them in chief."

Geoffrey nodded, "I do regret the situation but I was only informed of this shortly before we came into court and rather than delay matters, I asked Mr Davies to see whether there were any convictions that might be relevant."

David gave him a look that he hoped demonstrated he did not believe a word of this explanation. He had seen both prosecution counsel looking at a document together and now assumed it was a list of Helen's convictions. They were trying to ambush him!

He was granted a short adjournment to read the necessary paperwork and Isobel allowed him to speak to Helen, albeit solely about her criminal record.

Having read through the papers, he approached Helen outside the courtroom.

"Ms Rogers, I'm sorry I didn't get a chance to talk to you before you came into court. The judge has allowed me to speak to you now even though you are in the middle of your evidence."

He produced her witness statement.

"I have a copy of your witness statement here that you gave to your solicitors. It states that you have no previous convictions for any offence. However, according to the prosecution you have some 51 previous convictions for solicitation for the purposes of prostitution, two for carrying an offensive weapon, namely knives on both occasions, one offence of living off immoral earnings coupled with one offence of tax evasion for which you went to prison for twelve months. Is there any reason you did not mention these to us?"

Helen put on her most disarming smile and put her hand on David's arm, "Mr Brant, isn't it?"

David acknowledged his name and involuntarily returned her smile.

"These were all in the past, a past life of mine, in many ways the life of someone completely different. I wanted to forget them, so I could move on. I'm completely different now. I haven't been in trouble for over ten years. I became a Sex Therapist because of the problems I used to suffer when I worked as a prostitute. The convictions for Solicitation are very old and I'm sure you know they're an occupational hazard for a working girl. The offensive weapons were knives I carried for my own protection. Working girls meet a lot of unsavoury and dangerous types. The brothel keeping and the tax evasion were at the same time. I wanted to move away from street prostitution I got together with a few other working girls and rented accommodation to see our clients in relative safety. We shared the bills and our lawyers told us that because of that, we had to plead guilty to the living off immoral earnings charge. As for the tax evasion, well we didn't keep any proper accounts and we weren't as good about paying our tax as we should have been.

All that's over now. I keep perfect books. I don't work as a prostitute and I pay my taxes on time!"

David looked closely at her, "Thanks for your candour. It would have helped us though if you had told us before and we wouldn't be in this position."

"I'm sorry. I just didn't think anyone would raise them. I can't see how they are relevant."

They both returned to court and Geoffrey made his application. It was clear to David that Isobel was minded to allow it so he chose not to resist and only requested that he be permitted to ask a few further questions in chief about these matters before cross-examination. Geoffrey objected as strenuously as he could but Isobel accepted that the defence had been "ambushed, whether intentionally or not" and agreed to David's application. The jury returned to court and once Helen was seated in the witness box again, he asked her his last few questions.

"Ms Rogers, may I ask your age?"

Again Helen smiled at the jury, "I am 35 years old having turned 35 in January of this year."

"I understand that you have a number of criminal convictions, is that right?"

Helen turned to the jury, she was no longer smiling or confident, she now looked uneasy.

"Yes, it is."

"I understand you have convictions for solicitation for the purposes of prostitution, carrying an offensive weapon, living off immoral earnings and tax evasion. I want you to tell the jury about the background to these offences."

Helen asked the usher for a drink of water and dabbed a tissue to her eyes.

"I was born in Cumbria. When I was just 13, I was regularly abused by my father and his brother. They would beat me and force me to have sex with them. They raped me. They told me it was normal but I knew it wasn't normal but there was nothing I could do. It happened every week, sometimes more than once a week.

I told my mother but she slapped me across the face and called me a 'tart'.

I tried to tell my aunt, my uncle's wife, but she didn't want to know. The abuse went on for years.

I used to be scared of coming home, I played truant from school and stayed out until late with my friends. My grades at school suffered a lot.

The only person who was kind to me in my family was my grandmother, my father's mother. I could never tell her as I thought it would kill her.

Then when I was 15, she died. She was the last person I felt closest to in the house. I couldn't stand it anymore and I ran away from home and came to London.

I slept rough on the streets at first and tried to get work. After a year, I found that the only way I could make ends meet was to prostitute myself for money. I spent six years working on the streets. I was arrested for solicitation a number of times. I always pleaded guilty straight away, and once I paid the fine in the Magistrates Court, I had to go back on the streets to make money to live."

She dabbed the corner of her eyes and David noticed that even the stern-looking elderly jurors were listening intently.

"They were horrible times and I was beaten a lot by punters. I was hospitalised twice with broken bones. I started carrying knives for protection. On a couple of occasions I was stopped by Police officers who found the knives and charged me. I pleaded guilty to possessing offensive weapons.

I hated my life, and eventually to get away from it, I persuaded two of the other street girls to rent a house with me where we might be able to service a better quality of client. We were successful for a few years and made decent money. We were raided by police. We had shared our expenses and our barristers told us that meant we were guilty of living off immoral earnings. We hadn't got around to paying any tax so we got done for that as well, and I was sent to prison.

When I came out, I decided to change my life. I studied and became a Sex Therapist. I've never looked back, I've tried to forget my earlier life. Now, I try to help people and I always ensure my accounts are up to date and my tax is fully paid on time."

David had intended to ask a number of questions to elicit this information but it had flowed so freely and appeared to have been received so well, he decided not to ask any more questions. He thanked her and sat down.

Geoffrey gave his usual smile to the jury before turning to face Helen.

"Would you like a little time to recover, Ms Rogers?"

Helen dabbed at her eyes again and sipped the water.

"No, thank you."

"Let me ask you a few questions then. You have changed your life considerably since you were a COMMON prostitute?"

"Yes."

"After all, you no longer carry an offensive weapon?"

"No."

"You pay your taxes and no longer CHEAT the Revenue?"

"That's right."

"You no longer live off IMMORAL earnings?"

"No."

"You no longer CHARGE random men for sexual services."

"No."

"Sorry, is that actually correct?"

"What do you mean?"

"Well let's look at the services you offer, shall we. You provide sexual services don't you?"

"That's only a part of what I do."

"Yes, but it is a part?"

"Yes."

"And I presume you charge for your services?"

"Yes."

"How much do you charge?"

"Normally I charge a couple £200 for a 2 hour session. I charge single men £150 for that time."

"So the Defendant paid you £450."

"Actually, I gave Chas a discount. He told me he was struggling because he wasn't being paid his salary and he was still waiting for his compensation. I only charged him £100 for a session and in fact I never charged him for the third session."

"Chas?"

"Sorry?"

400

"You called him 'Chas'?"

"Well it's short for Charlie."

"Is that what you called him?"

"Sometimes, and other times I just called him Charlie."

"Very well, thank you for that. Let's move back to what you charged him. From what you have told us, you would have charged him about £200 for your services?"

"Yes."

"Presumably he wasn't like other clients?"

"What do you mean?"

"Well you gave him a discount and you spent the night with him, twice, according to you. Your relationship sounds very close?"

"I liked Charlie and I felt sorry for him."

"Were you more like friends than client and therapist?"

"He was always a client."

"In reality, weren't you closer than that?"

"What do you mean?"

"I suggest you were friends and you are willing to cover for him which is why you have given this evidence today?"

"No, that's not true, I've told the truth."

"You have produced your accounts in this case?"

"Yes."

"These are for Inland Revenue purposes because you don't want any more tax problems?"

"Yes."

"You did not charge him for the third visit, so why enter his visit in your accounts?"

"I probably made a mistake."

"Or is it that you are just covering for him?"

"No."

"Did you even see him on Friday, 15th June?"

"Yes, I did."

"You told us he stayed with you just two nights, the 8th and 15th June 2012?"

"Yes."

"So, it wasn't for the three Friday nights?"

"No."

"He did not stay the night of the 1st June 2012?"

"No."

"Tell us about the last Friday, 15th June 2012. How did he seem?"

"In what way?"

"Was he the same as usual or did you notice anything different about him?"

"Such as?"

"Well, you tell us, you saw him, we didn't."

"He just seemed normal to me. I didn't notice any difference."

"This last occasion was different to the others you tell us. He had some stirring, some hardness in his penis, as you put it, which was different to earlier weeks. As if something had recently occurred which had excited him?"

She paused, apparently thinking about the question before answering, "I don't know, I really can't say."

CHAPTER 45

THE PROSECUTION FINAL SPEECH

Geoffrey gave the jury his largest smile of the case. David amused himself with the thought that if it was any larger he would have literally been smiling from ear to ear. The rest of Monday had been spent on directions of law, now it was Tuesday morning and it was Geoffrey's final opportunity to sway the jury.

"Ladies and gentlemen, at the weekend, far removed from the concerns of this case, I was talking to my wife about the latest Hollywood films and she informed me that they are making a new film about Abraham Lincoln, the American President, starring the actor Daniel Day Lewis.

It set me off thinking about one of Lincoln's famous quotes, which you may consider applies appropriately to this case, namely, 'You can fool all the people some of the time, and some of the people all the time, but you cannot fool all the people all the time'.

All of you will not be fooled by what has been raised by the defence in this case. Throughout this case, the defence has tried to pour scorn on the prosecution case. There was even the suggestion that there was another potential killer, the other boyfriend! Really? Was there even a scintilla of evidence against him? The police properly investigated this case and concluded there was not. As you know, the prosecution has called him as a witness so you can assess the suggestions made by the defence.

Did he look like a killer to you? When he told you how much he loved Sheila Wright, did he look like he was lying? Did he look like he was someone who had made up a story to try and convince you he had nothing to do with her death?

Or did he look like, we suggest, a distraught man who has lost someone he deeply cared about?

You will remember the cross-examination he was subjected to. This is no criticism of my learned friend, he has his job to do as we all do. It was a vigorous, skilled cross-examination, which you would expect from such an experienced Member of the Bar, but did it come close to demonstrating that Mr Andrews might have lied to you?

We suggest not. Every possible allegation was put to him. Alleged text messages from phones were put, even though there is no evidence whatsoever, that he was the owner of the 3317 phone. He was questioned in minute detail about many matters, even about being ambidextrous, which he admitted, but he was adamant that he was not the killer.

He also made a comment to my learned friend, which you might think was the most important part of his evidence. When asked if he was the killer he said,

'I would never have come to this court to give evidence if I had killed her.'

Doesn't that make absolute sense. If he was the killer, surely he would never have gone willingly to the police station and declared that he was the other boyfriend. He would never have come to the Central Criminal Court, the most famous criminal court in the land, he would most assuredly not have set foot through the doors of this courtroom or travelled those long and often difficult steps into the witness box, if he had committed this murder. He would have hidden away, praying and desperately hoping that the police did not knock on his door one early morning.

The fact he came to this court voluntarily and gave evidence before you, knowing that it was going to be alleged by the defence that he was the murderer, was the most eloquent testimony of innocence you could have.

His evidence is there for you to judge, we doubt that you will find it wanting.

So who does that leave us with as the killer?

Certainly not her husband. We know he has the perfect alibi, he was on his way back to London from the Midlands when she was murdered. He was miles away from her. It could not have been him.

Was it someone else who might have a grudge against her?

No, there is no evidence of anyone else in that position.

Was it a random stranger who broke into the house?

No, you may think her position on the sofa suggests she knew her killer, she was probably close to him, at least in the past.

It leaves us with one possible killer - a man who was her former lover, a man who had suffered a terrible accident, a man who could no longer perform in the way that both of them wished. Did she taunt him with that? Did she raise it just one time too many and he, so frustrated with his condition that he had to see a former prostitute for help, finally cracked and killed her in a frenzy?

Let us put aside mysterious strangers, husbands, another lover and look solely at the evidence against the Defendant. When analysed after it has been strenuously and expertly tested by the defence, you may think that it is overwhelming and in many ways stronger now than it was at the beginning of this case.

I start with the obvious:

The deceased undoubtedly knew the killer. What was the Defendant's relationship with the victim? As we heard it had been an intimate one. As he told you in answer to his own counsel's questions,

'Did you love each other?'

He answered,

'Yes. We talked about her getting a divorce and us getting married.'

Did Sheila Wright really love the Defendant as he would have you believe? The answer probably comes from her friend Abigail Richards who she confided in. She told us in answer to my questions that Sheila Wright became bored with her husband and her marriage. I then asked her what Sheila did about this boredom. She answered that Mrs Wright told her,

'That she had met other men and had affairs with them.'

She had affairs with 'other men', plural, not singular. Did she really love the Defendant the way he wanted her to love him?

True my learned friend Mr Brant led Mrs Richards into saying that Sheila Wright loved the Defendant, but was it actually true? Sheila Wright apparently told her the following,

'She told me about two men. She said that both were younger than her and both were lovers'.

Then she told us, that Mrs Wright had said,

'They were both, 'virile and exciting lovers'.

Was it love she felt for the Defendant or simply unbridled lust?

In any event, what happened in that relationship? We know that the Defendant was involved in a terrible accident from which he received a crippling injury. That injury tragically took away his ability to have sex with.

Is that the key to what happened in this case?

How was their relationship at the time she was murdered?

Again, Mrs Richards, the 'confidant' assisted us. She told us that Mrs Wright 'said they met up twice a week and had sex at her house. That is until he had his accident!'

Then, Mrs Wright confided that the Defendant 'couldn't perform.'

No doubt, understandably, she felt sorry for him. We know she visited the hospital to see him, pretending to be his sister, but you may think this was a virile woman, enjoying and apparently needing illicit sex outside of her marriage. The Defendant could no longer provide her with that need.

Did Abigail Richards have it right when she told you, 'I think she'd gone off them both'

Was she looking for some other extra-marital entertainment?

Even the Defendant said something along those lines to his friend, Mr Bevan, who gave evidence. You may recall he was referring to a time after the Defendant's accident when he was delivering a chair to the Defendant's flat, he said the Defendant told him,

"That he thought she was getting a bit cold towards him, mainly because he couldn't have sex with her anymore."

The Defendant has not denied this, although he has suggested he was lying to Mr Bevan and in fact she was only getting colder because of his depression.

Why would he lie to Mr Bevan about that?

You may think the reality is clear, it comes from his own statement to Mr Bevan, Sheila Wright was growing colder towards him.

You will recall that there is clear evidence that Mrs Richards heard Mrs Wright on the phone at about 3:30pm talking to someone and saying she did not want to see him anymore. When she made a witness statement she said she thought that name was 'Chas', a name that the Defendant denies using and denies anyone called him by, but a name that his own witness, Helen Rogers, 'the Sex Therapist' says she called him by. Did Mrs Wright also call him Chas?

Of course, you will want to consider my learned friend's cross-examination on this point. Might it have been 'Chris' the name that Abigail accidentally used in Court.

You might think that was an act of desperation on the part of the defence. It is undoubtedly a coincidence that Mr Nicholas Andrews has a middle name 'Christopher'. There is no evidence he uses it instead of his first name and no evidence whatsoever, that anyone knows him by the abbreviated name, 'Chris'.

You may think this evidence is crucial. Mrs Wright had met young virile men for sex. One of them could no longer perform that vital function, so she no longer wanted to see him. He, on the other hand, still wanted to see her, wanted her to divorce her husband and marry him.

The defendant told us he did not know about the other boyfriend. How could he? Why would the victim tell him, when they were still in a

411

relationship? But did she let it slip sometime, or did he find out in some other way?

You may think it is understandable he was frustrated about his condition. He loved her, he wanted her to marry him. However, she did not want to see him again, as she told him in that phone call at 3:30pm and in that text she sent later at 4:13pm on 14th June 2012.

We then come to the 15th June 2012, the day of her murder. The evidence now becomes even stronger against the Defendant.

On his own account, he was on the way to see her and got on his usual bus and got off at the stop nearest to her home.

He obtained a phone top up card for her because he was going to present it to her. You may think that he clearly did not intend to kill her when he bought that voucher, otherwise why buy it? Something must have happened in the house after he gave it to her. Of course, he says he never gave it to her. Does he really expect you to believe he read out a 16 digit number on a busy, noisy London bus, through a mobile phone?

You heard that he claims that she phoned him at 10:50am that day and told him she did not want him to come round because she was seeing someone else and he then read the 16 digit code out to her. However, the flaw in that evidence is that there is no phone record of her calling or

412

being in phone communication with anyone at that time!

No, I suggest he was on his way to see her as he says he was. He was probably talking to someone else on the phone not Sheila Wright. Why warn her he was coming?

The Defendant agrees he was on the way to see her when he boarded that bus. We only differ on one factor, he says he got off at the stop nearest her house and then spent three hours ten minutes, aimlessly wandering around Clapham Common.

I suggest that makes no sense at all. The reality is, he got off at the stop nearest her address because that's where he was going. He had arranged to see her at about 12:00 but he was early, he would have got there at about 11:30am or so. She activates her top up voucher at 11:35am. The voucher he would have given her the moment he arrived, no doubt as some peace offering.

The timing is perfect. If he had given her the 16 digit number over the phone at around 10:51am, as he claims, surely she would have topped up her phone then and not 45 minutes later?

The Defendant was seen by Mr Callaghan entering the gate to her property. As Mr Callaghan told you, he saw a man entering her gate using a walking stick to push the gate open.

Was this another coincidence that he saw a man with a walking stick when we know the Defendant uses a walking stick? Or are there a number of murderers walking around the streets of Clapham Common all with black walking sticks?

Of course it is right that my learned friend suggests that because there was a light drizzle in London earlier in the day, it may have been a black furled umbrella that Mr Callaghan saw. It is right that Mr Callaghan did not seem as sure of his evidence on this point as he was when I asked him questions.

Also, it is true that there was a light drizzle in London, some 4mm of rain fell that day, but it wasn't raining at 11:30am and in any event, you might think that a black walking stick might even look like a furled umbrella from a distance. Isn't it more likely that what Mr Callaghan saw was what he first told you he saw, the Defendant's walking stick?

Mr Callaghan believes it was between 12-1pm he saw the man. He is undoubtedly wrong about the time. He was not looking at the clock and his timings do not match the evidence. That is not surprising, people regularly make mistakes on timings and the like.

Whatever the time, within half an hour of seeing the man, Mr Callaghan hears a scream coming from the direction of the house. Whatever, the defence may say about children's play grounds, you may think that was the last sound to emanate from Mrs Wright in that terrible moment as she saw the knife coming towards her, the knife that was plunged deep into her body repeatedly, until she was dead.

Now the defence no doubt will try to make some issue about the knife and understandably so.

There is no doubt that when I opened this case I told you that knife was the one that belonged to Abigail Richards and which she had lent to the victim that very day. It clearly is not, as Abigail Richards explained. I apologise for that, the prosecution made a mistake on that point which has been properly corrected.

You may be confused about the murder weapon. Where did it come from? Whose is it? The defence may suggest that the murderer brought it with him. Maybe he did, maybe it is a knife that the defendant took with him. Maybe there is a more simple answer, maybe Mrs Wright borrowed another knife from someone else that day because she did not think Mrs Richard's knife was adequate and did not want to tell her.

Please do not be misled by this knife. It is the proverbial red herring. It might be the murderer's, it might not be. We simply do not know. Because we do not know where it came from, does not mean that the Defendant was not the murderer, particularly when all the other evidence points towards him.

We have as a prime example the fact that his DNA was on the handle of the other knife. How likely is it that a housewife, who cleaned fanatically, would not have already cleaned the used knives in her kitchen, a day or so after the Defendant claims using it?

Surely such a house-proud person as Mrs Wright would have cleaned all the utensils in her home.

It is true that we cannot date DNA, it is true that there is a possibility that DNA can be placed on an object by secondary transfer as was explained to you by the expert witness, David Lawson, but isn't it the most likely explanation that the Defendant's DNA got on the handle when he touched it, searching for a murder weapon?

Was this because the victim had finally made it clear she did not want to see him anymore, or because she had taunted him with his inability to have sex, or because she had told him about the other boyfriend. We will never know. Nor do the prosecution need to establish these matters. It is no part of our duty to establish a motive.

What we do know is that the victim was stabbed nine times. She probably and mercifully died quickly. Because of the positioning of the wounds she was undoubtedly incapacitated quickly and there was little blood that flowed from the wounds and none that spurted from them. The murderer would not be covered in her blood and as we know, the Defendant was not, at least not so that it would be noticeable on his clothing when he boarded the bus home. He may have washed small splashes off his clothing as we heard the Forensic Scientist tell you may have happened. Again, we will never know.

We then have his journey home and the fact that, unusually, according to his neighbour, Betty Crawford, he left his flat that night and did not return.

Why did he leave that night?

He has produced his own witness, Helen Rogers, who states she used to be a prostitute, although she apparently still provides sexual services for money. You will have to determine whether her evidence is really credible. How many prostitutes stay the night with clients after they have paid for a two hour session? That will be a matter for you. Certainly Mrs Crawford thought it unusual for the Defendant to stay away on Friday nights and you may think, having seen her, she is not the type of lady to miss anything. She certainly seemed to keep a constant watch on what was happening next door.

Was Helen Rogers telling you the truth or was she providing a further favour for money? You will have noticed two points about her evidence that should cause you concern. Firstly, her account and the Defendant's accounts are not consistent. She says he only stayed the nights of 8th and 15th June, he says he stayed the night of the 1st as well. Did one or both of them forget the script at that point?

The other matter and more concerning one you may think, is why did he not say anything about her evidence until this trial had commenced? On his account, he knew where he stayed on the night of the murder yet, he never mentioned it in his prepared statement which he gave to the police before he was interviewed. He refused to tell the police about where he went that night and he never mentioned her name or the fact he visited her in his Defence Statement.

Was this all because he was 'embarrassed' as he claims? Would a man on trial for murder be so embarrassed about such a matter, a man who, after all, can joke about her 'hands-on' approach during his "therapy"? Or is it that he had not found someone to support his account yet and had to go running to a former prostitute to provide this evidence for him?

In any event, is it really supporting evidence? Ms Rogers states he left her flat at about 1pm. Why did it take so long to get back to his property in Clapham? He didn't return until about 5pm. Was that because he thought the police might be waiting for him because he knew what he had done?

We then have the evidence of his SIM cards. We know he had two SIM cards. The one he used to phone family and friends, which he used on the night of the murder after 8pm and the one he used to call the victim with.

He told us that the phone number of the missing SIM card ended in the number 83, the year of his birth. However, no numbers ending 83 appear on the telephone records that we have for Mrs Wright. Why? The only obvious answer is there was no such phone ending 83. This is yet another example of his lies.

What happened to this SIM card? It conveniently went missing. The SIM card that could establish whether his phone was the 3317 number or not just happened to go missing on the day of the murder!

You may think the obvious explanation is that it went missing because he knew it connected him to the victim, he knew what the last text from her said to him, he knew he had to get rid of it and he did, probably before 8pm on 15th June 2012, but certainly by the time the police arrested him at 4:52am on 16th June 2012.

What else is there ladies and gentlemen?

Possibly the most compelling point of all. He was arrested on Sunday 17th June 2012 at 4:52am. No doubt you will give him credit for the fact that he had just woken up, but look at what happened when he was told he was arrested for killing the woman he claims to have loved. He said nothing! He is told that he is being arrested on suspicion of causing the death of the woman he loves, a woman that, according to him, he did not even know was dead and yet he says nothing. Surely, he would have expressed some feelings of distress and asked how this happened? How did she die? But he said nothing. Why? The simple answer is because he already knew she was dead, because he had killed her.

Ladies and gentlemen, of course you will recall what I said to you in opening this case two weeks ago, it is for the prosecution to prove this case and to prove to you so that you are sure of the Defendant's guilt. I suggest when you put aside the smokescreens created by the defence in this case and analyse the evidence carefully, you can be sure and that there is only one proper verdict.

Guilty of murder.

CHAPTER 46

THE DEFENCE SPEECH

David looked at the jury and smiled, but did not even attempt to copy Geoffrey's wide grin for fear of suffering with lockjaw.

Geoffrey had given an impressive performance and David knew it would be difficult to follow, but that was how he usually felt at this stage of a serious trial when he was against a very competent opponent who could make a good speech. It was time to have a dig at the prosecution.

"Ladies and gentlemen, my learned friend began his address to you with a quote from Abraham Lincoln. You may be aware that before he was President, he was a lawyer and famous for a number of quotes. One such quote you may think is relevant to this prosecution, namely, 'It is better to remain silent and be thought a fool, than to speak out and remove all doubt'."

There were a few smiles from the jury who looked towards Geoffrey, who responded with his widest smile to date. They didn't hear Geoffrey mumble the word 'bastard' to his junior. David looked closely at the jury and noted that they were listening. *Good, they probably don't know* it's debatable whether that quote comes from Abraham Lincoln or Mark Twain!

"The prosecution in this case seek to dismiss the defence case on the basis of insulting you. Effectively, what Mr Lynch has just said, albeit in a very eloquent speech is, that you would all be fools, to believe the defence case and acquit this Defendant.

I am sure you will not fall for that overly simplistic approach. There are important issues to be dealt with here. As you have been reminded, a woman's life was taken, brutally. What you have not been reminded of is that the future of a man's life is now in your hands.

This is a serious case with grave consequences for Charlie Holmes and of course the evidence needs to be viewed seriously, not dismissed as if your only role is to rubber stamp a document presented to you by the Prosecution headed 'conviction.'

On 15th June, 2012, Sheila Wright, a mother of two young children, was murdered in her home. Her young children came home and saw her body and wrongly believing that she was still alive, tried desperately to revive her.

There is no issue in this case with these tragic facts.

There is no issue that she was murdered, or that

she was stabbed to death with that knife."

He pointed to the exhibit.

"The only issue in this case is:

Are you sure on the evidence that you have seen that it was Charlie Holmes who murdered her?

Mr Lynch has described this case almost in terms of a 'who-dunnit', pointing out potential candidates such as the husband and the other boyfriend and then saying they could not have committed the murder, therefore the inescapable conclusion is that it was Charlie Holmes who is guilty as if that conclusion is the only possible one.

You have been subjected to speculation upon speculation by the evidence called in this case and led away from what you should concentrate upon.

What is the evidence against Charlie Holmes?

Mr Lynch has valiantly tried to present the pieces of evidence in this case like pieces of a jigsaw fixing them together to try and make a complete picture titled, 'Guilt'. Sometimes those pieces have been carefully placed, on other occasions you may have got the impression he has been trying to hammer them in place. This is for a very simple reason, a large number of pieces do not fit!

I suggest that a careful analysis of the evidence does not prove guilt to the very high standard required in this case. That standard is deliberately high. You cannot convict Charlie Holmes unless you are 'sure' of his guilt. It is the same standard as 'beyond a reasonable doubt'.

This is not an Agatha Christie novel with my Mr Lynch playing the role of a Hercule Poirrot or perhaps a Miss Marple, revealing who the murderer is in the final scene with a convoluted presentation of the evidence.

This is real life.

We would all like to know who the murderer is. Every sane rational person would want to know who the murderer is and to see him or her punished. But equally, and more importantly in this trial, no one wants to convict an innocent man of the crime just because we are not sure about other potential candidates.

The defence are not in a position to say who the murderer was. We do not have the resources of the state to investigate the matter and send off forensic samples for analysis to try and prove who did it. Indeed, it is no part of the defence's function to provide you with a candidate. This is not like Television programmes where the defence comes up with the real killer.

This is real life.

I recall many years ago watching episodes of a television programme about an American lawyer, Perry Mason. Noticeably, he never made a final speech to the jury because at the last minute of the trial he would call a witness who would break down and admit to being the murderer. Sadly, that does not happen in the real world.

The defence do not know who the murderer was, it may have been Nicholas or 'Chris' Andrews or it might have been someone else, what I do say to you is, it was not Charlie Holmes.

In this case, the prosecution has made significant errors. For example, for a significant part of this trial they mixed up where the murder weapon came from, telling you convincingly, you might think, that it came from Abigail Richards. We only discovered they were wrong about that when she gave evidence. What other convincing, but wrong statements have they made which we cannot prove are wrong because we do not have the evidence available? I suggest that there is one major mistake here and that is their contention that Charlie Holmes was the murderer.

You will have noted how Mr Lynch's well-crafted speech asked large numbers of questions. I suggest that is understandable because there are a large number of questions still to be answered in this case. If the prosecution are still asking those questions at this stage then there is at the very least a reasonable doubt about Charlie Holmes' guilt.

Let us look together closely at the real evidence, not the evidence that the prosecution would like you to believe is there.

The starting point is that the whole of the prosecution case rests on circumstantial evidence. No one suggests they saw Charlie Holmes commit the murder. There is no direct evidence that he did. What the prosecution say is that you can be sure of his guilt because you can infer that guilt from the circumstances.

We have to be careful here. Circumstantial evidence can be good evidence but it cannot be mixed up with guesswork or speculation. To lead to a conviction the chain of evidence must be an unbroken chain of compelling evidence.

The prosecution say that they have that evidence and point to a number of factors.

Firstly, Charlie Holmes knew the victim Sheila Wright. Of course he did, no doubt countless others did too.

Secondly, Charlie Holmes had an affair with her. There is no disputing that fact just as we know Nicholas Christopher Andrews had an affair with her.

We have an unbroken chain of evidence to this point, far short of what is required. After this the

426

chain becomes weak and I suggest breaks under the pressure.

The third point the prosecution rely upon, Charlie Holmes had a serious accident which prevented him having sex. Again, there is no dispute he had a serious accident although there is evidence from Charlie Holmes and Helen Rogers that he was on the way to regaining some sexual feeling.

Fourthly, his relationship with Sheila Wright was cooling off because of his inability to perform. This is where the chain really begins to strain. Yes, there was a reference by him to his friend James Bevan that this might be the case, but Sheila Wright never seems to have said anything to anyone. Her confidant, Abigail Richards, thought she might be cooling against BOTH boyfriends, solely because she had not mentioned them in some time. Even she did not say that Sheila Wright had started to cool because of the inability to have sex.

Fifthly and now the chain is at breaking point, the prosecution suggest that the phone call from the mobile phone ending 3317, made at 3:30pm on 14th June, 2013,, and the texts to and from that phone at 4:12 pm and 4:13pm, were calls and texts associated with Charlie Holmes.

There is no evidence whatsoever that was the case. The highest the evidence goes to is Mrs Richards believing she heard the name 'Chas' used by Sheila Wright at 3:30pm. However, you will recall her evidence in court, she thought she heard 'Chris', which just so happens to be the middle name of Nicholas Andrews.

There is no other evidence whatsoever that the phone 3317 belonged to Charlie Holmes.

Sixthly, Charlie Holmes was on the way to see Sheila Wright on the day she died. Again there is no dispute that is right, However, the important question is surely, whether there is any evidence that he actually reached her address?

True he got on the bus which he would use to go to her address, true he got off at a stop that was closest to her address, but is there any evidence he was actually at her address that day?

There is none. As for the evidence of the bus, we are talking about a bus stop within 15 minutes or so of Sheila Wright's address. In Central London, 15 minutes covers a long distance.

Seventhly, and the chain now is at breaking point, the prosecution say that Charlie is seen by Mr Callaghan entering the gate of Sheila Wright's property sometime between 12 – 1pm on 15th June, 2012.

You will have noted the points in relation to this already. Mr Callaghan did not identify Charlie, he was never asked to stand on an identification parade because Mr Callaghan admitted that he only had a fleeting glimpse of the man and would not recognise him again. Also, the timing is wrong if it was Charlie. On the prosecution case, he would have arrived at Sheila Wright's house at about 11:30am if he had made his way there from the bus stop. However, 12-00pm fits in perfectly with the time that the mysterious owner of 3317 said he was going to visit Sheila Wright that day. Finally, there is no clear answer to whether he saw a walking stick or a furled umbrella. He clearly wasn't sure as he told you. He also apparently told the police it may have been an umbrella but that fact never made it into his witness statement for reasons best known to the officer in charge of this case, DS MacDonald. Maybe it was because, just like Mr Callaghan's timings, that piece of evidence did not fit the prosecution's case, so it was adapted to fit.

Eighthly, and desperately the Prosecution trying to keep the ever weakening chain together, rely on the Top up Voucher. However, the evidence of this does not assist them at all for two reasons. Firstly, if she didn't want him to come to the address, why did she ask him to get her a top up voucher? Secondly, the top up voucher was never found at Sheila Wright's address. Surely, if Charlie Holmes had handed over the voucher to Sheila Wright to top up her phone, the voucher would have been in the rubbish bin or on the coffee table in her lounge when the police arrived, yet no such voucher was found at her address.

On the other hand, if Charlie Holmes had read out the numbers to her over the phone as he states he did, then the voucher would never have found its way into Sheila Wright's address, which would in turn explain why it was never found there!

Mr Lynch did state that if she had received the number over the phone she would have been likely to activate it there and then, but surely that only applies if she had the right phone near to hand at the time.

She clearly wasn't phoning Charlie Holmes from her mobile phone. She could have been using another mobile phone in the house, an old one, her son's or her daughter's, we simply do not know. She could have written the code down and then been distracted before activating it 40 or so minutes later.

The ninth link in the chain is the Prosecution's claim about the DNA found on the other knife. As you heard, this really is a weak point. They state that you can be sure that was deposited the day of the murder. However, the evidence does not establish that at all. As you heard, we cannot date DNA. It could have been deposited the day before when Charlie Holmes offered to prepare the vegetables.

The prosecution is adamant that she would have

then washed that knife and that his DNA could not be found on it a day later. However, they ignore another simple fact. Charlie Holmes told you he OFFERED to cut up the vegetables and she declined so he put the knife back. There would have been no need to clean it in those circumstances and his DNA could easily have been found on the handle a day later.

The tenth link and again a weak one, is Mr Callaghan's evidence that he heard a scream within half an hour of seeing the man arrive at her house. As you heard, he originally thought it came from a school, which is in the same direction. It may well be that is where it came from. The Pathologist's evidence is that Sheila Wright was killed quickly, it may have been so quickly that she didn't have time to cry out. Even if it was her cry it does not point to Charlie Holmes being the murderer.

The eleventh link in the chain of evidence, which is now well and truly broken, is the prosecution's reliance on the fact that Charlie Holmes left his home address on the night of the murder. That may have been an important piece of the chain, if it wasn't for the fact that this was a Friday. As we heard, he did not see Sheila Wright at the weekends, nor did he contact her. It may be important evidence if he had never left his home on a Friday night. However, as you heard from Helen Rogers, he had stayed away the Friday before.

The prosecution attack the evidence of Ms Rogers, alleging that she has lied to you. But you saw her. Did she look like she was lying to you?

The truth is if he had persuaded her to lie for him in court, he would have had her provide him with an alibi for the time of the murder, not for Friday night. If he had got her to lie for him, surely they would have got their stories right and not made a mistake as to whether they stayed together on two or three Friday nights? Surely if they were going to lie they would have been word perfect and both given an explanation that he was with her until about 4:30pm, when he returned to his flat.

The inconsistencies in time do not support an argument for saying they have made up their evidence, quite the opposite, they are the inconsistencies that often appear in honest witnesses' evidence when they are asked to recall exact times.

Charlie Holmes has given an explanation for why he did not say anything before about this evidence. He waited because he was embarrassed. Is that too difficult to believe? A young man is embarrassed that he cannot perform sexually and that he has to see a Sex Therapist who provides sexual services for cash. You may think he tried to make a joke about her being 'hands-on' for the same reason, he was embarrassed. People often try to joke when they are embarrassed. We all do, even if we mostly fail.

The twelfth link, in this broken chain is the evidence about his SIM card. Mr Lynch considers it a coincidence that it just happens to go missing the day Sheila Wright was murdered. However, three points should be made about this:

Firstly, coincidences do happen, if they didn't we wouldn't have the word 'coincidence' in our language.

Secondly, there is no evidence that the SIM was lost on the day she died, it could have been lost on the Saturday or the Sunday.

Thirdly, who lost it? Charlie Holmes remembers putting the SIM card in his wallet. That wallet was seized by the police. As you are aware from the news reports on television and in the newspapers, it would not be the first time that the police have lost evidence!

The final link in the chain, is 'motive'. Mr Lynch rightly stated that under English law, the prosecution do not have to prove a motive, but you may think the absence of a proven motive goes a long way to demonstrating that the prosecution has not proven its case. That is why he suggested motives to you. As he put it to you in his final speech,

'Was this because the victim had finally made it clear she did not want to see him anymore, or because she had taunted him with his inability to have sex, or because she had told him about the other boyfriend?'

You will have noticed, there is not a shred of evidence to support any of those suggestions. They are speculative, mere guesswork and not based on any evidence you have heard. They have no proper place in your deliberations. The evidence does not establish that Sheila Wright did not want to see Charlie Holmes again. There is no evidence that she taunted him or told him about the other boyfriend or that he discovered there was another boyfriend.

People are not convicted on the basis of speculation and guesswork but on evidence. This link is not just weak or broken; it simply does not exist at all.

I suggest that the weak and broken links in the circumstantial chain of evidence are not strong enough to make you sure of Charlie Holmes' guilt, but it goes further than that.

You have two further important factors in this case to consider.

Firstly, you have the evidence of Charlie Holmes. You saw him take those, what Mr Lynch refers to as 'difficult steps' to the witness box. He didn't have to. He does not have to prove anything in this case. It is for the prosecution to prove that he lied to you. Indeed, if, having considered his evidence, you think he MAY be telling the truth, then the prosecution has not established so that you are SURE that he is guilty. Her Ladyship will remind you of this and also of the fact that he is a man of good character. There are no criminal convictions recorded against him and he is an honest, respected and brave fireman who has saved lives, not taken them. He is not someone with previous convictions for violence or dishonesty that might reasonably make you question his account.

I suggest you should consider his good character in his favour when you consider the evidence in this case and the allegation that he is a cold-hearted murderer.

Charlie Holmes was subjected to a vigorous cross-examination in this case and you may think he never wavered. He was never caught out in a lie or a half truth, and I suggest that goes a long way to establishing that he told you the whole truth.

Secondly, and finally, let us look at what is missing in this case. What would you expect to find in a case like this where a woman was brutally stabbed nine times?

There are two pieces of evidence that you would surely expect to find. You will recall the expert evidence in this case and indeed the reference to that French Pathologists famous principle, Locard's Exchange Principle, "every contact leaves a trace."

If Charlie Holmes was in that house THAT day, surely he would have left some trace to show that he was there THAT day.

There is no evidence that Charlie Holmes was ever in that property on that day. There were no traces of him going into the property. No fingerprints, palmprints or footprints in blood or dust, no fibres on the deceased's body or on the sofa, no traces of DNA around the door knobs, light switches, cups or saucers that were used that day.

Equally, if he had been the killer and stabbed her nine times, surely there would have been some blood on his hands, clothes or even his walking stick. Surely he would have left a bloodied print or a trail somewhere, but there were no such traces found anywhere.

Of course you have heard the prosecution experts in this case state that there wouldn't necessarily be such traces and no doubt you will want to consider their evidence carefully, but as Her Ladyship will direct you, you do not have to accept their evidence on this point. I suggest that common sense dictates that there would have been some traces of blood on the assailant in a case like this.

You have heard that Charlie Holmes' clothes were forensically examined. Not one drop or even a smear or microscopic trace of Sheila Wright's blood was found on them or any other item belonging to him including the walking stick.

'Every contact leaves a trace', keep this in mind during your deliberations members of the jury.

I invite you to consider that the obvious corollary of this principle is that if there is no trace, there was no contact.

In considering this aspect of the case no doubt you will want to consider where the assailant was when the attack occurred. The prosecution has always maintained that the assailant was seated to the right hand side of Sheila Wright's body. You will recall that the Pathologist, Mr Labaski, gave evidence that his favoured scenario was that the killer was in this position and because of the angle of the wounds he would have to be right-handed.

We know that Charlie Holmes is right-handed.

However, Mr Labaski did accept that the assailant could have been seated in front of her on the chair which was seen by the paramedic when she entered the room. He also accepted that the assailant could have been standing to her left and stooping. In those cases, the assailant could have been left-handed or, ambidextrous!

That leads me to the final point in this case, the murder weapon. Here is the piece in the jigsaw that simply does not fit the prosecution case, however hard Mr Lynch has tried to hammer it into place.

The prosecution has been at pains to say the murderer was right-handed and that Charlie Holmes is right-handed. You were told that in the opening by Mr Lynch. However, we now know from the Pathologist's evidence that the murderer could have been left-handed. We also know that the murder weapon was a knife specially designed for left-handed people. Namely, those working in a restaurant or perhaps behind the meat counter in a supermarket!

The Prosecution say you can be sure it was Charlie Holmes who murdered Sheila Wright, but this evidence suggests that the murderer was left-handed, or ambidextrous, and uses specialist knives. One person fits that description far better than Charlie Holmes, namely Nicholas or is it 'Chris Andrews'. You will recall he used his left hand to draw a plan of the victim's house, and then somewhat defensively claimed to be ambidextrous.

I cannot prove to you it was Mr Andrews or someone else, who murdered Sheila Wright, but as you know it is no part of the defence's function to prove anything to you. What I do suggest though, is that on the evidence you have heard you cannot be sure it was Charlie Holmes who carried out this crime, when there is another candidate who has not offered any provable alibi. In those circumstances alone I suggest there is only one proper verdict in this case.

Not guilty of Murder.

CHAPTER 47

DELIBERATION

Isobel adjourned the case until after lunch when she began her summing up. David listened carefully just in case the summing up needed correcting or any appeal points arose but apart from one or two minor errors the summing up was well-structured and fair.

Isobel dealt with the law and the evidence and then summarised the arguments of both Counsel. David was surprised, in his experience, most Judges became more prosecution-minded as time went on but Isobel, who had started out that way, was dealing with points fairly, for and against each party.

He mused to himself, *there is nothing more annoying than a fair judge! At least with an unfair one the jury may react against what the judge tells them to do, or there may be an appeal point, not here though.*

She had not finished her summing up by 4:15pm so she sent the jury away for the night. They all arrived early on Wednesday morning for a 10am start and at 12-32pm, after summarising the evidence, Isobel sent them to the jury room to consider their verdicts.

The first task that Isobel had directed them to do was to appoint a foreman. This proved surprisingly easy. Throughout the trial, Joseph Ward, a 64-year old Architect, who ran his own business, had gained a great deal of respect from the other jurors and he was quickly appointed. He took up his seat at the head of the table and the other jurors took up seats on either side of him.

Joseph asked for quiet and then told them how he was proposing to deal with their deliberations. "I consider it appropriate that we have a discussion about the evidence before we embark on any voting. I'm going to suggest that we start by using the prosecution's Chronology in the jury bundle and deal with conflicts of evidence when they arise. Does anyone disagree?"

No one stirred and he took them through the various points on the Chronology. "There seems to be no issues with the evidence of any importance until we come to 14th June 2012. Then we reach the first major one, whose phone was it that made the call at 3:30pm? The same of course applies to the texts at 4:12 and 4:13pm that day. I think we should deal with that issue first and I do have some ideas."

There was silence around the room and then Winston Amin, a 29-year old Building Society Cashier spoke. "Joseph, I think we may be going about this the wrong way. The issue as to whose phone made those calls is surely crucial to our decision. If it was Charlie Holmes who made the call and sent and received the texts, then he's undoubtedly the murderer. I think we should look at other issues first to determine whether it was his phone or not."

Alison Palmer, who was 27 and unemployed had noticed Winston on the first day of the trial and had made sure she sat as close as she could to him when she went for a coffee or lunch in the canteen. She beamed at him now, "I agree with Win. Those are the 'crucial' issues."

Winston smiled back at her. He had noticed her interest in him and was grateful for this support now, but he had no interest in her outside the jury room. He didn't find her large nose stud at all appealing.

Victoria Jones now joined in the discussion, she was a grey-haired widow and aged 63. Although she had no romantic interest she had found it easier to talk to Joseph and had sat next to him throughout the trial. She felt the need to support him now. She scowled at Winston and spoke in her most condescending voice, "We have appointed Joseph as the foreman, don't you think we should do him the courtesy of allowing him to act as one."

The comment did not elicit any murmurs of support and it was Joseph who decided to respond, "Thank you Victoria but I'm not pretending my way is the best way. It was nothing more than a suggestion. If others have better ideas, I am more than willing to listen to them."

Kevin Hargreaves, a 46 year old salesman was next to join in. He hadn't liked Winston who he thought had been too loud in the jury room, nor did he like Alison who dressed similarly to his 21 year old daughter, right down to the large nose stud. It was bad enough at home but in a courtroom! Nevertheless, he tended to agree with Winston and thought it only fair to say so. "The central point here is what the Defendant's relationship was like with Sheila Wright at the time she died. Surely we should concentrate on that?"

The discussions continued in the room like that for the rest of the day with different opinions being expressed as to the state of the relationship and at 4:20pm the jury were summoned into Court and sent home for the day.

The following day, discussions continued and became slightly heated when they discussed Charlie Holmes' bus journeys on 15th June 2012. Iqbal Mahmood, a 38 year old shopkeeper stated. "I don't believe his story that he read out a 16 digit number of a top up voucher over the phone. I sell the same type of voucher in my shop. If you make a mistake in one number you would have to start again. No I think he must have given her the voucher."

Members of the jury were already polarising into camps for and against conviction and this comment met with some raised voices from both camps, but then a hand was raised in the room and Joseph asked Jessica Wallace to make a contribution.

Jessica was a 32 year old secretary in a large company in Central London and this was the first contribution she had made to the discussion. "I pointed this out to Barbara when we watched the video. Did anyone notice on the video of his bus journey at 10:50am, when he sat down he appeared to be texting. I think he was texting the number of the voucher to Sheila Wright!"

Iqbal Mahmood was unhappy with the intervention and interjected loudly, "That is ridiculous. In any event, he told us he read it out to her and more importantly, the prosecution showed that not one of her phones was in contact with his at this time, so how could he contact her?"

Jessica remained calm, "I don't think we can be sure of that. The police seemed to have concentrated on Charlie Holmes right from the start. I don't think they properly investigated in this case. They never looked at any other phones in the house apart from the ones they said were Sheila Wright's. She may have used other phones belonging to her children."

Iqbal started to get more annoyed, he wanted to return to his shop. He had been working late at night whilst sitting on this jury and he was hoping this case would finish soon and he could return to normal work hours. "Alright, ignore the phones, what about that eye witness, Mr Callaghan. I thought he was a very good witness. He identified the Defendant. He saw the walking stick and he saw that the man limped. How many limping murderers are there in Clapham Common?"

Derek Smith, a 24-year old unemployed graduate of American Literature decided he had had enough of Iqbal. "Actually, Mr Callaghan did not make an identification of Mr Holmes. He said he had a fleeting glimpse of the person he saw. He wasn't really concentrating on him. I think the defence barrister did a good job of cross - examining him. Although, I question his knowledge of American quotations claiming a Mark Twain quote was by Abraham Lincoln!"

Everyone in the room looked quizzically at him, not having any idea what he was talking about so he carried on.

"I thought that it was established that Mr Callaghan could not describe the person he saw in any detail. The description he gave could have applied to probably half a million men in London! Callaghan couldn't be sure whether he saw a walking stick or a folded umbrella and I question whether he really saw the man limp. There wasn't time to see a limp.

Further I wasn't happy that he had told the police about the umbrella and they hadn't put that in his statement. It makes me very suspicious about the whole police investigation."

Iqbal was not willing to back down. "Alright, what about his SIM card? You didn't believe he just lost it?"

Jessica now interjected continuing to speak softly and quietly. "No I don't think he 'lost it'. I believed him when he said it was in his wallet when the police took it. After all, police officers do lose evidence."

Iqbal snarled but before he could say anything, Barbara Percy, decided it was time to support her. She was a 29 year old housewife and had become friendly with Jessica, having sat next to her throughout the trial. "I agree, a few years ago my younger brother was arrested by the police on suspicion of causing an affray. His lawyers asked the prosecution for a video from a CCTV camera that was in that area and which they said would cover the incident and show that he was telling the truth. The police said they had seized the video but had 'lost' it. I think they may have 'lost' the SIM card in the same way."

Victoria now joined in the conversation, "I am sure the police and the prosecution lawyers have not done anything wrong in this case. I am sure that nice officer, DS MacDonald, was truly trying to help when he was cross-examined by the defence barrister."

Winston had not forgotten Victoria's intervention the previous day when he had first spoken, he felt now was the opportunity to get his own back. "I don't think he was trying to help at all. He just tried to make the case against the Defendant stronger with each answer, even if the answer had little to do with the question.

I'm suspicious about that SIM card and the investigation as a whole. They did seem quick to arrest the Defendant and charge him. There seems to have been no further investigations of the other boyfriend and they even accepted what he said the moment he walked into the police station in the middle of the trial. No, I'm not impressed with this prosecution."

The deliberations continued as the jury dealt with all the evidence they had heard, including the evidence of Helen Rogers which caused some mirth. They then moved on to concentrate on the other boyfriend, Nicholas Adams.

It was Joseph who decided to take a lead on this subject. "I agree with the defence barrister that there are such things as coincidences, but there are some remarkable coincidences in his case. It is a remarkable coincidence that Nicholas Andrew's middle name is Christopher and that witness, Abigail Richards, thought she had heard the name 'Chris' used by Sheila Wright in that phone call at 3:30pm the day before she died."

Victoria looked carefully at him and then began to nod slowly.

Everyone was now listening closely to Joseph. "I've got a best friend who is called Warren David Bertram. He doesn't like the name Warren so he has been known as David since school. It's not that rare for people to use their middle names if they don't like their Christian names.

Also, I am very concerned about the murder weapon. There is no doubt it's a knife specially designed for left-handed people. It's the sort of knife that is more likely to be used in a restaurant or shop than in the home. How did it get there?

At 09:30am, Sheila Wright was asking to borrow a carving knife so it doesn't sound like she had a carving knife then. That knife must have arrived with the murderer. The right-handed Charlie Holmes was surely not going to carry a left handed knife to the house and why would he go there armed with a knife and bother to get her a top-up voucher at the same time. It makes no sense whatsoever. Further, Nicholas or Chris Andrews has no alibi. It's a little convenient that his alibi just happens to be abroad and isn't contactable during this trial. It's another one of those coincidences I just don't like. I'm not saying I'd convict Nicholas Andrews on this evidence, but I'm not saying I would rule him out either."

The room became silent as even Iqbal slowly began to nod in agreement with Joseph.

It was Kevin who broke the silence. "There is just one part of the case against Charlie Holmes that gives me concern and makes me think he did it."

All the other members of the jury looked at him closely now. He looked at them all in turn and added, "Let me tell you what it is."

CHAPTER 48

VERDICT AND AFTERMATH

At 3:30pm the jury was brought back into court and Joseph was asked by the court clerk whether they had reached a verdict upon which they were all agreed. Joseph replied in a firm voice, "We have."

"On count one of the indictment alleging the offence of murder, do you find the Defendant guilty or not guilty?"

Joseph paused for a few seconds, took a deep breath and looked towards Charlie Holmes in the dock.

"Not guilty."

"Is that the verdict of you all?"

"Yes it is".

David looked towards the jury and smiled, he then turned towards the dock. Charlie could not be seen. His head was in his hands and all that could be heard was the sound of loud sobs.

They were repeated in the public gallery. David looked up and saw his wife's old school friend, and mother of the Defendant, Anne Holmes, weeping and being comforted by close family members. His ex-wife Sarah had joined her in the public gallery without David knowing. Roger Wright was also in the public gallery. David noticed that he had his head in his hands.

None of them knew just how close the jury had been to convicting David, when Kevin had raised his concerns two hours before. He had been troubled about Charlie's story of spending three hours and ten minutes in Clapham Common. "I know the area really well. I just can't see why he would spend so much time there." Others had tried to persuade him that people did often spend a great deal of time doing nothing. Barbara had pointed out that she often spent hours in department stores without doing anything. "Why couldn't Charlie Holmes spend 3 hours 10 minutes in a park?"

Kevin had moved onto his next concern which was the bus CCTV. He had studied Charlie Holmes' journey back at 2:22pm and he was sure that Charlie looked anxious, "as if something momentous had occurred."

The jury had been provided with a copy of the CCTV and the facilities to play it in their jury room. On watching it again, some began to agree with Kevin, but most pointed out that the quality of the video was just not good enough to be able to clearly make out Charlie's facial expression. The few who had supported Kevin were persuaded by the majority that there was a reasonable doubt and soon even Kevin agreed that Charlie Holmes should be acquitted.

As soon as the verdict was reached David asked for Charlie's discharge from the dock and Isobel granted the application. Charlie still had to go downstairs to the cells for administration purposes but this time he knew it would be his last visit there.

David and Jamie waited 15 minutes for Charlie and then went to the cells to talk to him and congratulate him. Within a few minutes they were shown into a cell where Charlie was signing release papers from the prison.

David went forward to see him with his best smile. He was proud of the way he had conducted the case and happy that Charlie had been acquitted. Suddenly he froze and the smile was rapidly wiped from his face.

Charlie was smiling and saying thanks when he noticed David look at him. He looked down at the paper in front of him and smiled again. He had the pen in his left hand.

David recovered and asked the obvious question, "You're left-handed?"

Charlie didn't answer, he simply moved the pen to his right hand and carried on writing. "No, actually, I'm ambidextrous. I was really surprised to find that Nicholas Andrews was as well, I've never come across anyone else who is."

David closed the cell door behind him and Charlie. "Why didn't you tell us?"

"I didn't see the need. Anyway, the police were saying I was right-handed and I knew that a clever chap like you would spot that the murder weapon was for a left-handed person."

"How did you know about the knife?"

"Actually, it was a present I bought for Sheila, for when I helped her with the cooking. She never liked it though. She was right-handed and could never get used to it, but I've always preferred using a knife in my left hand..." He paused and smiled, "...when I'm cooking and I liked the handle on this one. You can get a firm grip."

He smiled at David before continuing, "I have to say David, I was surprised how long it took you to spot that the knife was for a left-handed person. I thought I might have to point it out to you at one stage."

David's face was ashen now. "Did you kill her?"

Charlie smiled and looked at David through cold eyes. "Now Mr David Brant QC, you know better than that. Of course I didn't. The jury has just proved that I was innocent, haven't they?"

453

David regained his composure. He didn't want to spend any more time in the cell with him. He simply said, "Charlie, you will be released soon. Your mother and your family are upstairs and THEY will want to celebrate your victory with you."

With that he turned and left the cell, with Jamie following closely behind.

As he left the court, Charlie's mother, Anne, approached him with Sarah. It was Anne who spoke through tears, Sarah just smiled and acknowledged him.

"Oh David, thank you so much. You were brilliant. If it wasn't for all the trauma and worry that I had, I would probably have enjoyed seeing you in action. Thank you so much for securing justice for Charlie."

David looked at her and smiled back, hoping not to convey his true feelings, "Thank you for your kind words. 'Justice for Charlie', yes I suppose that's what it will be called."

Sarah looked at him strangely, so he quickly added. "Charlie will be released soon. Life will be a little strange for him for a while. He's been used to being locked up most of the day and facing the possibility of life imprisonment. No doubt you will be ready for that."

With that and a shake of her hand and a nod to Sarah he made his way to Chambers.

Wendy was waiting for him there. "How did it go, another great Brant acquittal?"

"It was an acquittal, though I don't think I would call it a 'great' one."

It was Wendy's turn to look at him quizzically now and he told her the full story, seeing Charlie in the cell with a pen in his left hand and how Charlie admitted that the knife was his. Wendy listened silently and when he finished she added, "You don't know that he murdered her. He never admitted it. In any event, it's not the first time you've got an acquittal in a murder case."

"No, it's not, but it is the first time that I was convinced that he was innocent."

"David, just chalk this one up to experience and forget about it. You did an excellent job and ultimately the evidence was not there, otherwise the jury would have convicted.

Now, there are more pressing matters in Chambers. John Winston approached me and asked if I knew whether you were coming in. He needs to talk to you about Julian Hawker. Apparently, he's been arrested!"

CHAPTER 49

THE HEAD OF CHAMBERS

"You see sir, it's like this."

John Winston had come into David's room to explain the full details of Julian Hawker's arrest.

"Mr Hawker stopped waiting outside that pupil's chambers, as he said he would, but, unfortunately, he found out where she lived and started waiting outside her flat with bouquets of flowers and chocolates. She reported it to her Head of Chambers, Mr Lafferty, who said that she had suffered enough and advised her to contact the police.

The police arrested him on Wednesday night and he appeared before the Magistrates Court this morning. He was released on bail pending a full hearing. He'd like to see you. One good thing that I can say is he has paid his arrears of rent and he has recently been instructed on a big VAT fraud that may need a Silk to lead him. He was thinking of you. Shall I send him in?"

"Yes, thank you John."

A few moments later, Julian entered the room with his usual cheery grin.

"Hi David, I hear that you had another great victory in the Old Bailey. I've got some good news, I've paid off all my rent as you asked me to, I transferred the money today. I've also been instructed in a high value VAT fraud. It should last for 3 or 4 months and I'd like you to lead me."

David looked at him with an air of disbelief. "Julian, you've been asked to see me because of your arrest for harassing this pupil that we have discussed before. Natasha Bloomfield."

"I know David. She has taken it too far this time getting me arrested. For God's sake, I was only taking her flowers and chocolates to say sorry for hanging around outside her Chambers."

"You took them to her home address when you knew she had a Court Order out against you, preventing you from harassing her."

"Yes, but I didn't think she was that serious. Women will be women David. You know how they like to play 'hard to get', I suspect you've come across that a bit with the delicious Wendy."

David blushed involuntarily whilst becoming increasingly angry.

"Julian, you promised there would be no more of this behaviour. You promised me you would not harass this young lady anymore."

"Well, technically David, I said I would find another way home and would not go near her Chambers again. I was very specific, I didn't say I wouldn't go near her home address!"

David looked at him as if he was from another planet.

"You mean to say that when you gave me your word you were intending to go to her home address?"

"Oh yes, I know she will come round eventually, they all do. I suspect a few more nights staying outside her flat and she'll invite me in for a drink and then that will be that."

"Well, Julian, as Head of Chambers I do possess some powers that can be exercised without reference to Chambers Management Committee."

"Yes, David?"

"One of those powers is to act urgently in chamber's interests if I deem it necessary."

Julian looked at him with a curious expression, "Yes, and...?"

"I want you to go to your room, pack your belongings and leave this set forthwith."

Julian looked stunned, "You're not serious, you want me to leave just after I've paid my outstanding rent?"

"Oh yes" was the laconic reply.

"But David, I'm one of the most able barristers in this set!"

"I don't disagree, but tenants of these Chambers also require a quality you do not possess."

Julian now looked completely dumbfounded, "What's that?" he asked.

"A degree of sanity. Now get out. I don't ever want to see you in these chambers again. "

Julian looked as if he wanted to strike David, but thought better it, after-all David was stocky and strong and looked angry. He left the room muttering the single word, "Prick".

David looked out of the window of his Head of Chambers room, into the Inner Temple Gardens, across the old cobbled paths bathed in late afternoon summer light and smiled to himself. Now that the diplomatic niceties were over, that was a lot easier than he had imagined and a lot more enjoyable. Coupled with the fact that John Winston had also informed him that another murder case was on the way from a Solicitor's firm, who had specifically wanted the 'Head of Chambers' to conduct it, he thought to himself, *you know being Head of Chambers isn't that bad after all. I could quite get used to this.*

Books by John M. Burton

THE SILK BRIEF
The Silk Tales volume 1

The first book in the series, "The Silk Trials." David Brant QC is a Criminal Barrister, a "Silk", struggling against a lack of work and problems in his own chambers. He is briefed to act on behalf of a cocaine addict charged with murder. The case appears overwhelming and David has to use all his ability to deal with the wealth of forensic evidence presented against his client.

US LINK

http://amzn.to/1bz221C

UK LINK

http://amzn.to/16QwwZo

THE SILK HEAD
The Silk Tales volume 2

The second book in the series "The Silk Tales". David Brant QC receives a phone call from his wife asking him to represent a fireman charged with the murder of his lover. As the trial progresses, developments in David's Chambers bring unexpected romance and a significant shift in politics and power when the Head of Chambers falls seriously ill. Members of his chambers feel that only David is capable of leading them out of rough waters ahead, but with a full professional and personal life, David is not so sure whether he wants to take on the role of *The Silk Head*.

US LINK

http://amzn.to/1iTPQZn

UK LINK

http://amzn.to/1ilOOYn

THE SILK RETURNS
The Silk Tales volume 3

David Brant QC is now Head of Chambers at Temple Lane Chambers, Temple, London. Life is great for David, his practice is busy with good quality work and his love life exciting. He has a beautiful partner in Wendy Pritchard, a member of his chambers and that relationship, like his association with members of his chambers, appears to be strengthening day by day.

However, overnight, things change dramatically for him and his world is turned upside down. At least he can bury himself in his work when a new brief is returned to him from another silk. The case is from his least favourite solicitor but at least it appears to be relatively straightforward, with little evidence against his client, and an acquittal almost inevitable.

As the months pass, further evidence is served in the case and begins to mount up against his client. As the trial commences David has to deal with a prosecutor from his own chambers who is determined to score points against him personally and a co-defending counsel who likewise seems hell-bent on causing as many problems as he can for David's client. Will David's skill and wit be enough this time?

UK LINK

http://amzn.to/1Qj911Q

US LINK

http://amzn.to/1OteiV7

THE SILK RIBBON
The Silk Tales volume 4

David Brant QC is a barrister who practices as a Queen's Counsel at Temple Lane Chambers, Temple, London. He is in love with a bright and talented barrister from his chambers, Wendy, whose true feelings about him have been difficult to pin down. Just when he thinks he has the answer, a seductive Russian woman seeks to attract his attention, for reasons he can only guess at.

His case load has been declining since the return of his Head of Chambers, who is now taking all the quality silk work that David had formerly enjoyed. As a result, David is delighted when he is instructed in an interesting murder case. A middle class man has shot and killed his wife's lover. The prosecution say it was murder, frustration caused by his own impotency, but the defence claim it was all a tragic accident. The case appears to David to be straightforward, but, as the trial date approaches, the prosecution evidence mounts up and David finds himself against a highly competent prosecution silk, with a trick or two up his sleeve.

Will David be able to save his well-to-do client from the almost inevitable conviction for murder and a life sentence in prison? And what path will his personal life take when the beautiful Russian asks him out for a drink?

UK LINK

http://amzn.to/22ExByC

USA LINK

http://amzn.to/1TTWQMY

THE SILKS CHILD

The Silk Tales volume 5

This is the fifth volume in the series, the Silk Tales, dealing with the continuing story of Queen's Counsel (the Silk), David Brant QC.

Their romantic Valentine's weekend away in a five-star hotel, is interrupted by an unexpected and life-changing announcement by David's fiancé, Wendy. David has to look at his life afresh and seek further casework to pay for the expected increase in his family's costs.

The first case that comes along is on one of the most difficult and emotionally charged cases of his career. Rachel Wilson is charged with child cruelty and causing the death of her own baby by starvation.

The evidence against Rachel, particularly the expert evidence appears overwhelming and once the case starts, David quickly notices how the jurors react to his client, with ill-disguised loathing. It does not help that the trial is being presided over by his least favourite judge, HHJ Tanner QC, his former pupil-master.

David will need all his skill to conduct the trial and fight through the emotion and prejudice at a time when his own life is turned upside down by a frightening development.

Will he be able to turn the case around and secure an acquittal for an unsympathetic and abusive client who seems to deliberately demonstrate a lack of redeeming qualities?

UK

https://goo.gl/YmQZ4p

USA

https://goo.gl/Ek30mx

PARRICIDE

VOLUME 1 OF THE MURDER TRIALS OF CICERO

A courtroom drama set in Ancient Rome and based on the first murder trial conducted by the famous Roman Advocate, Marcus Tullius Cicero. He is instructed to represent a man charged with killing his own father. Cicero soon discovers that the case is not a simple one and closely involves an important associate of the murderous Roman dictator, Sulla.

UK LINK

http://amzn.to/14vAYvY

US LINK

http://amzn.to/1fprzul

POISON

VOLUME 2 OF THE MURDER TRIALS OF CICERO

It is six years since Cicero's forensic success in the Sextus Roscius case and his life has been good. He has married and progressed through the Roman ranks and is well on the way to taking on the most coveted role of senator of Rome. Meanwhile his career in the law courts has been booming with success after success. However, one day he is approached by men from a town close to his hometown who beg him to represent a former slave on a charge of attempted poisoning. The case seems straight forward but little can he know that this case will lead him on to represent a Roman knight in a notorious case where he is charged with poisoning and with bribing judges to convict an innocent man. Cicero's skills will be tried to the utmost and he will face the most difficult and challenging case of his career where it appears that the verdict has already been rendered against his client in the court of public opinion.

UK LINK

https://goo.gl/VgpU9S

US LINK

https://goo.gl/TjhYA6

THE MYTH OF SPARTA

VOLUME 1 OF THE CHRONICLES OF SPARTA

A novel telling the story of the Spartans from the battle of the 300 at Thermopylae against the might of the Persian Empire, to the battle of Sphacteria against the Athenians and their allies. As one reviewer stated, the book is, "a highly enjoyable way to revisit one of the most significant periods of western history"

UK LINK

http://amzn.to/1gO3MSI

US LINK

http://amzn.to/1bz2pcw

THE RETURN OF THE SPARTANS

VOLUME 2 OF THE CHRONICLES OF SPARTA

"The Return of the Spartans" is a sequel to "The Myth of Sparta" and continues from where that book ends with the capture of the Spartan Hoplites at the battle of Sphacteria.

We follow their captivity through the eyes of their leader Styphon and watch individual's machinations as the Spartans and Athenians continue their war against each other. We observe numerous battles between the two in detail, seen through the eyes of their most famous and in some instances, infamous citizens.

We follow the political machinations of Cleon, Nicias and Alcibiades in Athens and see how they are dealt with by the political satirist at the time, Aristophanes, who referred to all of them in his plays.

Many of the characters from "the Myth of Sparta" appear again including the philosopher Socrates, the Athenian General Demosthenes and the Spartan General Brasidas whose campaign in Northern Greece we observe through the eyes of his men.

The book recreates the period in significant detail and as was described by one reviewer of "The Myth of Sparta", is, "a highly enjoyable way to revisit one of the most significant periods of western history".

UK LINK

http://amzn.to/1aVDYmS

US LINK

http://amzn.to/18iQCfr

THE TRIAL OF ADMIRAL BYNG

Pour Encourager Les Autres

BOOK ONE OF THE HISTORICAL TRIALS SERIES

"The Trial of Admiral Byng" is a fictionalised retelling of the true story of the famous British Admiral Byng, who fought at the battle of Minorca in 1756 and was later court-martialled for his role in that battle. The book takes us through the siege of Minorca as well as the battle and then to the trial where Byng has to defend himself against serious allegations of cowardice, knowing that if he is found guilty there is only one penalty available to the court, his death.

UK LINK

http://goo.gl/cMMXFY

US LINK

http://goo.gl/AaVNOZ

TREACHERY – THE PRINCES IN THE TOWER

'Treachery - the Princes in the Tower' tells the story of a knight, Sir Thomas Clark who is instructed by King Henry VII to discover what happened to the Princes in the Tower. His quest takes him upon many journeys meeting many of the important personages of the day who give him conflicting accounts of what happened. However, through his perseverance he gets ever closer to discovering what really happened to the Princes, with startling consequences.

UK LINK

http://amzn.to/1VPW0kC

US LINK

http://amzn.to/1VUyUJf

Printed in Great Britain
by Amazon